MW00636395

# PLOWMAN

## HARVEST OF GRAIN AND INNOCENCE

Books by the Author

PLOWMAN:
HARVEST OF GRAIN AND INNOCENCE

Adelyn's Adventure Series:

In the Forest

In the Garden

On the Beach

# PLOWMAN

## HARVEST OF GRAIN AND INNOCENCE

Charles Bruckerhoff

Sequoia House Books™

Published in the United States of America by
Sequoia House Books™, Connecticut.

This is a work of historical fiction. The names, characters, places, and incidents portrayed in this book are the product of the author's imagination or are used fictitiously. Any similarity to actual persons, living or dead, businesses, companies, events, or locales is entirely coincidental and not intended by the author.

Cover design, book interior design, and typesetting by

Mario Lampic

Permission granted from

Rev. Dr. Scotty J. Williams for using his Prayer at the  United Nations' Permanent Forum on People of African Descent, on December 4, 2022.
https://scotty-williams.com.

Permission granted from

Dr. Oliver Tearle of Loughborough University for using his
*A Summary and Analysis of Sophocles' Antigone*, 2023.
https://interestingliterature.com/2021/03/sophocles-antigone-summary-analysis/

Library of Congress Control Number: 2023913443

ISBN 978-0-9905838-9-9 (hardcover)

Plowman: Harvest of Grain and Innocence
Bruckerhoff, Charles.

MDS 813.6
FICTION BRUCK,C PLO

[1. Suspense and adventure—Fiction. 2. Military—World War II—Japan—Vietnam—Afghanistan—Fiction. 3. United States—Politics and government—Fiction. 4. Friendship—International. 5. Family—Cultural and historical. 6. Faith—Judeo-Christian religions. 7. Education—reform.]

Printed in the United States of America
First edition: October, 2023
1 3 5 7 9 10 8 6 4 2

Give ear and hear My voice,
attend and hear My utterance.
Does the plowman plow all day to sow,
break open and harrow his soil?
When he levels its surface,
will he not scatter fennel and broadcast cumin
and set wheat in rows
and barley in plots
and spelt as a border?
For He guides him rightly,
his God instructs him.

— Isaiah 28:23

When he opened the fourth seal,
I heard the voice of the fourth living creature say,
'Come!'
And I looked,
And behold, a pale horse!
And its rider's name was death,
And hades followed him.
And they were given authority
Over a fourth of the earth,
to kill with sword and with famine
And with pestilence
And by wild beasts of the earth.

— Revelation 6:7-8

Blessed are they who cultivate:

Love

Spirituality

Honesty

Courage

Dignity

Loyalty

And

Resolve

FOR MY BEAUTIFUL WIFE AND BEST FRIEND, THERESA, WHO
GIVES SO MUCH TO ME AND OUR FAMILY, ALWAYS PUTTING
THE NEEDS OF OTHERS BEFORE HER OWN, AND TO MY FOUR
REMARKABLE SONS AND DAUGHTERS-IN-LAW, AND THE
LOVELY GRANDCHILDREN.

When you are inspired by some great purpose, some extraordinary project, all your thoughts break their bonds.

— Patanjali, India, circa 100 BC.

# Characters & Genealogy

## 1567 to 1615

**Sanada Nobushige (his original given name) Yukimura** was the ancient samurai warrior of the Sanada clan.

## 1934 to Recent Time

**Sanada Kenshin,** descendent of Sanada (Nobushige) Yukimura, is now leader of the Sanada clan.

**Haruki Sanada,** son.

# Hana Philomena Sanada's Family

**Akiro Sanada,** great great grandfather of Hana.

∞

**Sakura Sanada,** his wife, great great grandmother of Hana.

**Lieutenant George Washington Sanada,** son, great grandfather of Hana.

∞

**Philomena Bradley Sanada,** his wife, daughter of Craig and Stella Bradley, great-grandmother of Hana.

**Jonas George Sanada,** son, grandfather of Hana.

∞

**Audra Sanada,** his wife, grandmother of Hana.

**Evan Sanada,** son, father of Hana.

∞

**Isa Sanada,** his wife, mother of Hana.

**Hana Philomena Sanada,** their daughter.

# The Bradley Family

**Major Craig Alexander Bradley**, senior officer, recruited George Washington Sanada.

∞

**Stella Bradley**, his wife.

---

1st **Lieutenant Thomas Nelson Bradley**, son, KIA, Battle of Okinawa.

**Scarlett Bradley**, daughter.

**Philomena Bradley**, daughter, wife of George Washington Sanada, great-grandmother of Hana.

---

**Jonas Bradley**, Rifleman, deceased, ancestor who served in The Continental Army, under General George Washington, Spencer's Regiment at Valley Forge, 1777–1778.

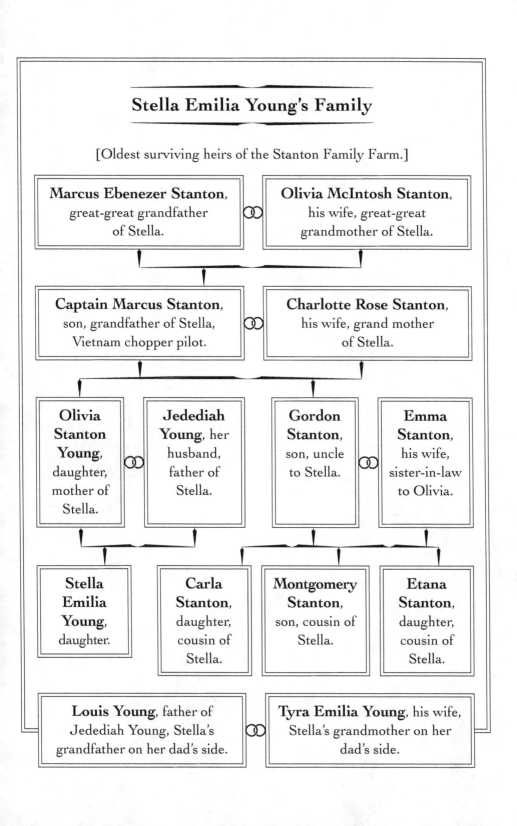

# Stella Emilia Young's Family

[Oldest surviving heirs of the Stanton Family Farm.]

**Marcus Ebenezer Stanton**, great-great grandfather of Stella.

**Olivia McIntosh Stanton**, his wife, great-great grandmother of Stella.

**Captain Marcus Stanton**, son, grandfather of Stella, Vietnam chopper pilot.

**Charlotte Rose Stanton**, his wife, grand mother of Stella.

**Olivia Stanton Young**, daughter, mother of Stella.

**Jedediah Young**, her husband, father of Stella.

**Gordon Stanton**, son, uncle to Stella.

**Emma Stanton**, his wife, sister-in-law to Olivia.

**Stella Emilia Young**, daughter.

**Carla Stanton**, daughter, cousin of Stella.

**Montgomery Stanton**, son, cousin of Stella.

**Etana Stanton**, daughter, cousin of Stella.

**Louis Young**, father of Jedediah Young, Stella's grandfather on her dad's side.

**Tyra Emilia Young**, his wife, Stella's grandmother on her dad's side.

# PLOWMAN

## HARVEST OF GRAIN AND INNOCENCE

## — 1 —

STELLA and Hana were born at St. Luke's Hospital, on a hot Thursday in June.

In Labor Delivery Room 731, Stella's mother, Olivia, gave birth first at 05:07. Jedediah Louis Young, Stella's father, full of love and wonder for his wife and their first child watched Olivia push the infant from her womb into the receiving hands of Dr. Anna Kaminski, the OB/GYN specialist. When Stella's head was out, she suctioned fluids from Stella's mouth and nose.

"Push hard once more, Olivia," she said softly.

Little Stella Emilia, with a bald head, came out fast, head to toes, into her world, wriggling. Kaminiski placed Stella on her mother's stomach, paused a minute to examine her, then clamped the umbilical cord in two places close to the navel.

"Jed, are you ready to start your daughter's life on her own?" Kaminiski asked quietly with a smile.

"My hands are a little shaky, but yes," Stella's father replied, taking the scissors.

Olivia watched as best she could, drearily, head tilted up from her pillow, showing some pain, but beaming with pride and joy.

Snip of the scissors.

Kaminiski gently massaged the baby's chest. Little Stella Emilia Young instinctively filled her lungs with fresh air—and wailed very loudly—for the first time in her life.

"That is the sweetest music in the world," Kaminski pronounced.

After a quick assessment of the still wailing newborn, now wrapped in a warm towel and cradled in her arms, Kaminiski handed Stella to the neonatal nurse, who was accompanied by several interns. Their task was to finish cleaning up Stella on a nearby radiant warmer, administer tests and monitor her vital signs.

Turning immediately back to Olivia, Kaminski waited for Olivia's ongoing contractions to deliver the placenta.

After receiving the placenta into a white plastic bowl, she said, "There. That's what I'm waiting for." Kaminski examined the placenta carefully for completeness and any other issues. "As natural and good as can be," she reported.

"I'll put in a few stitches where you have tears, and then it's over," Dr. Kaminsky added while stitching. "I'll check on you regularly, and the nurses and PAs will be here round the clock until you go home. Push that call button for help, and any questions."

Finished with the stitching, she continued, "For a first-time mom, you did good, Olivia. Congratulations, Jed and Olivia. God has given you a beautiful, healthy baby girl. Don't worry about her bald head. She will grow hair in time. Soon enough she'll have a full head of hair, probably light colored, like yours Jed." Mom and Dad smiled, kissed and cried tears of joy.

"Thank you Dr. K. You've been wonderful for us throughout the pregnancy and birth," Jed said.

2

Once Kaminski had completed her work with Olivia, she went to the radiant warmer to examine Stella once again. She consulted quietly with her neonatal nurse, and studied the stats flowing across the monitor. "Put a skull cap on her. Body temperature's falling a little. Keep me up to date, Nurse Sharma. LDR nurse, Linda Riley, is taking over cleaning up Mom. She's in great condition. Bring baby back to Mom as soon as possible and help her start nursing her baby." Walking toward the door, she said, "Olivia and Jed, your prenatal classes just ended. You are now officially parents. Love and care for your beautiful baby girl. I'll be in 733, next door with your best friends, Isa and Evan Sanada. You'll soon know about their newborn."

Kaminski checked her iWatch. "Good timing," she said, while opening the door to exit LDR 731. A few steps later, she opened a door and entered LDR 733, where Isa and Evan were waiting.

Inside 733, another neonatal nurse, Zxun Chén, was measuring how much Isa's cervix had dilated. "Four centimeters, the diameter of an Oreo cookie," she reported. This was troubling to Kaminski because there was no difference since the last check.

Evan was sitting in a chair next to Isa's head where she lay on the hospital bed.

"Hi, Isa and Evan," Kaminiski greeted them. She went to Isa's bedside, put her hand on Isa's shoulder, and assured both Evan and Isa that everything was going well. "We have a delay with the dilation of your cervix, but nothing to worry about. I can administer a drug, Pitocin, intravenously, if needed. We just have to wait. We will work patiently with your body and your baby for this delivery."

3

"Nurse Chén, let's review the stats." The nurse walked with Kaminski to the monitor. They studied print and digital reports from when Isa was first hooked up to the monitoring system until the present.

Returning to Isa's bed, Kaminski, holding up an internal fetal monitoring device, told her and Evan that she was installing an electrode onto the baby's scalp to monitor its heartbeat while it was still in the womb. Working and explaining to the parents, to keep them calm, she said, "This procedure was covered in your prenatal class. You might find it gets serious now, because it has a tiny wire that I will screw into your baby's scalp. Presto, it's in place. I hear the heartbeat. It's good," she said. "Now, both of you take a deep breath and relax. Everything in life is ongoing, different in its own way and time. Labor of love and purpose is our God-given destiny. We are going to bring your baby into this world when your body is ready to deliver."

Evan kissed Isa's cheek and held her hand. The contractions of her womb continued at closer intervals and with increasing intensity. The pain caused Isa to grimace.

Kaminski sat at a desk to monitor all incoming data. Nurse Chén watched the monitors, talked soothingly to Isa and reported her observations to Kaminski.

Three hours later, Kaminski injected Pitocin into the IV. From that point on the baby's movement through the birth canal increased, but not to Kaminski's satisfaction. She squeezed her fingers and hand into the birth canal around the baby's partially visible head. Reached its neck with her fingertips, hooked the umbilical cord and loosened one wrap from around its head. She paused, listening to the fetal heartbeat. "It's got another wrap

4

around the neck." Kaminski had kept her hand on the baby's cheek on the off chance there would be another wrap. She smoothly hooked and loosened the second wrap.

"Heartbeat is returning to normal. Nurse Chén, be ready. This baby's coming into the world, now."

Moments later, at 08:07, Isa delivered little Hana Philomena Sanada into Kaminski's waiting hands. Then lifted her onto mom's stomach. When she had completed cleanup of the baby's airways and eyes, Kaminski reported, "She's weak from the umbilical cord problem, but healthy otherwise."

With Hana resting on her mother's stomach, Kaminski paused, double-clamped the umbilical cord and cut it with the scissors. "No time to waste." Little Hana let out a mild wail. "Nurse Chén, put the baby on the radiant warmer, administer tests and monitor her vital signs."

Kaminski received the placenta and inspected it. "All's good, Isa. Your baby girl will be fine after Nurse Chén's care. Now, I'm gonna put some stitches in to help heal your tears."

When she had finished the stitching, Kaminski stood up, looked at Isa and Evan and said, "Congratulations. Hana is going to surprise you from this day forward. You are now parents of a beautiful little girl. Love her and care for her. She will bring you much joy over the years. Born with a head full of coal-black hair."

They all laughed.

With tears in his eyes, Evan said, "Thank you for all you did for us, Dr. Kaminiski."

"You are most welcome, Evan and Isa. All I did was catch your baby before she fell on the floor. Isa did all the hard work. I'll check on you and the baby regularly while you're here. Nurse Chén, or another neonatal nurse, will be here 24/7. And the rest of the Maternity Ward staff. Use the call button for help. Again, congratulations."

Kaminski excused herself and exited the room.

As time and events unfolded, Hana and Stella became the best of friends, sisters in life.

# — 2 —

NINE years passed.

Hana had spent many weekends with Mom and Dad at her grandparents' home in the country. One Saturday morning, she awoke early, cleaned up, and walked out of her second-story bedroom into the hallway. Straight ahead was a door she hadn't noticed before.

"Have to ask Grandad if that's another closet, bedroom, or what," she promised herself. Then, walked down the stairs, dreamily, into the kitchen.

"Good morning, Grandad," Hana said. "Mom and Dad are sleeping in. Where's Grandma?"

"She's working on a pesky computer virus in the office. She's hoping she doesn't have to take it to the repair shop. She said we should eat breakfast without her, because fixing the computer might take a while. Mom and Dad will eat after they get up. How did you sleep last night, Hana?" Grandad asked.

"Wonderful. I kept the windows open all night. Bright stars and moon. The frogs did their croak-croaking and the insects buzzed their crazy music. Lightning bugs flashed their yellow buns everywhere. Put me to sleep, for sure," Hana replied.

"I slept great, too. Like a baby. Now, let's eat breakfast," Grandad said, while bringing two cups of apple juice and two plates of egg sandwiches with melted cheese on toast to the kitchen table. "Have a seat, Hana. Looks like you have something on your mind?"

Hana pulled out her chair and sat down, while smelling the fresh-made sandwich. "Thank you for making breakfast. It smells yummy. This is one of my favorites. And you always cook it just right." Before taking a bite, Hana said, "You are so good at reading my mind. How can you do that, Grandad? Yes, I'm curious about something. What's behind the door across the hall from my bedroom? I didn't notice it before this morning."

Grandad chuckled, recalling how much Hana loved a mystery, then said, "Your Dad can tell you lots after he gets up. But I'll start. Behind that door is a stairway to the attic. Your Dad and his friends often played games, read books, or studied up there. Evenings, rainy days, when they couldn't play outside. You'll find lots of fun things to do up there. Eat up and be on your way."

Hana finished the egg sandwich, wiped her mouth with a napkin, and carried her plate and cup to the sink.

"You and Grandma are always so good to me. Thank you. Now, I'm going to explore the attic," Hana announced. She rushed to the stairway and flew up the steps to the second floor.

From the bottom of the stairs, Grandad said, "Hana, when you open the door to the attic, there's a light switch on your left. Flip it on, and the stairway and attic lights will come on. Same switch is at the top of the stairs."

"Have fun. If you need anything, call for me," Grandad added.

8

Hana flipped on the light switch and walked up the creaky steps to the landing, halfway to the attic floor. She paused. An unfamiliar sensation came upon her. Something strange, eerie about the attic?

"Silly girl," she chided herself. She dismissed the strange feeling and climbed to the top of the stairs.

The long, narrow attic room was immediately inviting. Hana discovered all kinds of board games. Lots of sports equipment. And found a huge bookcase.

From a section with children's books on the bottom shelf, she pulled out *The Hundred Dresses*, written by Eleanor Estes and illustrated by Louis Slobodkin. Hana opened the front cover to see her grandma's name written with her fine script on the title page. *Audra*.

A leather armchair was across the room. She sat in the chair and began reading the book, realizing her grandma had read the same story in this very book. Possibly at the same age as she was.

For years and years afterwards, the attic would be Hana's favorite place to read, relax, and reflect on life.

A private, fanciful room she would soon share with her best friend, Stella.

— 3 —

THE girls, now twelve, were enrolled as first-year resident students at the Stanton Academy for Humanity, whose theme was Agriculture from the Dawn of Civilization. On a Saturday afternoon in September, they returned home to visit with their families. That evening a family dinner was held at Stella's home.

Her mom, Olivia Stanton Young, had invited Hana's grandparents, Jonas and Audra Sanada, and Hana's parents, Evan and Isa Sanada. Stella's grandparents on her mom's side, Marcus Stanton and Charlotte Rose Stanton, and Louis Young and Tyra Emilia Young, Stella's grandparents on her dad's side.

The previous March, Stella's dad, Captain Jedediah Young, had been deployed to Afghanistan. Everyone missed him terribly, and worried for his safety, especially Stella and Olivia. Family dinners, held at least once each month, were a warm and loving comfort for all.

Olivia made the girls' favorite meal, lasagna with meat sauce, lots of ricotta and mozzarella cheese. Also, a lettuce salad with homemade Italian dressing. Isa made barley soup. Tyra brought tiramisù for dessert, Jed's most-liked sweet dish. Jonas brought two bottles of Chianti Classico.

"The table's set," Olivia announced. "Let's all sit down to dinner."

11

When they were seated, Olivia said a prayer over the meal.

"Father in heaven, we gather here again, a family for dinner, as we do once each month. We thank you for this food to sustain our bodies. We thank you for our good health and spirits. We ask your blessings upon our parents and children, that they will be guided by your love for all humankind. We ask also that you watch over our much-loved son, father, uncle, and husband, Jed, my love, and return him to us soon, safe in body and soul."

"Amen," all said.

A reverent pause.

"Help yourselves," Olivia said.

"'Pass the plates of food to the right,'" Hana said.

The girls laughed at their inside joke.

"What's that about?" Jonas asked. "Did I miss something? A joke in there, somewhere?"

Still laughing, Hana explained. "Sorry, Grandad Jonas. Yeah, it's a mealtime rule at the Academy. Otherwise, with the twelve or more kids, and the Family Parents, we'd have a mash-up, something wicked."

"I see," Jonas said. "I heard your lunches are with twenty-four kids. Twelve each, non-residents and residents, right? Boys and girls. That's a huge sit-down."

"Yep, Grandad Jonas," Stella answered, while spooning lasagna on her plate. "Avoid disaster: always 'pass to the right.' Our school food tastes great, because it's homemade. We take turns with food prep and kitchen work. On a schedule. We get to know so many different kids and Family Parents. Every year, we move into a different Family House with new Family Parents. We're in the Gilmore House this year, with Desmond and Kiera Gilmore. 'One Dozen Stars,' it's called. All girls, first-through-sixth-year

12

students, mixed up, with four girls to a dorm room. A great big family. So fun."

Stella added, "There's the instructors and neighbors, too. They all got their own occupations, many neighbors are farmers, but all use a big part of their day to help us learn what's behind their work. All the history, science, discoveries, math, literature, research methods, famous inventors and authors, on and on, art and music."

Isa asked, "What are your studies like?"

Stella answered, "Oh, Grandma Isa, that's the best of all. Hana and I are in *Ubiquitous Water Faucets: Where Does Our Water Come From?* with Mr. and Mrs. Walker every day now, studying Glacier Pond. They've told us that, soon enough, we'll be turning that pond upside down to see what's in there. Our first year with the Walkers, we get to own a portion of the pond for life, shore to shore, and help take care of it for our whole life! We learn about that job in the sixth-year study area, *Your Stewardship and Husbandry of Glacier Pond.*"

"Really cool," both girls said.

Hana added, "Yeah, along with snorkeling, diving, drilling and all the rest outside, inside, underneath, and all turned inside out, upside down."

The girls laughed and chanted, "What the devil is going on here? Figure it out," which Stella explained is the key question driving the learning process of the Walkers.

Hana continued, "There's applied math, science, chemistry, microorganisms, and more thrown in. All about Glacier Pond every day. The Walkers also run a research company, 'Happy Humus,' that helps property owners manage the quality of their soil and water for lawns, gardens, and farms."

13

The girls could talk non-stop all night about their school.

"Sounds to me like the Academy knows how to help kids learn, and love learning, too. That's what we pay our taxes for, right, Louis?" Jonas asked.

"You bet," Louis replied. "I'm impressed, and very glad for you, Stella and Hana. Would have loved that as a kid. By the way, I understand the Family Parents sometimes put on meals from their ethnic cuisine. What dishes have they served at the Gilmore Family House?"

"Yeah," Hana replied. "Desmond and Kiera Gilmore are Irish—Desmond from Ulster and Kiera from the Scottish Highlands. Their specialty dishes are fantastic. Stella, you were on kitchen duty. What did we have that Sunday?"

"Oh my God, unforgettable, to make and to eat," Stella replied. "For breakfast: Scottish porridge, that's like our oatmeal with strawberries, blueberries, and jam on top. For lunch: Cullen skink. Yeah, sounds weird, I know. It's smoked haddock, and a thick potato and onion soup, and so good. And for dinner: haggis, that's ground-up turnips, potatoes, meat, oatmeal and onions—without the drams of Scotch whisky, though. That's the adult version. And mashed potatoes and carrots.

"I talked about the Scottish Sunday Feast with Dad when he called last. He's so excited for us at the Academy. And hopes I make a Scottish Feast for all of us when he gets back next year. I said, 'I will for sure, Daddy,'" Stella said.

When dinner ended, the whole family helped clean up the table, dining room, and kitchen. Dishwasher was loaded. Large pots and fragile glassware, Olivia and Isa washed by hand in the sink.

"Olivia, thanks so much for having the dinner here tonight," Tyra said. "We'll do it next month. I'll float ideas

14

for what we want in a week or so. Maybe Cullen skink or haggis," she laughed.

"Works for us," a chorus answered.

"Mom?" Stella said, "Can I stay the night with Hana and her grandparents?"

"It's okay with me. Have you asked Jonas and Audra?" Olivia asked.

"Did you ask them, Hana?" Stella asked.

"Always okay with us," Audra answered for Hana.

"Yeah, yeah, yeah," the girls said in one voice.

Good nights and goodbyes said, the family dinner party ended and all motored home. Hana and Stella rode with the Sanadas to their country home.

Next morning, the girls slumbered in their beds, with no hurry to get up. Besides, they heard rain falling on the roof and windows. Nothing outdoors today.

They talked about Stella's dad, Jed. How much she missed him. How she and Mom handled the worry and stress with him being in the war zone. And stuff Stella and Olivia did to keep up their family life, like sending "care packages" with Jed's favorite foods to share with his buddies. Writing letters, texts and having FaceTime calls, sometimes during our monthly family meals.

"Mom and I so like the dinners we have together with the whole family, like last night. That was my grandma Isa's idea when Dad was first deployed. It's the best of family life, family love," Stella said.

From a radio broadcast downstairs, a local meteorologist gave the day's forecast: "Expect temperature in the low 60s with thick clouds and rain, all day, at times heavy. Low-lying areas may have some flooding. Your garden and lawn will love this. Drive safely."

15

They walked downstairs wearing PJs. Hana's Grandma Audra wrote a note, taped to the fridge: "Morning H&S, Glad you slept in. Help yourselves to breakfast cereal, juice, fruit, yogurt, toast, or whatever. We both have doctor appointments. And some shopping to do. Be home late afternoon. Love you both!"

Over a breakfast of juice, yogurt, fruit, and buttered toast, they talked about their friends from the Academy, girls and boys. How fun they were. Keenly competitive in sports and learning. Sam, one of the new first-year boys, fit in really well. Smart and cute.

Stella cracked a smile. In her clever way she mimicked Hana's mother, Isa, with an inside joke: "Be careful what you wish for, Hana Philomena Sanada." Then she shouted, "Gotcha!"

"Unfair. I got no interest in him. You're bad, Stella Young!" Hana shot back laughing.

"Hey, with rain all day, how 'bout we go up to the attic?" Stella proposed. "You said there's tons of stuff to rummage through. From our grandparents and great-grandparents. Play a board game or two. Kick back and listen to the rain. Crank up some music. Pass time." Then, she slipped in another funny, "Whaddya say, Hana Philomena Sanada?"

"You win, Stella Emilia Young. Again," Hana said with eyes rolled upward and a feigned grimace. Then, "Yeah, I like that idea. Let's clean up the table and do it."

On the way upstairs to the second floor, Hana grabbed Stella's arm to stop her and said, "Did I ever tell you about the first time Grandad Jonas said I could go in the attic?"

"No. Another one of your secrets?" Stella asked laughing.

"Well, it scared the bejesus outta me. 'Bout peed my pants. Was only nine," Hana answered.

Hana stopped Stella again at the second-floor hallway, lowered her voice, and got serious, "Grandad Jonas opened the door. It creaked pretty loud. Pitch black inside. He said, 'Go on, Hana. Go on in. Turn on the light. There's a switch, left side.'"

"So, I looked down and there was the first step, barely visible," Hana continued. "I put my weight on it. The board made a low groan. I felt a little nervous. Scared, actually. I put my hand up to switch on the light and I felt this little furry thing. It moved and 'eeeked.' I pulled back my hand and screamed bloody murder.

"Grandad Jonas looked in, said matter-of-factly, 'Just a bat. Nothing to worry about. Been meaning to clear them out of the attic since last winter.' Like it was nothing at all!" Hana exclaimed. "Well, the bat scared me big time. But it also taught me to watch out for surprises. Don't freak out. Gets you nowhere." Then, Hana turned and clawed at Stella's neck, "G-r-r-r-r-r-r!"

"Ahhh!" Stella gasped.

"Gotcha good, Stella Emilia Young!" Hana laughed.

"You're a devil girl!" Stella parried playfully.

With that they ran down the hall to the attic door. Hana opened it. Dark inside. She stepped back, bowed gracefully to let Stella hit the light switch, and lead the way.

"No way I'm going first!" Stella laughed. Then, she smacked on the switch. Raced up to the landing halfway. Bounded up the last steps to the attic floor.

"Bats beware! Devil girls here! Tada!" Stella shouted in the attic.

Hana said, "Wow! You can be crazy scary, Stella. Honestly, the attic has always been a tad eerie and spooky to me, on cloudy, rainy days especially. And that's when I usually go up here ... to relax. Weird, ha?"

# 4

STELLA looked up, around, and observed, "With raindrops softly hitting the roof, it's so peaceful in here."

They stood at one end of a long, narrow room. A large, oval, braided rug covered the hardwood floor. The ceiling was steep-angled, with the 12:12 pitch of the roof. A small single-sash window was on each end wall.

Hana pointed, "There's my favorite brown, leather wingback chair. I curl up in it and read books for hours. There's another one just like it in the family room."

Hana walked to the chair and rubbed dust off the cool, smooth leather seat with her hand. Sat down. Pulled the last book she was reading from under the seat cushion, *A Wrinkle in Time*, a sci-fi novel written by Madeleine L'Engle. Started reading where she left off.

Stella noticed, scattered around the room, were boxes of toys, board games and jigsaw puzzles. From at least three generations of Sanadas. A guitar and saxophone were propped against a tall, mahogany bookcase running the length of the room, organized and filled with titles for both kids and adults. A toy piano with brightly colored keys sat on a low flowerpot stand. In an opened steamer trunk, a rugby ball was balanced atop shoulder, elbow, and knee pads, old cleats, beginner and advanced skateboards, generations of molding baseball bats and gloves, and helmets for different sports.

19

Looking up from her book, Hana said, "My daddy wrote his name with a black magic marker on all the sports equipment."

"My daddy, too," Stella said, touching the rugby ball. "On almost every day when he was home from duty, he'd take me outside to play ball. You remember. 'Cause he always got you over to practice moves with us."

"Yeah, for sure," Hana said. "Uncle Jed is so thoughtful, so kind, loving, and determined to make us the best. I miss him, I love him, too."

Stella, now in a melancholy spirit, thinking about Daddy so far away, fighting in a war, walked over to pick up the saxophone. When she grabbed it, her forehead hit a teetering large wooden box and knocked it from the top shelf. The box bounced off the rugby ball, crashed against the piano, making a shockingly loud clanging noise. Was launched from the steamer trunk, turned ungainly, to rest on the floor. Landed right side up, amazingly, intact, on the rug.

"Jeez! What could be more incredible," Stella exclaimed, reflexively backing away.

She stooped to pick up the box. Wiped a thick layer of dust off the top. Faded and scratched red letters on the lid identified it as *The Army Company First Aid Case, Nov. 1916, Bakers Pure Drug Co. LTD, Plymouth*. A perfect cube. Twelve-inch sides, bottom and top made of maplewood. Sanded smooth, sealed, and hand-rubbed with several coats of tong oil. Corners were intricate dove-tailed joints. The top had two heavy-duty brass hinges, and was kept tight-shut with a solid brass clasp, bearing "Made in England."

"Huge. Heavy. Ancient. From England. How cool is that? Awfully weighty for a first aid kit," Stella mused.

"Daddy taught us first aid for all kinds of injuries, but we couldn't have lugged this monster box around."

That got Hana's attention. She stopped reading. Laid her book upside down on the rug, opened at the last page she read. Went over to where Stella stood holding the box at her stomach with both hands.

"That box never caught my attention before. Where'd it come from?" Hana asked.

"Top shelf of the bookcase. Here," Stella pointed. "It went crazy down when I bumped it with my head," Stella explained.

"Do you really think it's a first aid kit? Maybe something else stored inside?" Hana guessed.

"I dunno," Stella replied. "Should I open it? Hana Philomena Sanada! Did you put a freakin' bat in here?" Stella playfully accused.

"No, Stella, honest. Would be a super joke on you, though. Ha ha. Open it, and let's see what's so heavy."

Stella shook the box. Nothing moved inside, like it was stuffed full of something. "Weighs a ton," she guessed. Stella paused, wondered what could be inside the box, pursed her lips, then flipped up the tight-fitted brass clasp. The lid popped open with a loud, strong force.

"Oh my God!" The girls said reverently at once.

Stella was awestruck, "Look at the title. *Wartime Journals of Lieutenant George Washington Sanada with Major Craig Alexander Bradley*, all printed in his super fine script. Hana, it's your grandfather's writings from World War II!"

Hana added, "Your great-grandfather's gonna be all over it 'cause he's in the title. Mom always said that's when they met, and our families started!"

"Yeah," Stella affirmed softly, now lost in thought. "My mom, too, but gave no details about it."

Stella knelt down and sat the box on the rug. She delicately lifted from the top a manila folder, not tied together, with the title written on the cover by George Sanada over the date "April 5, 1945." Stella laid the folder on the rug between her and Hana. She closed her eyes and thought, "I feel like a priestess in long-ago Mesopotamia, or Minoa, on the island of Crete, opening ancient parchment scrolls, the people's sacred texts!"

She turned over the cover and delicately flipped each document. There were many loose papers with journal entries inside. Yellowed pages smudged with fingerprints dirty from the field, handwritten notes in pencil on loose pages. Whatever writing paper the author could get. Flight and luggage tags and tickets. Military orders. Certificates for training on equipment. Flight training records. Rifle and pistol qualification and competition targets. Awards and citations. Letters from home, and from buddies in the field. The day, month, and year for this folder written at the top of each page or scrap. She closed the folder without disturbing any documents.

Stella carefully lifted all of the bundles out of the box and placed them side by side on the rug, in the exact order she found them.

"Hey! Look at this!" Stella exclaimed. "At the bottom of the box there's a separate bound manuscript, *A Glimpse into the Troubling Vietnam War and the Grave Aftermath Going Forward*, Captain Marcus Stanton. Oh my God! That's Papa! He never talks about that war. The dates show he started writing the journal when he got to Vietnam on April 10, 1968, and the last entry before leaving on April 30, 1975. This is surreal! My Daddy's fighting in a war now!"

A badly tarnished, Sterling silver, St. Jude Thaddeus medal fell from the manuscript to the floor. Picking it up, Stella asked, "How does this religious medal fit into the journals from Papa? And the whole story?"

She and Hana got up and ran downstairs to bring up a second wingback chair. Placed both chairs to face each other. They sat down not saying a word for some time. Eyes closed prayerfully. Wondering what the journals would reveal.

Using the first bundle as their sample, the girls concluded that every separate bundle was a collection of journals for a particular period. Each bundle was marked for an alphabetical series and tied together with hemp twine. Every entry in the journals had the day's date on all pages, numbered, in sequence, from page one for each bundle in a series. Some pages were updated with later entries with dates, adding more details in the margins and between the lines, and additional pages slid in.

"Stella, I'm thinking we've seen enough for now. We should put all the bundles back in the box exactly where they were. Return the first folder back on top of the stack where it was. Close up the box until we have a plan to study the journals."

"Good call. I'm with you, Hana," Stella said. Stella placed the bundles back in the box with the same care as when she took them out, and closed the latch. Hana and Stella stared into each other's eyes. Hugged with joy.

Stella mused, "Hundreds of pages. The small handwriting, smudges, writings in margins and between lines, updates over time. We can't risk losing anything or messing up the order of so many loose pages."

Hana added, "We gotta be careful not to lose or misplace anything. Whatever we do with the journals, it's gotta be done right, and will take a lot of time."

Stella offered, "I have an idea, Hana. We write this into a book about our grandparents."

"Can we do it?" Hana asked. "We're only 12."

Stella replied, "There's plenty young writers did it before us. So, we won't be the first to try it. S. E. Hinton, Jake Marcionette, the Guptara brothers, just a few."

"Where'd you get all that?" Hana asked.

"One day, I was talking with our English instructor about my love of writing. Mrs. Benedictus told me about the authors who published as kids, some younger than us. She urged me to 'write, write, and keep on writing. That's what writers do.' Said she'd help me."

"Okay. I'm with you, Stella," Hana said. "We got school work, games, and chores to do on most days. So, we do this in our free time, Wednesday and Saturday afternoons, and on Sundays."

Stella added, "Let's talk to Mrs. Benedictus and ask her to guide us as we comb through the journals. I think she'd love to help. Then, recommend how we write it up. What genre and style to use. She can help edit our writing. Maybe she'd let us do this for our sixth-year writing project?"

"For sure," Hana agreed. "This is gonna take a while. We can't rush it. We get her guidance. I'm already feeling anxious."

"And we want to tell our folks first thing," Stella noted. "It's the wartime stories of our great-grandparents and one grandparent, my papa, who's still alive. I'm gonna talk to Daddy about this on the very next call. He'll be amazed at what we're doing. Oh my God. Gotta be done right," Stella concluded.

Late Monday afternoon, the girls met with Mrs. Benedictus and explained what they had found in the grandparents' attic. She was a professional writer before she joined the Academy. Still writing and publishing poems, short stories, and novels.

"My guess is, you got a real treasure in those journals," Mrs. Benedictus said with great enthusiasm. "I am delighted you asked for my help. I will give you all the guidance I can. You are both exceptionally good writers for first-year students. I think you can do this.

"My great-uncle kept a diary his whole life. Called it *The Diary of Dominick Cornelius Benedictus*. Dom and his wife, Maria, were talented painters of social realism, focused on American working-class men and women in daily life. I turned it into a short story when I was your age," Mrs. Benedictus said and then asked, "How will you tackle the research and writing?"

Stella began, "First, we find out what's in the journals, and keep them in their original order. We start by reading aloud to each other, from the first page of the first journal to the last entry of the whole collection. Maybe Hana starts. And I'll take notes. Then, me, and Hana does the note taking. We go on like that until we get to the end of the last journal. Second, we begin writing. Maybe this could be our sixth-year writing project?"

Mrs. Benedictus was listening.

Hana added, "We talk about the stories. Fill in details we get from our grandparents, or from the library or online. We record all our questions. We'll need a big space to spread out all the pages. Thought we'd take the box of journals to the Academy's library. Ask the librarian, if we can use one of the conference rooms. We meet there next Saturday afternoon, same time, for a couple hours. And the following afternoons on every Wednesday, Saturday, and Sunday until we get finished. Might take a couple of years."

Mrs. Benedictus smiled approvingly, proud of the girls' expert planning, and said, "You have the right outlook. An excellent plan. You have time on Saturdays at 2:00 p.m., right? Get permission from Brother Peter to bring the collection to the library this weekend. I'll join you there. We'll get a long table, maybe two or three together, and take the journals apart, delicately, piece by piece. See what you got. Then, over time, we'll modify your plan for plowing through it. As for the sixth-year writing project, that's a ways off, but you've signed up for it today and planned out your project nicely. Gives you plenty of time to research, write, and edit. You turned over pure gold here. Go for it. Coauthored manuscript. A first for the Academy. I'll see you next Saturday at 2:00 p.m., girls."

The trio met on the following Saturday, as planned. With expert guidance from Mrs. Benedictus, they painstakingly separated and organized the loose pages, intact journals, scraps and bits.

The entire contents of the first aid box was laid out in chronological order on three oak tables. Ready for research and writing.

"Wow," Mrs. Benedictus proclaimed. "There are so many documents and journal pages with so much striking detail in the entries! From the little I've chanced to read so far, you have an incredible story to tell. Congratulations. This is a great find.

"I asked Brother Peter to keep this meeting room door locked at all times. That prevents any disturbance of the layout. He'll gladly open the door whenever you make time to work on your project.

"Any time you want my help, you know how to find me. Good luck. A lotta work here, but deeply personal. You're gonna love this. I'm confident you'll finish the writing for the sixth-year project with ease. After graduation from the Academy, I expect we'll take up writing and editing to publish the book. It's going to be a great story, but will require a whole new level of work. I'll help you then, also."

With those parting words, Mrs. Benedictus excused herself, and left the conference room.

Stella and Hana stood in silence gazing at the wide array of original source materials, perfectly organized on the library tables.

"Hana, I broke the news to Papa Marcus last Sunday when we had dinner together," Stella began. "He, Grandma Charlotte, and Mom were instantly happy for us. Papa was aware of George Sanada's journals, but had never read them. Once he got to Vietnam, he decided to write his journals for the family's wartime records. He will help us at any time. When I told Daddy on our weekly call, he said, 'That's my girl! You and Hana will do great work. I can't wait to read your book. Update me on every call. I love you Stella.'"

"Yeah, I told my grandparents, and Mom and Dad of our discovery on Sunday, too," Hana said. "They were so pleased that we want to write up these stories. No one had ever read them. They guessed, since it's about these great wars, it takes a while, a generation or two, for curiosity and comfort to 'spring up,' as Grandma Audra said.

The girls looked away from the journals spread out on the tables, and into each other's eyes.

Stella said, "I can't wait to look into our past. Find out what that tells us about us now, and our future."

Hana said, "I'm so glad I have you, Stella, my sister."

"Hana, same here. You're my bestie. We start next Saturday at 2:00 p.m. We don't stop until the whole story is told," Stella confirmed softly.

# — 5 —

IN 1567, Sanada Nobushige was born in Japan. When he was three years old, Nobushige's parents and clan taught him to follow the way of the samurai, a word that means "those who serve" in English. Like all samurai, he would be loyal to his lord, and place honor above his own life.

He attended a school for samurai children that was located in a nearby Buddhist temple. Over time, Nobushige mastered archery, horseback riding, spear throwing, unarmed combat, the jujutsu system. And how to plan and execute battles.

To develop his character and virtues, Nobushige's teachers assigned him many readings in poetry and history, and taught him how to write and count.

At the Buddhist temple for samurai training, Nobushige's 12 peers were amazed by his cool prowess, and applauded his natural talents for leadership, tactics, and camaraderie.

On the playing field practicing fighting, young Nobushige could see better than anyone how a training battle was going, and devise tactics "in the moment" that led his team to victory.

By his twentieth birthday, Nobushige was a highly skilled samurai warrior, and his father began taking him into battle.

Throughout a samurai's life — women as well as men — they practiced being honest, kind, frugal, and caring for family members, especially their parents, grandparents, and great-grandparents. The samurai's code of conduct, is called *bushido*, which, translated into English, means "the way of the warrior." Their service included fighting against enemies with the weapons of that era, bow and arrow, spears, swords and knives, and practicing martial arts for highly skillful use of their weapons.

Samurai were not only warriors. They were well educated, knew the Japanese culture, influenced the culture extensively, and were skilled in financial matters.

For his feats in battle, Nobushige became known as "a hero who may appear once in a hundred years," and the "Crimson Demon of War."

Sanada Nobushige became the leader of his clan, called the Sanada.

In 1615, during the last Battle of Osaka against a longtime foe, the Tokugawa, Nobushige's forces were outnumbered by thousands of enemy soldiers. The fighting was fierce. Nobushige fought valiantly alongside his men, but eventually knew that his forces could not win the battle. Exhausted, Nobushige told his enemies he could fight no longer. They should sever his head from his body, in keeping with the samurai custom. A Tokugawa samurai killed Nobushige with his Katana sword.

The bloody battle was over.

In 1868, when the feudal era ended in Japan, many samurai warriors put down their swords and used their deeply instilled code of conduct, vast historical knowledge, and rare self-discipline, to help lead Japanese culture and society into the modern era.

The Empire of Japan began in 1868. By the first three decades of the 20th century, Japan's imperial conquests ranged from Manchuria in the north to the jungles of New Guinea and nearby islands to the south. In the the western region, Japan threatened India and the Gilbert Islands in the South Pacific.

Growth of the empire required massive amounts of new resources—land for crops, coal and oil for energy, minerals for making iron, steel, and other metals, and especially, people to serve the emperor and the generals.

Plus one thing, above all: unlimited power.

Question authority? Resist the conquering forces?

Lose the gambit.

Fortunates suffer a quick death.

Thousands of years had passed since the dark beginning of conquests by absolute rulers.

Wherever the long arm of tyranny rules, with legions of yes-men all too willing to carry out commands, the only path offered to the conquered is surrender to fear, powerlessness, poverty, slavery, or servitude.

Ordinary people might survive, but they live only as slaves.

The vanquished lose loved ones, land, homes, grain stores, and other material possessions. They are stripped of God-given rights, and may lose their cultural traditions as a people. They suffer merciless abuse, indignity, torture, and death.

Since the beginning, untold millions of people the world over have endured that awful fate.

Escape from tyranny rarely occurs, and succeeds only with grave risk, and a hair's-breath margin.

Beyond the architects and functionaries who forced the new order on Japanese people, there were other people who believed that a government must respect the God-given rights of the governed—life, liberty, and the pursuit of happiness. They had studied historical documents of earlier civilizations, and notably, the United States Declaration of Independence and Constitution.

There was one samurai warrior, Sakamoto Ryoma, who dreamed of different principles for the reform of Japan. The time had come, he believed, for Japan to abandon the caste system, where rights and privileges are hereditary, not based on personal merit. He was inspired by democratic principles of government in the United States and England, notably that "all men are created equal."

On this foundation, Sakamoto drew up an eight-point plan to modernize Japan.

He was assassinated by foes in 1867.

In the lead-up to WWII, dictators in Europe were on the same march for ultimate control of the world.

# — 6 —

DURING an entire fall term, Mr. Ulysses Mortimer Harding, headmaster for the Stanton Academy for Humanity, searched for a talented young theater director. He wanted an experienced producer with a strong background in classical theater and 19th-century English literature.

If Harding found one to his liking, this talent would charge up the students for classical English literature during the spring term, and beyond.

It was now December, a week before Christmas break. His search was not going well, and he confessed to the headmistress, Mrs. Victoria Boyington Graves, that he might instead have to go for someone offering a more pragmatic career focus, like field studies on deadly microorganisms. The kids loved getting their hands dirty on outdoor assignments. And that topic would match the academy's science studies to a tee.

Still, Harding was always determined to add richness, depth and novelty to the students' learning. His inner spirit told him that gutsy classical and English literature would put one more jewel in the Academy's crown.

"Do schools teach classical literature anymore?" he mused.

"Doubtful," Victoria weighed in.

Harding's cell phone rang with a FaceTime call.

"Harding here. Who's this?"

"Darius James, responding to your ad in The New York Times. You're searching for a 'talented young theater director and producer with a strong background in classical theater and 19th-century English literature.' I'm interested."

"Thanks for calling, Darius," Harding said. "That's a great name, and you have a strong voice. Darius the Great. King of Persia from 522 to 486 BC. What did you say your surname was? Sorry, but I'm practically deaf."

Victoria laughed aloud.

"James. Darius James, Mr. Harding."

"Got it. Like William James. But Darius James," Harding said and shifted to the interview. "I'm interested, too. Tell me something about yourself that no one would ever guess if they saw or read reviews of your work as a theater director and producer. Don't hold back. Take as much time as you want," Harding said. "I'm putting my cell on 'Speaker,' so the headmistress can take notes and weigh in."

"No problem,"Darius said.

"Here goes. I'm a twenty-seven-year-old man who grew up on the streets of Brownsville in Brooklyn, NY. My mama was a crackhead and prostitute. Died when I was seven. My daddy didn't leave his name. Never heard about him. There was a building for elder care nearby run by the Little Sisters of the Poor. The Sisters took care of me, especially Sister Clare. Gave me food, clean clothes, and a place to sleep in bad weather. Good people, those nuns."

"I'm with ya. Keep goin'," Harding threw in.

"One day when I was twelve, I was walking down Rockaway Avenue. Up ahead a gang was heading my way for no good. I'd seen what they did to people. There was a door to a used bookstore. I dove in. The owner, an old man, at first thought I was with the gang. He threw back a Black Betsy, committed, ready to fire. The look on my face told him different. His name was Isiah Goodman. So kind. Said I could wait in his store till the gang was out of sight. And I should find a book to read. I didn't have a clue how. But the Sisters had taught me to read and write, and I loved learning. After walking through several aisles, I pulled down a thick book with faded gold lettering, ragged boards, and slightly yellowed pages. There were long notes written in pencil in the margins of most pages. Written in the most beautiful script. Two dollars was written on the inside of the front board. I didn't have a dime. Isiah was at the counter sorting his mail. I laid the book on the counter. He bent over to look. Showed amazement. He opened the front board, and slowly fanned pages. He had the most prodigious nose and enormous, black, shaggy eyebrows."

"'What's your name, young man?'" Isiah asked.

"'Darius James.'

"Isiah continued, 'Hundreds of people have come in here over the years, and most want a trashy novel from the Free Books Box just inside the door there. Fact is, they probably ran out of toilet paper. But, Darius, you picked up *The Complete Works of William Shakespeare*. Do you know what you got your hands on?' Isiah asked paternally.

"'No,' I answered, 'but from the titles inside, the pictures and the handwritten notes, I thought it must have

35

been important for somebody to read. Maybe if I read it, I'd find out why.'"

"'Get down!' Isiah commanded. 'That gang's circling back,'"

Time elapsed.

"'Okay,'" Isiah sighed with relief. "'They're gone for now. You got a home?'"

"'No,'" I answered, "'but the Catholic nuns, Little Sisters of the Poor, give me food and clothes. They take me to church, teach me how to pray to God, have good manners, respect myself and others. Lots of good things for daily life.'"

"'What about your parents, brothers and sisters?'" Isiah asked.

"Just me," I said.

"'See that big leather soft chair in the back of the store?'" Isiah asked.

Yeah,'" I said.

"'Take your book,'" Isiah directed, "'go back there, sit for a while and read. I'll call you when I get the mail and bills sorted.'"

"I sat in the chair reading the first section, 'Life of William Shakespeare,' until I noticed it was getting dark out. Walking back to my safe place for the night would be risky."

"'Okay, Darius. Come up here,'" Isiah said. "'I checked out your story with the Sisters and they spoke very highly of you. Polite, honest, ambitious to improve yourself — extremely rare on these streets. Then, I called my wife to talk with her about you.'

"'Darius, we would like to take you into our home in Queens. Treat you like family. Adopt you. Our children

36

have all grown up, got jobs, and kids of their own. We have plenty of rooms in the house. Good schools in town. A Catholic elementary and high school right across the street. What do you say?'"

"'Oh my God! I say yes! Thank you.'"

"Isiah Goodman gave me the first hug of my life. I cried."

"'Lights out. Let's go home, Darius. Bring Shakespeare, too.'"

Harding said, "This is one great life story, and you're only twelve. Keep going."

"Mr. Harding," Darius explained, "I'm a self-made man. Had love and great care from very dear friends, Sister Clare and the other nuns, and from my loving, adopted family, Isiah and Ruth Goodman, my real parents. I love them so much. I came from a tough place, but lots of others have, too. Some from much worse places. I harbor no regrets. I look to God and the Bible for living a good life. I hope to help others in need. My parents sent me to Carnegie Mellon University for Directing and Theatrical Production degrees. I did well. I'll send you now, if you approve, several recordings of my work and print and non-print reviews."

"Not necessary, Darius. Mrs. Grace found your Facebook and LinkedIn pages right after you repeated your name for me, She sent me the links. I've been poring through the posts and reading your resume while you answered my grand tour question." Harding answered.

Long silence.

"Mr. Harding?" Darius asked.

"Hold tight, Darius. You probably noticed on the FaceTime screen, that your interview audience grew over time. Mrs. Grace took the initiative to invite other people on the call. School's on Christmas break, so everybody's hanging loose. We have the Family Parents, Gordon and Emma Stanton, and also a sampling of students. Say hello to Darius James, everyone."

"Hi, Mr. James!"

"Darius, I will call you tomorrow about our decision and the terms and conditions for working in the Academy. Oh, one more thing. Why are you applying to the Academy for Humanity? You were working notable off-Broadway venues in the City, getting rave reviews," Harding continued.

Darius said, "I'll answer directly and personally, as before. My wife, Cherice, is expecting our first child next February. She's a board-certified veterinarian, but waiting to open her own practice until we get our family started. As for me, I got the directing and producing career well on the way. Plenty of connections. I want to be a good husband and father to my child. The constant pressure of shows and the rat race of the Big Apple would mean I'd have little time for the baby and Cherice. If I can bring my talents to the Academy for Humanity—with its themes, style, countryside location, and religious foundation—it would be the opportunity of a lifetime. I could make good on a promise to give back to others."

"You got a good foundation, Darius. Tell me, would you and Cherice be comfortable living in Eridu Springs, our small town in New England? Gets cold here, and snowstorms are common in the winter, sometimes bury us," Harding cautioned.

"Yes, for sure," Darius said. "Cherice's parents live in northern Wisconsin, so she's used to the climate. Thanks to her, I love the fullness of the seasons. There's a saying, 'if you chop your own wood, you're warmed twice.' My father-in-law, Anders Olsen, taught me that lesson one cold morning at his woodpile."

"Wisdom of the Northwoods, for sure," Mrs. Grace softly said in the background.

Mr. Harding closed the call with, "Thank you for applying to our school, Darius. I mean that sincerely. Is 10:30 a.m. tomorrow a good time to get back to you on our decision?"

"Yes, it is. Thank you," Darius said.

"Great. I'll call you then."

"Okay," Darius ended the FaceTime call.

Mr. Harding said to the Family Parents and students, "Talk about the candidate, Darius James, during the rest of today. Mrs. Grace will put us all on a Zoom call at 9:00 a.m. tomorrow so we can make our decision. Thank you for your help. Thank you, Mrs. Grace, for taking care of important details," Harding said.

Victoria responded with, "I can't wait to see what Darius does for our school."

Next morning on the Academy Zoom call, Harding got right to the point — he never wasted time — and said, "Tell me any concerns or reservations you have."

Silence. A screen full of windowed, smiling faces.

Harding continued, "Did we find our theater director and producer, with a strong background in classical theater and 19th-century English literature?"

"YES!" everyone on the Zoom call shouted.

"Alright! I agree. Later, I'll offer Darius the usual generous salary with the benefits package, starting in January and continuing until either party chooses to end it. Could be a long time. We'll add free lodging and utilities in the Stanton Cottage. They'll have ample room for their family."

As promised, Harding put through a FaceTime call to Darius, telling him of the school's decision to hire him, the salary, and benefits, including free lodging and utilities in the Stanton Cottage.

Darius was very pleased with the offer—overjoyed, in fact. He introduced Cherice on FaceTime to Mr. Harding and Mrs. Grace. He and Cherice would move in December 26th, the day after Christmas, and he'd be ready to begin work January 10, when the students returned from Christmas break.

"Hold your horses, Darius," Harding was chuckling. "Let's talk some more about your plans and needs between now and your arrival. Your salary started today. Let Mrs. Grace know the banking details, tax info, and the day you and Cherice will arrive. The Cottage will be open, keys on the kitchen counter. Oh, by the way, Mr. Goodman's nose is nothing compared to my honker. Wait till you see this prodigious specimen," Harding put in. In the background, Mrs. Grace shrieked with laughter.

"Back on topic, Darius, you'll take the month of January to visit with other staff, students, and parents. Look into the labs, library, hook up to the Internet, and so on. Get a good feel for the Academy's people, style of learning, and the curriculum. The Academy's not a run-of-the-mill public school. When you get settled in, let me know. Soon after, I'll give you the grand tour of the Stanton campus. Merry Christmas!"

"Merry Christmas to you all, too," Darius said, ending the call.

# — 7 —

THREE hours before sunrise in late January 1934, twenty-eight members of the Sanada clan had gathered up their personal possessions, basic tools, preserved food and garden seeds. Everyone, young and old, had agreed that they would rather escape Osaka, risking imprisonment, torture, and death, than continue living as serfs for Imperial Japan. When their first steps had been taken, they saw the faintest light of dawn shining on them that morning from the eastern horizon.

The air was a chilly thirty-five degrees, and dark gray puffy clouds were slowly passing overhead. In spaces between the clouds, a silvery moon, stars, and planets shined through, guiding and lighting the streets for the intrepid clan. Wind blew stinging sleet into their bare faces.

Months before leaving, their leader, Kenshin Sanada, had made a reconnaissance of rugged, unsettled regions in Japan, where they might resettle.

When he returned from each expedition, he called together the adults to meet in secret late at night. They talked quietly, openly, about their family history. How to protect their beliefs, religious preferences, customs, and traditions and obtain justice and happiness for their children and grandchildren. But mostly, they discussed how to live as free people.

They formed an oral pact to escape Osaka, to hide for an uncertain period of time and seek an unknown future, hoping that one day they would come out of hiding to help reform Japan.

Once satisfied that he had found a suitable location, Kenshin divided the route into even segments for progress, rest, and recuperation. He then ventured back and forth on the route, with six trustworthy allies, securing and hiding provisions, mainly food and clothing, at the end of each segment. At the final cache, he compiled food, gardening tools, blankets, yarn, leather for assorted uses, and fabric for making and mending clothes.

When Kenshin had the escape route and provisions in place, he set about planning the best strategy, policies, and a departure date.

On that fateful night, he collected his family—in utmost secrecy. Kenshin had each adult and teen memorize the route they would take, only telling them of one segment at a time. He also gave them a false route, in case anyone was captured. They carried—hidden in their clothes—a sheathed Japanese tanto dagger for personal defense, and self-sacrifice in case of discovery. They would not betray their clan if captured or tortured.

He ordered all teens and adults to walk alone, as individuals, in a long strung-out line. If accosted, the adults and trailing teens were on a mercy trip to care for sick relatives. All families would travel along different streets in the city to help prevent guards from recognizing them as a group.

Dressed as peasants in varied, dark clothing, they slowly, secretly, escaped on foot from Osaka, their ancient homeland. They carried their belongings in shouldered rustic baskets and cloth packs. Men, women, and teens escaped, some carrying infants. Adults, children, teens, and the elderly, all who were fit for the rigors, stepped away unseen through dim light and silence.

Once they reached the countryside and were safely out of the city, Kenshin drew the clan together in a secluded apple orchard at the end of the first segment. The moon was down. Dim light from the heavens shone through passing wispy clouds.

Kenshin ordered the adults to take a full accounting of all members. Missing from their number were: one fourteen-year-old girl, Haruko, and one nine-year-old girl, Sachiko. "We wait here and rest for one hour," Kenshin commanded. "Be prepared to fight or flee on my orders. Everyone, draw your knives. Scouts, expand into the perimeter." The clan scattered around, crouching down to hide in silence and balancing gut-felt fear of discovery, torture, and death with a firm resolve to protect their family and live free.

Moments later, Haruko stumbled out of the brush along the orchard edge, and walked, heavily overburdened, into their midst. She had Sachiko in a fireman's carry across her shoulders. The nine-year-old's body had been mutilated horribly and was bleeding out. Haruko's parents and Kenshin helped ease the child's body down to lie across her mother and father's laps. She was still alive. With her last breath, Sachiko looked at her parents and mouthed, "I kept our secret." Her parents and their family choked, hugged, trembled, and wept in silence.

Haruko, through streaming tears, told Kenshin, "Sachiko and I fell back from the adults. We were traveling together until we heard crowds of rowdy, drunken, soldiers coming our way. We decided to split up, walk on different streets, and each find a hiding place as soon as possible. I hid in a garbage cart and covered myself as deep as I could. The soldiers passed by, and didn't know I was there. I waited and waited, until well after the soldiers were gone. I crawled out and searched for little Sachiko." The teenager fought to breathe through immense upheavals in her chest from crying. "She had hidden in a garbage cart, too, but a neighborhood dog sniffed her out for the soldiers. I found her clinging onto a light pole, trying to stand and walk. I carried her here as quickly as I could."

Overcome with exhaustion and extreme sorrow, Haruko collapsed into her parents' arms.

"You are the noblest of warriors," Kenshin said softly, affectionately to Haruko, while hugging her parents and Sachiko's parents. "We are proud of you for saving our family."

A pause.

"Everyone, help bury our precious, innocent Sachiko, in the best grave we can make for her. We will continue our journey after praying for her soul."

Through the dim light of dawn, they snuck single file, as before, out of the apple orchard into a gossamer-thin fog. They resumed their northeasterly trek, segment by segment, skirting towns and cities on remote footpaths, unknown to many locals.

At one point, they followed a high, meandering ridge on a ledge of rock. Takashi, one of the elders, rolled his ankle on a loose stone, lost his balance, and fell to his death into the deep, rocky gorge. His wife, Fumiko, had been right behind him. The clan stopped, and those nearby, hugged and consoled Fumiko. Kenshin walked back from the lead

44

position to hug her and express his deepest sorrow for Takashi. The clan sat, grieved, and sobbed quietly for some time. Then, at Kenshin's signal, they continued walking.

One morning, a third tragedy visited the clan. A young couple, Tasuke and his wife, Ishi, were expecting their first child. Ishi was still early in her pregnancy. For two days, spots of blood appeared intermittently on her underclothes. She consulted Inu, a physician. After examining Ishi, Inu prescribed rest. When Inu told Kenshin about Ishi's condition, he informed everyone that they would all rest at this location for some time, hoping and praying that Ishi's bleeding would stop. However, the bleeding worsened. The following morning, Ishi miscarried, had unstoppable hemorrhaging, and died. Losing Ishi and their baby, hit Tasuke hard. The clan gathered around the young, grief-stricken husband. The men and women hugged him, prayed with him, and gave countless assurances that they would help him through grief and recovery. The next morning, Kenshin organized a burial party. At midday, the clan said a final goodbye to Ishi and her unborn baby.

From the start of the journey, Kenshin had employed his six trusted allies as scouts, and they knew the whole route. Three scouts went ahead of the main party, and three hung behind, on the lookout for threats, especially military camps and mobile patrols.

Late one evening, a forward scout rushed back to the clan and reported to Kenshin, "A patrol of six soldiers caught us by surprise. I slipped away unseen. They're interrogating the other two scouts now."

Kenshin turned to the clan and said, "Would one of you give me your tanto knife?"

45

Haruko stepped forward, "Use mine, and God bless you."

Kenshin bowed to her, took the knife, and slid it under his belt next to his own tanto. He and the scout rushed to the interrogation scene. Kenshin, pretending to be drunk, stumbled forward, mumbling the traditional Japanese song "Kokiriko Bushi." Swaying and staggering, he got within arm's length of the soldiers, which allowed the captured scouts to stand and take a few steps away.

The Japanese patrol leader pressed the muzzle of his Nambu pistol on Kenshin's forehead, and ordered, "Back up, drunken old peasant! You'll all be shot for treason! Starting with you." Instantly, Kenshin transformed into a whirling, samurai warrior. The knives in his hands severed the leader's head from his body. In the next heartbeat, he dispatched the two soldiers standing on either side in the same manner. Taking their cue from Kenshin, the scouts instantly attacked and killed the other three soldiers without a sound. The scouts rolled the bodies into a gully, covering them with tree bark and limbs. Then, they all returned to the waiting clan.

Kenshin, bowing, returned the tanto knife to Haruko and said to everyone, "We must not waste time here. Follow us quietly, at a fast pace." He and the forward scouts turned and led the clan to rush away into the black night.

The remainder of their journey proceeded with no crises.

The Sanada clan walked for several months, stealthily and often in darkness with dim light from the stars, planets, and moon.

They paused to rest at times.

In addition to eating the cached provisions, they caught fish from streams, gathered edible wild grains, and discretely took bits of food from farmlands. In the worst weather, they took shelter under trees, in caves, and under rock ledges. They avoided remote farms in the countryside, rural villages, and small cities, skirting far around the large metropolitan areas of Tokyo and Yokohama on the eastern coast.

Their destination: the Japanese Hida Range of mountains, a sparsely populated wilderness near the western coast of Honshu, Japan's main island.

They arrived in the foothills of the Hida Range at noon in heavy fog and drizzling rain. After a rest, they walked on a narrow animal trail bordered by a stream. Up and up they trekked, crossing and recrossing the stream over boulders and logs, clambering at last onto a wide rock ledge. Several feet away, was a narrow, secluded entrance to a large cave. By good fortune, the cave had an opening in the ceiling above the back wall. This natural vent allowed a constant flow of fresh air from the entrance, and channeled smoke from fires for cooking, drying, bathing, and warmth.

Partway up a rugged mountain in Japan, the Sanada clan dared to live, with their God-given rights, according to their beliefs and ideals.

Kenshin called the clan together at the mouth of the cave and asked all to join in a devout prayer. "My family, thanks be to God for bringing us safely out of Osaka, a city-turned-war-machine, to our new home in the wilderness."

"We have vowed to:

"Observe our commandments from God, and the sacred rites and ceremonies.

"Protect as unalienable our rights from God: freedom of religion, speech, assembly, and the right to keep and bear arms. Keep our children and elderly safe and comfortable.

47

Protect everyone in our families from harm. Fight against all enemies. Destroy them, if need be. Welcome friends and relatives into this life. One day, build a better Japan, and a better world. My family, we embarked on a frightful journey for freedom, marked as deserters and traitors. We knew at any moment we might be captured, tortured most cruelly, and killed.

"Our innocent little Sachiko, surrendered her life on the first day to save us all from a horrible fate. We lost a husband, Takashi, in an accident, and a wife, Ishi, in a miscarriage. God rest their souls.

"We walked day and night, ill-clothed, in miserable weather, full of fear. We harbored in our hearts and souls the fervent desire for a better life for ourselves as individual men and women, for our children, for our children's children. For Japan. For the world.

"Throughout time, many other freedom-seeking people, the world over, have risked everything for self-determination.

"Many suffered horrible deaths, defeat, and slavery.

"We achieved where most failed.

"My family, today is not the end of our journey, or suffering. Only God knows what lies ahead for us. We pray for the strength to prevail against hardship, illness, injury, and threats from enemies.

"Thank you, my family, for trusting me to bring us here.

"It is a good place.

"May this mountain, and God above, give us safety and security now, in a world consumed by hellish war."

"Amen," the clan said reverently together.

Far from Osaka, the Sanada clan lived, illegally, secretly, in an unmarked cave east and high above Toyama Gulf.

48

Every day at dawn, teams of twelve plus one, took turns walking in secrecy down the mountain. All day they foraged for food, plowed, weeded, raked, planted, and tended their crops along a tributary of the Himekawa River. At twilight they walked back up the mountain, carrying the day's harvest on their backs.

Their life was full of the utmost caution. Every second was dangerous. Yet, they lived as a free clan, and they would have life no other way.

# — 8 —

FOURTEEN years had passed by since the girls were
born.

On a Saturday morning in July, Stella arrived to stay
with Hana at her grandparents' country home.

After lunch, they practiced soccer on the front lawn
until 3:00 p.m. Today, the girls were determined to train
both feet to shoot the ball equally well, as the distance and
circumstances on the field demanded. Again and again,
from different locations, they took turns driving the ball
into the goal.

"Yeah! Yeah," Stella shouted after her last successful
shot.

Hana followed with, "Woo-hoo! Yeah! Stella, great
practice! This fall, we're gonna have a winning season at
the Academy."

Then, they went to the garden, where the grandparents
were working. Raked leaves, hoed and pulled weeds, vines
and stems from the garden's edge into a large pile. Used the
wheelbarrow to move decaying material to the compost bin.

Stella had helped tend this garden every growing season
for as long as Hana could remember. And she and her
mother, Olivia, had often stayed over at Hana's house in
town and here at her grandparents' house in the country.
Many weekends and during school breaks, off and on,

Hana also stayed at Stella's house in town with her mother and father. They were family.

The sun had been unseasonably hot and shining brightly through hazy clouds all day, burning their skin. The air became thick with humidity.

"It's terribly hot. Don't think I can work much longer in the garden," Grandad Jonas said while helping the girls load the garden debris into the compost bin.

Grandma Audra added, "Yeah, for sure, my clothes and gloves, even my socks and sneakers, are soaked with sweat. Let's drink a cup of cold water from the cooler and pack it in for today."

Hana said, "I'm totally wiped out."

An enormous, cannon-loud thunderclap startled them mightily. The lightning strike, close by, signaled a violent storm was approaching rapidly.

The gardeners looked at the sky all around.

Grandad Jonas noted, "A direct hit on the Taegels' giant white pine, our neighbor to the southwest. Hope Archer, Hera and their alpine goats are okay. Now, it's flaming like a monstrous candle. Look at that blazing tree! Less than a half mile from here!

"Run to the house, now!" Grandad Jonas shouted over a second lightning strike and horrifically loud thunderclap.

"Run as fast as you can, everybody. Go, go, go! Come on, Grandad," Grandma Audra shouted as she led the way.

Hana and Stella followed her out of the garden. Grandad Jonas trailed. The sunlit day turned into the darkest night with fast-moving charcoal clouds covering the sun, and overspreading the land.

All of a sudden, a high-speed west wind roared through the valley, whipped and thrashed trees, filled the air with sticks, leaves and dust. Marble-sized hail fell by bucket loads from charcoal-black, swirling clouds, now tinged with pink and green.

Hana saw the grassy path ahead bouncing hailstones everywhere. Stella held her hand over her head as a shield against the pounding hail.

When the gardeners reached the safety of the porch, the hailstorm slowed, stopped, and faded into a torrential rainstorm. Giant raindrops fell furiously from the sky, splashed wildly on impact. Visibility was a scant ten feet. The front yard became a shallow lake filled with floating hailstones.

To the west, a jagged white-yellow streak of lightning ripped down from turbulent dark clouds. Instantly, the ancient burr oak tree on Winston and Mary Hancock's dairy farm ignited. Huge exploded, airborne limbs fell out of the sky, burning and smoking to the ground.

Thunder blasted deafeningly loud.

"Sure hope the Hancocks are okay. Glad we're on the porch. Not much more we can do," Grandad Jonas said.

"Just now IM'd the Hancocks and Taegels, 'Anybody hurt there?' Waiting." Grandma Audra shouted. "Good, both farmers are fine, wondering about us."

"I'm okay," Hana said.

"Me too," Stella answered.

Grandad Jonas chipped in, "I feel lucky to have made it here in time. Woof! Glad we're all good."

"Where'd that thunderstorm come from?" Grandma Audra asked, still short of breath from running.

Hana said, "Wow, a thunderstorm is so fascinating! Nature's force. So fast, so powerful and fierce. It nearly blew me over. And the hail beat down on my head."

"Yeah, no kidding. If I wasn't so hard-headed, I'd be a bloody mess," Stella said, laughing along with Hana, at her self-deprecating humor.

"We're lucky we ran to the house when we did. Standing in an open area, like the garden, a lightning strike can kill people," Grandad Jonas said. "Thunder and lightning: you don't touch metal buildings, step in wet grass, and you get under a dry shelter immediately."

"I left my gloves and garden tools in the wheelbarrow!" Hana exclaimed.

"Mine are next to yours," Stella said.

"It's fine. You had no time to go back and grab 'em," Grandad Jonas said. "And, I left my wicker basket with all my tools on the boulder by the arbor. When the storm's over tomorrow, you guys can get it all. We'll clean up the tools, dry 'em and wipe 'em down with linseed oil, so they don't rust."

"Yeah. Alright," Hana said.

"Oops!" Grandma Audra said. "We just lost power. Quick. Let's go inside and set out the oil lamps, candles and flashlights. It's already evening time. This power outage could last all night. If it's not back on by morning, we'll start up the generator."

With the emergency lighting in place, they worked together to prepare a dinner of salad greens, cold lunchmeat sandwiches, condiments, and Grandma Audra's homemade lemonade.

Hana had just finished eating her dinner, when she said, "Ooowee! I'm really tired."

Then, she yawned wide and long.

"Me too," Stella said, breaking into a wide yawn and holding back laughter.

"You two've been nodding all through dinner," Grandma Audra said, laughing. "You've got to be tired from morning chores, soccer practice, and working in the garden."

"I'm finished for the day, too," Grandad Jonas confessed. "Mowing the lawn and orchard, garden work, racing against the raging storm. I'm hitting the hay soon as we get the table cleaned up. What do you say, Grandma?"

"Yeah, I'm for it," she replied.

"Excuse us," Hana said. "We're going to bed now."

Hana and Stella stood, gave both grandparents a tight hug and kissed their cheeks.

On the way out of the kitchen, Stella said dreamily, "I'm so lucky. I love you both to pieces."

"We love you so much, Stella. Sweet dreams," they said together.

"There's a flashlight on the nightstands," Grandma Audra said.

"I will clean up the table," Grandad Jonas said. "And turn in."

The girls walked slowly, tiredly up the stairs, cleaned up in the bathroom, pulled on their pajamas and crawled into their twin beds.

Later, Grandma Audra checked on them. Hana was fast asleep, head under her pillow, with no covers on. Stella had covered herself head to toe in a comforter, and was sound asleep.

Grandma Audra checked that the flashlights worked and closed the door.

# — 9 —

STELLA woke up at dawn the next morning and lay under the covers of her bed with her PJs on, head poking out on the pillow. She listened to raindrops pitter-pattering on the roof and windows.

A solemn spell passed.

Looking through the window on her side of the bedroom, Stella muttered, "I miss you, Daddy." Tears welled up in her eyes and ran down her cheeks. She squeezed her eyelids shut, her breath choppy as she sobbed, weeping openly.

Hana threw off her covers, rushed to Stella's bedside, and knelt on the floor. "My dear sister. I'm so sorry, Stella." She put her arms lovingly around her sister's shoulders, hugging her tight. She rested her head on Stella's chest, listening to her fast-paced heartbeat pumping with much sorrow, *Thump thump . . . thump thump . . . thump, thump.*

"My dearest friend, I love you," Hana said. "Your Daddy was so kind, so loving. Always ready to help. . . I've loved him, always." Raising her head to look into the young girl's eyes, Hana said, "Your Daddy is in heaven and very proud of you, sister." Stella wrapped her arms tightly around her sister's neck. Tears poured from their eyes, ran in streams together across their shoulders. The girls swayed slowly back and forth as they felt the greatest sadness and cried as if their hearts would break.

Seventeen months ago, on a Friday morning in spring, when Stella was twelve years old, her first year in the Academy, halfway around the world, her father, Captain Jedediah Louis Young, US Army, 10th Mountain Division, 2$^{nd}$ Brigade, died in battle in Kandahar Province, Afghanistan.

Early Saturday evening, Olivia, hearing the knock on the front door, peered through the glass to see who was there. Backed away, and screamed loudly. "Oh no! No, no, no! Not my Jed! Please God, not my love! Not my life! Oh my God, no, please, no!"

Stella raced from her bedroom, where she was reading. She hugged Mom tight, they both sobbed loudly, raining tears.

Stella was now an inch taller than Mom.

When Jed was first deployed, Olivia had told Stella that this horrible news could come to their home. They prayed together nightly that it would not, and for Daddy's safe return.

She explained to Stella what would happen, though, if that day came. Unthinkable. Unbearable. They would need each other more than they could ever imagine.

Stella put Mom's arm around her left shoulder and held her hand. She wrapped her right arm tight around Mom's waist, and guided Mom to the couch. Both sat there, hugging, crying, and shaking uncontrollably. Stella's tears poured out so heavily, she could barely see. Eyelids swollen. She kissed Mom's cheeks and forehead and hugged her very tight.

Stella stood and slow-walked back to the front door, waited there, weak-kneed, tears streaming on her face. Feeling she might get sick or faint at any second.

Her hand reached out with a nervous movement. Turned the knob. Pulled the door until fully open.

Mom was sobbing loudly. With a side-glance, Stella saw Mom rocking slowly back and forth on the sofa, hands on her cheeks. Staring straight ahead.

Then, Mom stood next to Stella, stiffened up, arms wrapped around her. Loving mother and daughter braced for the worst.

They looked through thick tears to find outside Evan and Isa Sanada, their parish priest, Brother Blaine, and three uniformed army officers.

"Pardon me, are you Olivia Young?" the lead officer said in a kind voice.

"I am," Olivia answered.

"Thank you, Mrs. Young. May we enter?" the lead officer asked.

"Yes," Olivia answered, feeling weaker with every passing second.

Once the notification team had entered, Evan closed the front door, then led everyone into the living room.

The lead officer said softly, "Let's all sit down."

Evan and Isa sat on the sofa, either side of Stella and Olivia. The others took the love seat and wing chairs.

"Mrs. Olivia Young, I am Major Benjamin Sawyer. I served with Jedediah on mission assignments, recon, and combat patrols in Afghanistan."

"Yes, Jed often mentioned you in his FaceTime calls, letters, and texts," Olivia said quietly, without emotion.

Major Sawyer continued, "We always talked of our families back home. He spoke lovingly, of you, and Stella, and your extended family. We shared our latest family pictures every week. Attended religious services together. Prayed to God that we end this war. Send all our soldiers home." He took a deep breath, then continued, "As Jed lay dying, his last words to me and the medic were, 'Please send all my love to my wife, Olivia, and my daughter, Stella. Tell them, I will wait for them on the other side.'"

Olivia knew these words were from her Jed, and not made up. He had told her that, if the time came when he had to say a last goodbye to her and Stella, it would be with these exact words.

Major Sawyer took another deep breath, then continued, "With me today are Evan and Isa Sanada, your relatives, Brother Blaine, your parish priest, and my assistants, Lieutenant Harold Blakely and Lieutenant Moodus Garvey. The commanding general of the Army wants me to express his deep regret that your husband, Jedediah Louis Young, was killed in action in Kandahar, Afghanistan, yesterday. He and his unit were clearing out an enemy stronghold when they were ambushed. Captain Young selflessly returned fire, covering his team. He pulled three badly wounded men to safety, before suffering a mortal wound. The commander extends his deepest sympathy to you and your family in your loss."

The other words said by Major Sawyer, sincere, comforting, official, and reassuring, were lost in the fog of overwhelming grief.

Major Sawyer and the lieutenants expressed their sincerest condolences to Olivia and Stella, and all present.

Assured them of 24/7 on-call service from Major Sawyer, for any concern.

Evan led the army officers, with tears in their eyes, to the front door. Thanked them. Said, "We will be in touch." Closed the door and returned to the sofa.

The little family gathering stood and tightly embraced Olivia and Stella. Brother Blaine O'Neil, OFM, a modest Franciscan friar, approached, and stretched his exceptionally long arms wide to embrace them all, quivering, overcome with sorrow. They cried and trembled and cried and swayed and cried more.

Silence reigned for a time.

"Let us bow our heads and pray." Brother Blaine said, while tightening his arms around the tiny mission. Lifted his head to heaven, his heart pounding so heavily with sorrow he felt it might burst. Closed his eyes. Took a deep breath. Began with a soft and gentle voice.

"In nomine Patris et Filii et Spiritu Sancti. Amen.

"Lord God Almighty, maker of heaven and earth. You gave us Your Son, Jesus Christ, whose death on the cross saved us from eternal death—that would have separated us from you, our God, forever.

"Our loving husband, father, captain, and brother, Jedediah Louis Young, left earth yesterday, a valiant soldier, who perished in war. Forgive him of any sins. Welcome his soul into your arms. Grant him peace in heaven forever.

"Bestow upon Olivia, his loving wife, and upon Stella, his loving daughter, your grace, now and throughout life. Grant them, and all gathered here in your name, the courage to continue their own life's journey.

"Our life on earth is, naturally, a crooked journey, fraught with suffering, pain, and sorrow, but also blessed

61

with joy, happiness, and your abounding love. The choices we make along the twisting, gnarled path make us who we are in your sight, Lord.

"You gave us life and blessed it with faith, hope, and charity, liberty, and the pursuit of happiness. God, bless us with your grace. Cloak this precious family in your love. Guide them. And bless them.

"The beautiful memory of Jedediah shall remain in our hearts and minds forever. Amen."

For the remainder of the evening and way into the night, the little mission sat hugging, crying, talking in the Youngs' living room. One after another, they recalled many things they remembered about Jed. He seemed to be sitting in the living room with them.

His preference for getting things just right. He gave and gave to people in need. He always asked youngsters he met where they were headed, what their life goals were. Coaxed them to do their best in all things. Reminded them to stay away from bad habits, bad things, and bad people. He did the same for Stella and Hana, which always made them smile lovingly. His spontaneous gift of blue and sarcastic humor, drew sheepish smiles among the experienced, and sometimes shocked folks who didn't know him well.

God's blessings came onto them as the night wore on. Fresh tears poured from their eyes. More and more, each was moved by loving thoughts about Jed, pride in his achievements, his love and devotion to Olivia, Stella, his mom and dad, all the family, friends, and God.

As the sun rose in the east to herald a new day, the entire mission lay asleep, sprawling on the sofas, soft wing chairs, or the carpeted floor.

Brother Blaine awoke first, with a start. Sat up from his make-do bed on the floor. "It's Sunday!" he mouthed silently, checking his watch. "Ten after five. I have to say Mass in twenty minutes!"

Buckled on his sandals. Brushed lint and wrinkles out of his brown habit of penance with his hands. Adjusted the cincture around his waist. Paused, as his fingers touched each knot, to solemnly recall his vows of poverty, chastity, and obedience.

He found Evan asleep, curled into the sofa's arm. Touched his shoulder, while putting his index finger on his lips for silence. Whispered in Evan's ear, "I have to say Mass at 5:30 for St. Ann's Parish. I'll return as soon as I can."

Brother Blaine left the house through the front door without disturbing the others.

JAPANESE forces attacked Pearl Harbor, on the island of Oahu, Hawaii. just before 08:00 on Sunday morning, December 7, 1941. They destroyed nearly 20 American ships and 300 aircraft. And 2,400 American soldiers and civilians died in the attack.

The next day, the United States of America declared war on Japan.

— 10 —

THREE years, three months and 29 days later, at 0800 Saturday morning, April 5, 1945, Major Craig Alexander Bradley walked casually into a Japanese American internment camp in a western state, the third and last camp on his short list of well-researched camps to visit.

Major Bradley had volunteered for a top-secret mission to help end the war with Japan. The major had served his country loyally with distinction for years, lately flying P-38s in Europe.

He was in this camp to find the best copilot for the mission.

In the depths of his soul, he believed that, throughout history, leaders and governments had been necessary for civilized life and protection and defense of people, societies and cultures. But over and over again, leaders and governments had bungled national and international affairs. Or became tyrants and stripped God-given rights from the people they ruled.

At great risk, freethinking people had to carve out a good life, somewhere, somehow, often clandestinely, in defiance of their rulers.

Now, war was worldwide, again, threatening civilization, human life, all life.

Major Bradley had a personal stake in this mission. On February 19, 1945, he and his wife, Stella Bradley, received the tragic news that their twenty-three-year-old son, 1st Lieutenant Thomas Nelson Bradley, had been killed on the first day of the Battle of Okinawa. "This horrible war must be brought to its end," he vowed, once again, silently, pursing his lips.

The day was sunny, mildly warm, with a chilly breeze from the northwest. Week-old, muddied, blotchy snow covered the ground.

A late spring was unfolding.

Major Bradley walked through the heavily guarded, barb-wired compound. Looked at kitchens, dining areas, outdoor toilets, laundry facilities, housing, hospital, parade ground, guard towers. He wanted to get a sense for the place, who was here, and who could best help him.

Japanese men, women, and children, some in family groups, walked about on errands, to visit friends, or for physical exercise.

A sign for "Apartment Family Housing" pointed to a large horse stable with 12'x16' horse stalls inside. Bradley looked in an open door. A single light bulb on an electric wire was nailed on a ceiling joist over each stall to light a family's whitewashed, cramped room. The inside of the barn and surrounding area reeked of dried horse dung and urine.

A small wood stove by one wall served for cooking and heating in winter. Insulation was tar paper on the roof and exterior walls. Poor ventilation year round. Shared bathrooms, showers, and laundry rooms were in separate buildings.

There was no privacy.

"What have we done to these loyal, American citizens?" Bradley pondered quietly.

At the baseball field, in the center of the camp, the major sat down on crude bleachers, halfway to first. A group of energetic young lads, all Japanese, were playing baseball. They had, surprisingly, professional-grade equipment and uniforms provided by the camp commander and company soldiers. Family and friends, especially young girls, sat in the bleachers nearer to home plate, loudly cheering on the players.

Bradley was immediately impressed by the pitcher for the Oakland team. The coach had installed him for the final three innings. His style was smooth from the first to the last step. Rhythmic. Powerful. Three up and three down, all strikeouts, and from the look of it—curveballs, knuckleballs, and fast balls. Driven skillfully into the strike zone. The catcher's mitt had to be burning. Pitcher and catcher were a great battery.

Bradley had been a catcher for the Army's West Point Black Knights before being commissioned as a second lieutenant. He was good at suggesting, signaling, and reading pitches.

Game over, Oakland 5 to Berkeley 1. The crowd and players erupted, "Hurray," and congratulated the winning team.

Bradley noticed that the young man, the ace pitcher, was about the same age as his late son, Thomas. That thought took his breath away, and tears of sadness welled up in his eyes. He prayed for his son's soul, his own loss, and felt deep sorrow for his wife and two daughters, who were grieving at the family home, back east, alone. Wiped his eyes dry on his sleeve.

A middle-aged Japanese woman walked from the outfield along first baseline toward Craig. Her thick, long black hair was roughly styled in a traditional vertical mage, a bun, held in place with a comb up front and several hair-sticks through the sides. Her badly worn shoes, dress and sweater were clean, but drab and ill-fitting. She carried two bamboo steamers with rice hanging from a milkmaid's yoke.

"Ancient ways merging with modern times here," Bradley mused.

Her walk and bearing told Bradley she was accustomed to a better life before being sent to this concentration camp. "So sad what our government has done to the Japanese people. Our own American citizens," he reflected.

The woman stopped in front of him and said: "Good morning, Major. Can I help you?"

"Good morning to you. Yes, you can. What is your name?"

"I am Sakura Sanada. My husband is Akiro Sanada. We are from Osaka, Japan, originally. Our ancestors came to America in 1865 and worked on the transcontinental railroad in Utah and Nevada. By 1928, my husband and I had worked hard, saved money, and created a national clothing goods business in San Francisco.

"Today, we are interned in this camp. We have lost everything. We do not live with regret. We made America our new homeland. We are American citizens. We will rebuild our company in America, Sanada Clothiers, one day soon. God willing."

68

Bradley had been briefed on the Sanada family by headquarters when he arrived at the camp and explained his purpose for visiting. Their son, George Washington Sanada, 24 years old, was first on the list of prospects for the major's mission.

"I'm looking for a bright, patriotic young man, who can help me end the war with Japan."

Sakura thought about the major's stark interest for a while. Out of the blue! Many of her relatives remained in Japan. For years she had corresponded with them regularly by mail. She learned that one family disappeared years ago, never to be heard from again. Then, all correspondence with Japanese relatives ended on February 19, 1942.

Now, she had no idea where the clan was living. No idea of marriages. New children. Who had died. Who was serving in the Japanese military. Nothing. And at present her country of origin was at war with her adopted country.

Sakura was a beautiful, smart, and talented woman. She spoke Korean, Chinese, Vietnamese, English, and Japanese fluently. She could do anything, far better than most American women and men could do. Her love for her husband, for her son, for her family in America, and in Japan, was sacrosanct. Yet, America was her country. America was her homeland.

In camp, Sakura, her family, and friends, kept up on world and national news as best they could by reading newspapers provided by officers at headquarters. Untold numbers of lives were lost and mangled every day. So much of human life was at stake the world over — all the hopes and dreams for mankind's innocents, the littlest children alive today and those not yet conceived.

"Major, what's your name?"

"Craig Alexander Bradley. Please call me Craig, Mrs. Sanada," he answered politely.

She had powerful, knowing eyes. A strong woman. "Call me Sakura," she said directly. She lifted her gaze from the major and looked to the eastern horizon, where the sun rises.

Sakura began, "Dawn signals a new day for our world. To live, to believe in God, to till the soil, to harvest the grain, to bake bread, to cook family meals, to weave wool and cotton, to bathe, to love, to birth newborns, to struggle, to heal, to pray, to fight, to die. Never-ending 'fields to plow and plant,' as God made the lifework of humans.

"Every dawn is a new beginning. One can never know what it portends. We do our best. Sometimes it's less than what we should do, because of circumstances beyond our control. We accept what comes, work with our fate, hampered as we are here. Armed with our trust in other people, our strength, our hopes and dreams, and our faith in God," Sakura said tranquilly.

She paused there.

Thoughts of her family in Japan, and here in America, her friends, her husband, Akiro, their son, George; their destiny, and the grave uncertainty about the major's interest. All streamed like a murky, tepid, wild river through her mind, her body, and whirl-pooled deep into her soul.

She shivered, though the chill breeze had ended when their talk began.

Solitary tears swelled in her eyes. A droplet flowed slowly down her right cheek to stop under her chin.

Time passed by.

Sakura's dark brown eyes looked deep into Bradley's.

"Major Bradley," Sakura continued, "we are proud descendants of Sanada Nobushige, leader of the samurai clan from medieval Japan. We honorably served Japanese people, society, and culture for hundreds of years. Samurai is a way of life, a code of behavior rich in tradition, honor, culture, beauty. Lives in our soul.

"We will not serve bad leaders or false causes. We will fight against enemies who are determined to destroy us and this great country.

"Wars begin and, in time, wars end.

"Let's hope and pray this war ends soon. And we win.

"In this camp? There is little Japanese Americans can do to help.

"Today, we Sanadas, do not espouse the code of warfare badly corrupted in our medieval past. Nor by the current Imperial military regime.

"Japan's leaders have twisted the art of the samurai.

"Retaliate, strike, kill, never negotiate, is their way.

"For what? Tyranny, greed, slavery, rape, murder, more territory, resources. The leaders have shamed us and destroyed relations with our friends and allies around the world.

"Is government any different here in America? For Japanese Americans now? I think not. For other Americans? I don't know. I question what I'm told, what I read, and what I see.

"We need less government. Too much government by hasty, indolent, cruel, or stupid people, explains where we are today.

"Look at this abominable place. We were rounded up from our homes, lost everything, shipped to one camp then another, and penned in here like cattle. Our clothes are the worse for wear. Food is not fresh and is not like food in Japan. Water smells. Unclean toilets and baths. Live in a horse stall.

"We are proud Japanese American citizens.

"No. We are proud American citizens!

"We named our only son, George Washington Sanada, after General George Washington, because, like a true samurai warrior, he risked all personal gain to lead the Continental Army, and fight for freedom against the British Empire. And won."

Sakura looked away.

Paused.

Sakura said slowly, softly, prophetically, "Last night, I dreamed that a mournful Holy Man ran into a cathedral with blazing torches in both hands. Hurled the firebrands onto the marble floor, where they spat fire and sparks, and billowed acrid, black smoke.

"'Beware! I am the herald of doom!' the Holy Man proclaimed stridently.

"A full moon shined in the dark heavens.

"The Holy Man raced to the altar, where a single metal goblet sat. With both hands, he grabbed up the giant, golden chalice.

"'Satan's rite conquers all in this darkening house of prayer! It is meant to be,' the Holy Man pronounced. His gaze was transfixed on the cup as he raised it to the heavens.

"Sinister forces controlled him. With extreme downward power, the chalice tipped in his fiendish hands and poured out more human blood than ever flowed in time.

"This monstrously hot, red bloodstream ran out the door and upon the land everywhere!

"'Oh my God, please help us,' I shouted, as I ran up to the altar.

"I tackled the Holy Man onto the Nero Portoro black marble floor of the sanctuary. He was diabolically possessed. Tortured. Riven-faced. Bleeding from his eyes, nose, ears, and mouth. Divided in purpose by opposite forces. Now one, now another spirit ripping into him. A horribly ravaged mind, body and soul.

"We struggled. Rolled back and forth on the floor. Dark thickening blood slathered everywhere. One man and one woman, struggled, sloshed around in a satanic, surreal sauté. Hoping to right the chalice for mankind's survival. Stanch the blood flow.

"An ugly power beyond us cut short our might. I took hold of his forearm to stop the chalice from pouring out any more blood. To no avail. The thick, boiling blood poured out with even more energy. Flowed into a hundred streams. Nothing could stop it. All life was flowing away. I was trembling, writhing, and screaming.

"My husband awoke to put his loving arms around me. Hugged me calm. The nightmare slowly faded away.

"George remained asleep, thank God.

"Time stood still.

"Hear my call, Major Bradley.

"Pikes, arrows, and swords of the past were deadly. The guns and bombs of today are horrific, on a monstrous scale. What lies ahead? We don't know. We can only hope to do the right things. And pray to be saved from an awful end. We want to live, do good deeds, make things, fix stuff, plow the fields, plant, and harvest the grains, create beautiful art, music and inventions, right wrongs civilly, bring children and grandchildren into the world, care for parents and grandparents, and love one another, again and again. As God intended."

Time passed by.

Sakura's tears had dried. Her chin was set. She breathed deeply.

"Major Bradley, I've said my piece, as we Americans say. Thank you for hearing me out. Follow me to our place in camp, where you will meet my husband, Akiro, and our son, George. And then we will talk about your request over dinner," Sakura said.

## — 11 —

ᕼARDING'S cell phone lit up at 8:30 a.m. with a
FaceTime call, as planned, from Darius James. He
immediately said, "Perfect timing, Darius. What's your
schedule look like? Can you do the tour today, 9:00 to
2:00-ish?"

"Yes, Mr. Harding. I was thinking I'd meet you at your
office in 15 minutes or so."

"It's a warm, sunny, winter day. Perfect. School's
underway. See you then. Bring an appetite," Harding said.

"Okay," Darius signed off.

When Darius had walked up from the Stanton Cottage,
Harding was waiting by his two-door, green 1960 Studebaker
Lark Regal. Firmly shook the young man's hand. Harding
said, "Great to see you in person, Darius. You got a good
handshake. Get in, and hold on."

Behind the wheel, Harding started, "My first car. Love
at first sight. I was discharged from the Army at Fort
Leonard Wood, Missouri, in '64, and headed home on a
Greyhound bus. She was a standout on a used car lot, in
East St. Louis, a stopover, across from the bus station.
Hopped off the coach, walked up to the salesman, and paid
for her in cash. Drove myself home. Ride's a little bumpy
now. Needs new shocks. Squishy breaks. But she runs
great. Only wants a regular change of Pennzoil, filters,

75

topped-off fluids, and grease jobs. How's the cottage suit you guys?"

"Cottage?" Darius replied. "It's a whole house! Great. Plenty of room for storage. Three bedrooms. Beautiful kitchen. We love to cook. Lots of lawn, shade trees for summer days, and walking trails. We love it. Thank you."

"So glad to hear that," Harding said. "You and Cherice are the first to live there since we had it renovated last year. Sat for years unused. That's the original Stanton home. Was built in 1775, beginning of our War of Independence. Not much more than four walls, a wooden floor, and a roof. Ebenezer Stanton left his wife, Anna, and joined George Washington for the Battle of Bunker Hill in Boston. I've got lots more on that subject for the tour, but first, how are Cherice and the baby?"

"According to her OBGYN specialist, as good as or better than can be expected. We got the names picked out, walk every day that's nice out. Set up the baby's room with furniture yesterday. Got a ton of baby stuff from a shower her mom gave two weeks back," Darius answered.

"Great news. First childbirth is full of mystery and scariness. Not much parents can do except pray, and let the little one come headfirst, hard-kicking and screaming into its world. We'll keep up the prayers for you guys," Harding said.

"Thanks. We're doing our best," Darius responded.

Harding, in no hurry, began the tour with a history lesson while they sat in the Lark.

"A few years ago, the Academy for Humanity was a fully developed, operating private school, with our unique curriculum, policies, faculty, students, and so on. Our campus was an old abandoned wool mill in Eridu Springs,

76

near St. Ann's Church. We were living hand to mouth, but proud of our little school. Then, a day came I will never forget.

"An elderly couple paid us a visit. I knew them from church, where they were very active in supporting families living in poverty. The gentleman asked Mrs. Graves if they could talk with the principal. We don't have a principal, so Mrs. Graves brought them to me. Marcus Ebenezer Stanton and his wife, Olivia McIntosh Stanton, wanted to help support our school.

"Marcus explained that he and Olivia read the Congressional Record regularly, and last week found the American Children's Learning Act in its pages. Marcus explained that the ACLA bill had opened all kinds of new ways to support children's learning across the country. Allowing America's citizens to invest in our future, our children.

"I had read the bill, too. In fact, on the previous evening, the Academy's board had discussed what this bill might mean for our school. We ended the meeting resolved to take advantage of the bill. At the next board meeting, I'd present a plan of action.

"The Stantons knew the ACLA, chapter and verse.

"Olivia, wife, mother, grandmother, and great-grandmother of the family, recalled the key elements. The bill created a huge public/private partnership. Tax-deductible donations for children's education were welcomed by billionaires and ordinary folks. The bill opened floodgates of philanthropy in America. Had the fewest regulations. Best of all, it granted tax-paid vouchers for America's children under eighteen years of age. Their parents and guardians had freedom to use the vouchers for home schooling, or to send their children to a charter, parochial, private, or public school of their choice."

"'About time,'" Olivia and Marcus declared together.

"Olivia added that eligible options for schools must demonstrate that their curriculum respects the United States Constitution and Bill of Rights, as written and intended by the Founding Founders. The facts of American history. The uniqueness in world history of the American heritage and laws. That America, from its beginning in the late 1700's, has come to recognize and welcome different ethnic and racial groups, and the historical, moral, and legitimate customs, and traditions of the people.

"They believed that the public schools of late had failed our children, especially poor and disadvantaged children, regardless of national origin, religion, or race. Fostered hostility between people instead of unity. Public schools had become political platforms for progressive, communist activists since the 1920s. There were too many complicit, stupid, or duped state and federal lawmakers and regulators. Degenerate teachers' unions and teachers. Self-righteous and ignorant school administrators. Wrecked our American education system. For what? More control by anti-American zealots over our children, their learning, their morals and character, and our nation's future.

"The activists were ripping out America's keystones: the Bible, Constitution and Bill of Rights. Mocking Judeo-Christian religions, morals, and values. Teaching the kids that America has been bad from the start. Racist. White elitism. Ill-founded to the core.

"The communists trash-mouthed factual, logical argument. Refused to allow differences of opinion. Scorned traditional beliefs. Showed contempt for practicing Jews,

78

Christians, and other faiths. Disavowed the rightful, beliefs, traditions, and customs of any groups they detested. Disrespected our American flag.

"Lately, they'd brought immoral fringe groups into schools to groom children for pedophilia, gross sexual perversion, sex trafficking, self-mutilation, non-binary or genderqueer sexual identity, medical and surgical sex changes, and lewdness as 'the new normal.'

"'And that's only my short list,'" Olivia concluded. 'No! We, and many Americans across this beautiful land, have had enough of their decadence! Too much, in fact! Tolerance of depravity is not a Christian virtue and is not mentioned in the Constitution. No! We believe in the Constitution and the Bill of Rights, charity, justice, mercy, prudence, honesty, and the rule of law.'"

"I thanked the Stantons and said that we saw the plight of schools in America the same way.

"Marcus acknowledged that Olivia has always been better with words: very direct, thorough, and truthful. They had talked about this issue many times over their seventy-five-year marriage.

"Marcus explained that they were the heirs of the local Stanton Family Farm. With this new legislation, they wanted to give the land, farmhouse, barn, all the outbuildings, plus a substantial monetary sum, to the Academy for Humanity. They'd watched this small school become the most dynamic opportunity for learning anywhere.

"Their two grandsons and three granddaughters graduated from the Academy in recent years. Their grandsons became fine young men and their granddaughters became very successful young women. They were so proud of what the grandchildren became as adults.

"'Congratulations Mr. Harding!' Marcus said. 'This gift, and all the other donations it may help you garner over time, is to help grow and develop the Academy for Humanity into the premier learning platform for American youth.'"

"Mrs. Grace was in tears. She hugged Marcus and Olivia. I came close to tears myself. I thanked them both, hugged them, shook their hands. We talked about their wishes for the Academy. I explained that I would take care of all the paperwork on our end. Would have it ready for signing by the date they set. Then, I invited them to attend our upcoming Board of Directors meeting, the next evening."

Darius was awestruck, "Oh my God. What a beginning!"

"Yes, indeed. A miracle. Unbelievable generosity. Only in America. At the Directors meeting, we renamed our school, the Stanton Academy for Humanity. Its central theme became: Agriculture from the Dawn of Civilization. The kids call it Sustainable Farming on Steroids."

Harding hit the switch, the Lark's engine fired right up, and he pulled onto the pavement. Leonardo da Vinci Drive, called "the Loop," was a one-lane, three-mile roadway along the perimeter of a wide ellipse in the center of the campus. Students and faculty walked the Loop on their way to and from study areas. Resident students walked around the Loop to hang out after dinner on Saturdays and Sundays.

Harding was rolling on with a lead foot, Darius noticed. As a soon-to-be father, he suddenly became aware of his mortality. He held on tight with both hands.

"I'm taking you first to Glacier Pond," Harding announced. "Spring fed. Runs from northwest to southeast.

80

Narrow on both ends, wide in the middle. Drains headwaters for a stream at the southern end. Stretches over 100 acres. Crystal clear. Deepest hole is just over 95 feet. Great for landlocked salmon and trout fishing. Formed and filled by receding glaciers 15,000 years ago. A puddle compared to many such lakes around the world, but we got a nice, little one. There she is."

Harding turned a sharp right onto a dirt lane and made a hard stop with the Lark, and nearly launched both of them into the lake.

"Ever drive one of these contraptions, Darius?"

"No. But I was a valet for an upscale restaurant while in college. Drove everything on wheels. Never saw a car like this one. It's been a while since I drove a stick shift, but I could probably do okay."

"Alright with me. You drive for the rest of the tour, maybe always. I'll ride shotgun so we don't die on the campus tour," Harding said with a jovial laugh. Then, he picked up the office key from the floor and put it in the ashtray. It had flown off the front seat with the hard stop.

Darius cracked a smile. He was beginning to like Harding, the way he liked Isiah Goodman, early on. Both were old enough to be his grandfather. He wondered about that association. Darius never knew his biological grandparents, dad or mom, or any other blood relatives. He was always amazed at the joy in his wife's face when she saw her mom and dad again, after only a few days or weeks being away.

"Our child will have a family," he vowed to himself. "I can't wait to watch my family grow."

Harding continued talking while both got out of the car. "We're at the middle of the lake on the western

81

shore. Brought you here first, because the Walkers, Sam and Clara, husband and wife team, set up this site years ago for pond science. They're both accomplished chemists and biologists who left high-paying jobs in industry. Now, they bring true science to our students. We matched their previous salaries after seeing what they could do for us.

"Mr. Harding, maybe give me an impression of *how* they work with the kids?"

"Better, here come the Walkers." Harding introduced them. Right off, Sam and Clara said how glad they were to meet Darius, and how pleased they were to have him on the faculty. Then, Harding asked them to talk about the content and style of their work with students.

"Sure," Clara started. "And please, Darius, come visit with us in the lab and field, any time. No advance notice needed. Watching the kids in action is incredible. Right now, they're working in the lab analyzing pond substrate samples they gathered yesterday.

"We provide six perspectives on *Applied Science: A Case Study of Glacier Pond*. One for each year at the Academy.

- *Ubiquitous Water Faucets: Where Does Our Water Come From?*
- *Aqueducts Through Time.*
- *Plants Living in and Near Water.*
- *A Little Matter of Air, Water, Storms, and Soil.*
- *The Curious Lives of Animals in Glacier Pond.*
- *Your Stewardship and Husbandry of Glacier Pond.*

"These perspectives concern the entire pond, historically, as an ecosystem above and below the water level.

"I'll begin with *Stewardship and Husbandry* for now. It's for sixth-year students. This final study area shows where we take all first-through-sixth-year students.

"We begin with first-year students, by formally granting swaths of land to small groups of five to six, an acre of surface area in size, rectangular. The Academy's lawyer sets it up as a lifetime ownership for each group—with responsibilities, including when they return after graduation.

"Different groups will own the same section over the years, but their scientific studies will vary over time. So, they all have a different focus.

"A bronze plaque, like this one here," she said, pointing to one, mounted on top of a large stone, "gives the exact coordinates for this particular section. Same on the east side of the pond. You can see the other marker stones placed all around the pond from where we're standing."

Gesturing with her arms, and with a good measure of excitement, Clara explained, "Each section starts twenty feet away from the west shore here, runs through the pond, to the east shore, and goes another twenty feet on land. Overall lengths and widths of the grants vary, depending on where they're at on the pond. As do the depths of water, muck, and other substrates on the bottom."

Sam continued, "Each group owns their section, is responsible for it, and they work together on their project. One of the first things they do is name their section. We create a formal deed with the name of their section, and their names, with signatures, sealing land ownership.

"You will see them out here in all kinds of weather, early morning to late evening. Camping overnight. They might be taking core samples, like yesterday, from the bottom substrate through the ice in winter, or spring, summer or fall. If they are out here, we are, too.

"We have a first-rate indoor lab. And every team member has a fully stocked science tool kit, with a microscope. And there's an electron microscope for the entire science study area."

Clara returned spritely, "The focus of the project for all levels of students is always macro and microscopic life forms, and relationships in their environment. The natural world, in their section, is their oyster.

"Living and dead organisms, native, foreign, or invasive, animals, plants, bacteria, protozoans, humans, spiders, fish, deer, snakes, turtles, worms, birds, snails, lizards, raccoons, butterflies, slugs, water, soil. Basically all living and dead things found in their section, or visitors."

Clara's eyes were very exciting to watch. Smiling broadly she said, "Over the six perspectives, they will identify, photograph or sketch, catalog, and estimate population sizes of the plants and animals they find, and determine the quality of the ecosystem in their section for supporting life. Is it healthy or unhealthy? For all, for some? Make hypotheses about causes of issues. Do experiments. Test hypotheses. Report results. They take steps to improve their section over time, if warranted."

"What activity do the students especially like?" Darius asked.

"No doubt, exploring in the pond, deep as possible, even in winter. Something about the alien world underwater fascinates them. Summertime session is a blast!" Clara said, laughing.

Sam, who spoke more seriously, though still engagingly, said, "There's a healthy dose of chemistry in our curriculum, and the students often remind us of that fact. And math, history, statistics, scientific method, logical reasoning. 'Mr. Walker, where does it end?' they always ask. I say, 'Learning has no end, only a beginning: starts with an observation. And a question to answer. Then, leads you on and on.

"'Check out this list of questions raised by Leonardo da Vinci in his notebooks.' They haven't heard of it. I give them copies of the questions he posed in the 1400s.

"Never fails to awaken their desire for unbounded personal inquiry.

"The startup question for the groups is always the same, 'What the devil is going on in our section of Glacier Pond?'

"Three months after the sixth-year students began the final study of Glacier Pond, their work ends. They submit their findings, and get to read the reports of previous investigators of their pond section, and make comparisons. We conclude with one day for summary, critique, and recommendations for improving the different studies.

"A second day is an all-day applied science conference for the students to showcase their work to fellow students, faculty, staff, and parents. From time to time, students have their articles accepted for publication in a professional journal, trade magazine, or newspaper. Although publishing articles is not an objective."

Harding confessed, "That's a great thumbnail sketch. We've barely scratched the surface of their curriculum, and the Academy style of instruction. As you visit other studies on campus over the next few weeks, Darius, you'll see many variations of this style."

Clara was not finished. She jumped in again, "At the Stanton Academy for Humanity, we cultivate curiosity, inquiry, ingenuity, commitment, and zeal for learning among faculty and students. We don't follow the bell-driven, piecemeal, lockstep routine of factory-type schools. Students in each of the six studies of *Applied Science: A Case Study of Glacier Pond*, spend three months with Sam and me, and the other ten instructors for *Glacier Pond*. We work hard every day, get to know, trust, and respect each other. Follow the Academy's Monday-through-Saturday schedule, with half days on Wednesday and Saturday."

Harding concluded the talk with, "Instructors are experts in their fields, practicing professionals outside of the Academy, and passionate about learning. They meet with the large group of fifteen to twenty enrolled students at the start, and occasionally later on. But more often, hold focused labs and study sessions with small groups of three to five students.

"The face-to-face meetings are great for enriching learning. They take place in labs, the library, technology center, the barn, the field, any place where resources at the location best support the learning process.

"Instructors at the Academy work mainly as 'clever guides' for students. They set students free, driven to learn, learn, and go on learning. Faculty give ongoing guidance, know their subject matter, and are wizards to the students. They encourage the youngsters to use their time wisely, take initiative, and do their best in all studies.

"Nobody's a slacker," Darius noted. He was a good listener. Their talks about the content and style of instruction at the Academy reminded him of basic truths about his personal learning experience on the streets of Brownsville, with the Sisters, and with the Goodmans. He would not have survived a minute if he was a "slacker." The street gangs would have "got" him.

Today's glimpse of the Walkers' content and style, "clever guides," as Harding called them, convinced Darius that the Academy was the place for him to give back.

Sam and Clara excused themselves, because they had to check up on the students' progress and do prep work.

Going back to the car, Harding took the passenger's seat, Darius the driver's. The Lark pulled away smoothly. Harding directed Darius to the campus barn on the northern tip of Leonardo da Vinci Drive.

"Mighty fine driving, Darius. If you like, you can take over that job. I drive the Lark alone, mostly. My maneuvers can be a little rough on passengers. My grandkids get a kick out of riding with me to the hardware store. They like the ice cream shop along the way, too. Playgrounds and more. My wife, Sarah, prefers to drive us in her car wherever we have to go," Harding explained, laughing.

# — 12 —

SAKURA Sanada led Major Bradley to their home in the horse barn. Akiro Sanada was sitting on the stoop at the doorway to their stall. When he saw Sakura bringing Major Bradley along, he stood and bowed.

"Major Craig Bradley, this is my husband, Akiro Sanada."

"A pleasure to meet you, Akiro." Bradley said.

"I've invited the major to dine with us," Sakura explained.

"Come inside," Sakura continued with a bow.

"You two can get acquainted while I go out to get some things, and prepare our dinner. Normally, we eat in the mess hall. But not tonight. That food is not fit for a guest, such as you."

With that said, Sakura bowed and hurried away.

"The Sanadas are the same age as Stella and me," Bradley noted silently.

Inside, Bradley saw a small wooden table with three wooden stools, a crude sink, cook stove, and several wooden boxes arranged into a makeshift cupboard. One wall had a cotton sheet hanging, ceiling to floor, on a wire, covering a twin-sized bed for Akiro and Sakura. On the opposite wall, a sheet hung ceiling to floor, covering George's cot.

Bradley learned that Akiro was a huge fan of baseball especially, the San Francisco Seals, a minor league team in the Pacific Coast League.

Akiro taught George his first pitching lessons when he was six. They played pitch and catch daily in a vacant lot near their home. He took George to the Seals Stadium for home games. A highlight was the 1935 final game of the PCL Championship Series, where the Seals beat the Los Angeles Angels for the title. Akiro grew more and more lively, telling about the baseball games he and George went to. The lad was not only a fan, but also became a talented Bay Area Little League pitcher.

They saw Joe DiMaggio play his last game in the 1934–35 season for the Seals, before joining the New York Yankees.

Akiro. a loyal sponsor of the team, arranged for them to meet Joe in the dugout after the game. Talked baseball. Joe signed his bat from that game, and gave it to George. Then, he reached into his cubby and drew one of his home run balls, recovered from a previous game. Signed it, gave that to George, too, and said, "Good luck, kid. Hope I see you on a ball field some day."

While in the dugout, George struck up a conversation with Win Ballou, pitcher for the Seals, who showed George essential pitching grips. Handed the ball to George for him to try each of the grips. "We're gonna do better than that," Win said, when he recognized the kid's quick learning and keen interest in pitching. Win jumped up from the bench, and grabbed Joe Becker, the team's catcher. Joe got behind home plate, all suited up. Joe DiMaggio grabbed an umpire's face mask and chest protector and played Bill Klem, The great Old Arbitrator. Win took George out to the pitcher's mound. "Play ball!" DiMaggio announced. The pros got a kick out of coaching George for the next two hours. They fine-tuned his style for throwing the curveball, "Uncle Charlie," knuckleball, "fingernail ball," and four-seam fastball, "heater."

When the four of them returned to the dugout, Akiro thanked the Seals players, and told each to visit the Sanada Clothiers. He and Sakura would design custom-made suits for them.

"Those were the glory days," Akiro said sadly, looking into Bradley's eyes.

While the men were talking baseball, Sakura returned from her foraging trip to friends in camp for provisions she didn't have. She immediately set to work preparing their dinner.

The aromas were heavenly. Bradley hadn't had a home-cooked meal in too long. He knew that Sakura had made a special effort, at high cost, to get the ingredients and table setting pieces she wanted for their dinner. The camps did not cater to the Japanese diet, family life, or customs. Bland army food was served, cafeteria-style, in several huge mess halls. Three shifts of 500 men, women, and children were rushed through each hall for daily meals.

The door to the Sanadas' horse stall opened, and in walked the pitcher for the Oakland team.

Akiro, bowing, spoke first. "Major Bradley, this is our son, George."

Sakura, her eyes teared up, bowed and said, "Major, did you guess from our conversation at the ball game, that this young man would be our son, George?"

"Honestly, no. I was so caught up watching his style. He is a great pitcher. Akiro told me about his coaching from the Seals' players."

"Mighty fine pitching, George. I'm very pleased to meet you," Bradley said, shaking his hand.

"Shall we sit for dinner?" Sakura asked with a bow.

George bowed, pulled up a sturdy, wooden box from under his cot for his seat. The box stored his baseball equipment.

Akiro, Sakura, and Bradley sat on the stools.

"My gosh," Bradley said, looking at the table setting of bowls filled with hot, savory food, silverware, teapot and cups, and tablecloth. "This is a beautiful feast."

"You are our special guest," Sakura said, bowing. "We haven't had that pleasure since leaving San Francisco." Her eyes still teared up.

"My dear wife, were the onions so strong to make your eyes cry? Is there sadness in you?" Akiro asked kindly with a bow.

"No, no, not the onions," Sakura answered, bowing in turn. "We'll get to that after dinner. Please. Let's eat."

Sakura described the dishes for Bradley. "Here we have onigiri, a rice ball wrapped in seaweed. This bowl has miso soup, with vegetables, seaweed and tofu. And the main dish is oyakodon, which translated, means, the parent-and-child-rice-bowl. It has bite-sized chicken thigh pieces, soft-cooked eggs, peas, sliced onions, and a soy-sauce-based broth soup. It's served over white rice in a bowl. Please enjoy."

During dinner, Bradley learned that, like his mother, George spoke several languages fluently.

The Sanadas spoke matter-of-factly about their clothing business in San Francisco. The forced move from their home to an "Assembly Center." Then, transfer to this "Relocation Camp." Their new friends here, camp life behind barbed wire, and constant MP guards.

92

At Bradley's prompting, George discussed his studies and life goals before the uprooting, the Oakland team's record this season, and his fun times with new friends. Like his father, he lit up talking of things he was passionate about.

Everyone in the family missed their home, old neighborhood, friends, and their thriving clothier business.

When dinner had ended, Sakura removed the bowls, utensils and tablecloth from the table, wiped the table top clean, and sat down.

"Thank you so much for this delightful dinner," Bradley said.

Akiro and George bowed acknowledgement to Bradley. But they noticed this unusual behavior of Sakura. Normally, when eating in the stall, she would pick up the tableware and begin scrubbing the pots, platters, dishes, and all. Ask George or Akiro to go out for a bucket of water or to toss scraps. Not tonight.

Bowing, Sakura began speaking in a quiet voice. "Akiro, my dear husband, and George, our loving son, Major Bradley has a special request of us." Tears flowed in rivulets down her cheeks. "Major Bradley, would you please continue?"

"Yes, Sakura, thank you," Bradley began quietly, using her first name, hoping that would help the family absorb his request as sincere.

"I came here to search for a young Japanese man, with talents and trust, far beyond the ordinary. George was one of several in camps like this one, whose records showed they could probably do the job. All the others were good young men, but George, you stood out in the records. Then, after meeting you and your parents today, you're my top pick.

"Akiro, I met Sakura at the baseball field, earlier. We discussed things of common interest. When I found out her surname, I told her why I was here and that I would like to discuss this request privately with you, Akiro, and with you, Sakura, and with you, George.

"I will be going on a mission soon to help bring the war with Japan to an end, hopefully. I can't tell any more details. If you consent, I promise to do all in my power to bring George back home to you, safe and sound, so help me God."

Bradley took a deep breath and paused to let the Sanadas consider his broadly stated request.

"This is so very unusual," Bradley continued. "Please do not share this request with anyone. There isn't much time. Talk it over as a family tonight. If you have questions, I will try to answer them now. If not, I'll return tomorrow morning at 1000 hours for your answer. There is no time to spare."

"Major Bradley, if we say yes, when would George leave?" Akiro asked with a bow.

"Three days from today, I'll return, and George will go with me," Bradley said softly.

Akiro, Sakura, and George stood and bowed.

"Major Bradley, we will have an answer for you by 1000 hours tomorrow morning," Akiro said.

"Thank you. Your consideration alone is all I can expect, and for that I am extremely grateful," Bradley said, and shook hands with them one by one.

George led Bradley out the door. Then, he went back in.

Bradley walked to the officer barracks, and knew he was in for a long, restless night. But first, he had some phone calls to make.

Next morning, Bradley commandeered a jeep, and picked up two MPs. He drove them up to the guard house, got clearance, and pulled through the entrance gate of the barbed-wire camp. He parked the jeep a few yards inside the enclosure. From there, the three of them walked to the Sanadas' home in the horse stall. The eyes of many Japanese internees followed them. Each was wondering what to make of this unusual event.

Time was 1000.

George opened the door. Bradley had the MPs wait outside beyond hearing, and entered.

"Good morning, Akiro, Sakura, and George," Bradley said, in the same hushed tones of the previous evening, while bowing respectfully.

The Sanada family bowed.

Akiro spoke first, "Major Bradley, this has been a most difficult request for us to consider. Yet, we are honored that you asked. George is our only son, and we love him dearly. He has proven to us that he is not drawn into the camp ways of many youths here. In a short time, some of the other youths have grown to disrespect their parents and elders, turned away from our traditional family life, our customs and religion, even our Japanese food. Concentration camp life is bad for Japanese people, especially families and children."

Sakura said, with eyes swollen from crying, "Major Bradley, we talked about your request all through the night, and only a few minutes ago, made our decision. Our hearts say no. . . . Our minds say . . . yes, because . . . George said it best, 'If I can help end this war, how much better is that than remaining in this concentration camp, with no idea of where our life is going. Staring through these barbed wires every day. Doing nothing for ourselves, for America, our homeland, for freedom.'"

George stood between Akiro and Sakura. The little family, with tears in their eyes, hugged each other tightly.

Then, George kissed his parents, stepped back and bowed most respectfully. Turning around, he said, "Major Bradley, I will go on the mission with you. My beautiful mother and my strong father give their full consent. What should we do next?"

Bradley, much honored and relieved, said, "Thank you, Akiro, Sakura, and George, sincerely. As I said last evening, I will return three days from now. I have arranged for all three of you to travel with me to a new place. You won't know where, until we arrive, but I believe you will be pleased. So, when that day comes, at 0700 hours, please have your belongings packed up. I will have the MPs escort us to the gate. From there our travels begin. As army ways go, this is totally unorthodox, but I am radical when it suits me. An American, like you, I back down from no wrong or evil force."

The Sanadas bowed, and all put their arms around Bradley.

Sakura said, backing up slightly, "Your eyes speak of trust, kindness, and love of your family back home. This war has had an ugly, heavy toll on all of us Americans. God be with you Craig, and God with you, George, our dearly loved son."

Akiro said, "Son, we are so proud of you. Major Bradley, we will be waiting when you arrive."

George opened the door. Bradley shook George's hand, felt the steely firmness of the young man's commitment to serve his country. And the power behind his "burner."

96

"Thank you all. See you soon," Bradley said.

Outside the Sanadas' horse stall, Bradley ordered, "Okay, MPs, we got more work to do before sundown. Move out!"

When Major Bradley returned three days later, George let him in the door of their horse stall. Inside, Akiro and Sakura held small suitcases in their hands, ready to go. George picked up his suitcase and looked at Bradley.

"We're ready, Major Bradley."

They were escorted to the guard shack by the MPs. Two jeeps were parked nearby. Bradley and the MPs loaded the suitcases into one jeep. Bradley got behind the wheel of one jeep, with George in the passenger seat. Sakura and Akiro took rear seats in the second jeep, with the MP guard as driver.

"To the command post," Bradley ordered.

The commanding officer of the camp was waiting on the front steps of the headquarters building.

"Major Bradley, take my family car to the airport, the black Chevy deluxe parked over there. Keys are in the switch. It's got a full tank of gas. One of the MPs will ride along to bring it back here. Good luck. And thank you, George, Akiro, and Sakura Sanada. We are honored to have your help. We will take good care of you."

'Thank you, sir. Much appreciated," Bradley said.

The MP opened the trunk of the Chevy, stored luggage for Bradley and the Sanadas, and got behind the wheel. Bradley rode shotgun, and the Sanada family sat in the back seat. The Chevy's tires threw up dust, and sped away.

At a nearby airport, they boarded a troop transport aircraft. Several hours later they touched down at the Fort Ord Army Airfield, Monterey Bay, California. While the pilots taxied to the hanger, Bradley told the Sanadas what he had arranged for Akiro and Sakura.

"Welcome back to California! I'm extremely pleased that the brass allowed for this exception to the rules. We've landed at Fort Ord. Two jeeps are waiting for us. One will take you, Akiro and Sakura, to the base and the other will take George and me to our conference room to prepare for our mission. I wish we could have more time for saying goodbye, but it's wartime—we don't."

Two MPs driving the jeeps had already unloaded the luggage from the plane and were waiting, engines running. Bradley and the Sanadas exited the plane. George hugged and kissed his parents. Bradley shook Akiro's hand, and hugged Sakuro and Akiro.

"I promise to take the best care of George. In the meantime, you will live on the base in an officer's cottage, with commissary privileges, just inside the guarded entrance. Two MPs will be stationed in the gatehouse 24/7 for your protection and needs. Enjoy your new home."

Final goodbyes were said.

"George, are you ready?" Bradley asked.

"Yes, Sir," George answered.

They climbed into their jeep and were off.

Akiro and Sakura watched them leave, then took seats in the other jeep. The MP drove them to their cottage on the base.

# — 13 —

FEBRUARY was cold and windy in the Eridu Springs area of New England. First week, a winter storm, with temperatures hovering around freezing, dumped twenty-seven inches of wet snow.

After the storm had passed, the Academy's students, Family House Parents, neighbors, and staff cleaned up walkways and drives. Local farmers with snowblowers, or with snowplows mounted on their trucks, made short work of the heavy, white stuff.

That night, hard-blowing, cold winds dried out the snow and created high snowdrifts that again buried the Loop, driveways, and walking paths.

A 5:00 a.m. Saturday morning notice from Mr. Harding informed the campus via IM, that snow clearing would begin, once the wind tapered off at 3:00 p.m., following the weather forecast.

"Study sessions are canceled for today. Hunker down with a hot beverage and your favorite author. Enjoy being snowbound, folks. Our campus is a beautiful winter scene. Really cold out. Brilliant sunlight. All buildings are open as usual for the intrepid. Let somebody know where you're going and when you'll return," Harding recommended.

Cherice read Harding's text at noon, then looked out the kitchen window of their cottage. "Darius, we usually take our daily walk on the orchard path about this time, but I say we take a 'snow check.' What about you, hon?"

Darius stepped out of the bedroom, where he had prepared for their walk. Had on heavyweight canvas duck pants, a red plaid, long-sleeved flannel shirt, and thick wool socks.

"Yeah, Sweetheart, been thinking about our walk. Seems better if we do it tomorrow. You said the baby kept you awake all night, squirming and kicking?"

"Yeah. I'm so tired. Gonna lie down now for a nap."

"While you're catching some Zs, I'd like to run over to the library and do more research for my project. Be back in an hour or so. Are you okay with that, dear?"

"Yea, but put a throw on me, please, before you go?"

Cherice was already snuggled into the sofa, nearly asleep, with four pillows for comfort. Darius grabbed the down comforter from their bedroom and gently settled it over her. He bent down and kissed her cheek. "I'll be back soon, dear." Cherice was fast asleep. He pulled on insulated rubber boots with gaiters, over his socks and pant legs. Slipped into a heavy insulated parka. Put on sunglasses. And stretched a black, wool watch cap on his head.

When Darius opened the front door to the cottage, the wind hit him full in the face. He tightened up all buttons and zippers, pulled up the hood, and snapped the collar in place.

The trek to the library was a short distance. He sighted it from the porch to get bearings. Trudged ahead through blustery wind and hard-packed snow drifts. Opening the wide library door was a challenge, with the hard-blowing wind. Next instant, he stood in the vestibule, shook off

100

snow, and removed his boots for drying. Hung his coat and cap on the coat tree.

Once his vision adjusted from the bright sunlight and frigid blast of winter's wind outside, he looked around and saw he wasn't the only one to seek out the Stanton Library for reading and research. There were many students, and some faculty, at the tables, or coursing through the stacks. Their winter wear, stacked to dry around the vestibule, was dripping melted snow and ice into pools on the speckled terrazzo floor.

The Stanton Library followed the hallowed tradition of all respected libraries: silence, whisper only. Once inside, like in St. Ann's Church, tradition, thick walls, and the massive, oak doors held at bay the raucous world outside.

"Good to see you again, Darius," Brother Peter Kingsley, the librarian, quietly greeted him from the front desk. "How was the walk over here?"

"Marvelous," Darius joked in a hushed voice, with a big smile. "Brisk, fresh air, pelting snow, and high snow drifts. But at least I'm awake."

"Let me know if you need any assistance. We'll be open till 5:00 p.m.," said Brother Peter.

Darius headed, stocking-footed, to where he usually did his research: the Classical Literature and the English Literature sections. On the way, Lucia Benedictus opened the door of a windowed meeting room, and motioned for Darius to enter.

He walked in and closed the door. "Hello, Lucia. What brings you out on this blustery day?"

"I want to show you something," she said. Darius saw that Stella Young and Hana Sanada were also in the room.

101

He'd been introduced to them previously. Lucia motioned to the girls, and said, "You know Mr. James?"

They nodded, "Yes."

Lucia continued, "Darius, what you see spread over these three library tables is the sixth-year writing project that Hana and Stella are doing as coauthors. It's still at the research stage, but really has promise." Gesturing to the girls, Lucia asked, "Would you explain to Mr. James what you got here?"

"Sure," Hana volunteered eagerly. "These are the journals that our great-grandparents wrote when they served in World War II, and later one grandparent wrote in the Vietnam War. They were closed up in a box in our attic ever since. One day, a few weeks ago, we were in the attic, and Stella accidentally knocked this box off the shelf."

Pointing to the box, Hana continued, "Marked on top: *The Army Company First Aid Case, Bakers Pure Drug Co. LTD, Plymouth.*"

Stella picked up the discovery tale, "Yeah, like, I had no idea what hit the floor. Was big and heavy. Hit the floor with a loud bang. Missed my foot by a whisker. When I popped the top, this handwritten title page stared up at us. We were totally astonished," Stella put her index finger on it: *Wartime Journals of Lieutenant George Washington Sanada with Major Craig Alexander Bradley.* "Both our great-grandparents!"

Hana jumped in with, "Then, Stella carefully goes down through the many pages and manuscripts to find this large journal at the bottom of the box: *A Glimpse into the Troubling Vietnam War and the Grave Aftermath Going Forward,* by Captain Marcus Stanton."

"That's my papa, my grandfather," Stella said with obvious excitement. "He's still with us. We asked Mrs. Benedictus to advise us with turning the journals into a story. She agreed, and accepted our proposal to do this for our sixth-year writing project. At this point, we've organized everything chronologically, read all the entries, taken tons of notes, and listed our questions. We've met here every Wednesday, Saturday, and Sunday afternoon since the discovery. For the past several weeks, we've been writing. We use half days, Sunday afternoons, holidays, evenings, and vacations—until it's finished," Stella concluded.

"Now I understand why Mrs. Benedictus asked me to join you," Darius said. "What a treasure! I'm intrigued— hooked, in fact. Would you mind if I read the journals, too?"

"Not at all," Hana answered.

"And we'll take all the help you can give us," Stella added.

Darius took the next hour reading randomly selected pages of the journals. The last journal, about the Vietnam War, held his attention longest of all. He flipped between journals to compare later material to the earlier entries about WWII.

"I'm all in," Darius summed up. "There's something here that I've been looking for since arriving at the Academy. Thank you so much for pulling me in, Mrs. Benedictus. We've chatted off and on about the theater project due to begin next month. These journals have drawn everything together for me. They planted a seed, and answered my prayers. Stella and Hana, thank you so much. I will help you every way I can. We'll talk further next week. Contact me with any questions."

Lucia explained, "The door to this room is locked at all times. Whenever you want to work on the journals, Brother Peter will let you in."

Darius said, "This is a godsend. Thank you all. Please excuse me, but I need to get back to the cottage and check on Cherice."

"No problem, Mr. James," Hana said. "We're glad to have your help. You know where to find us."

"Same for me," Lucia added.

"Hello to Mrs. James from us," Stella said.

After leaving the meeting room, Darius went to the Classical Literature stacks. He pulled down *Antigone*, a play written by Sophocles in or before 441 BC. Still today, Sophocles is considered the greatest of all playwrights since antiquity. Darius checked out the volume with help from Brother Peter, then stepped in the vestibule, dressed for the cold, and trudged home to be with Cherice.

# — 14 —

FLIGHT ORDER

6 JUNE 1945.

EQUIPMENT: Experimental Northrop XP-61E Black Widow photographic reconnaissance version. Unpainted.

PILOT: Maj. Bradley, Craig A. 548th Night Fighter Squadron.

LOCATION: Western Pacific.

DEPARTURE: 0100 HOURS JST.

CLASSIFIED: Top Secret Reconnaissance Operation.

MISSION: Photo reconnaissance, Japanese military installations: Kagoshima Fukuoka, Nagasaki, Kokura, Hiroshima, Osaka, Nagoya, Tokyo, Ishikawa and Aomori.

FINAL DESTINATION: Vladivostok, Russia.

WEATHER FORECAST (next 24 hrs.): Sunshine with clear skies starting at 0500 JST. Turning partly cloudy at 1600, then increasing clouds, with rain likely in northwest mountainous region.

TEMPERATURE: 50 degrees Fahrenheit.

VISIBILITY: 5 miles.

WIND SPEED: 13 mph northwest.

God Speed.

# — 15 —

MAJOR Craig Alexander Bradley climbed into the pilot's cockpit of a modified Northrop XP-61E Black Widow, two-crew fighter, unarmed, unpainted aluminum skin, specially adapted photo-reconnaissance aircraft.

Second lieutenant George Sanada got into the copilot's rear cockpit. Sanada was Bradley's navigator—he was now a trained pilot on the Black Widow, an expert at map and compass work, Japanese language, geography and history of Japan, and a skilled radio operator, translator, and camera technician.

Both wore G-1 leather flight jackets with dark brown mutton collars.

"Welcome aboard, George. We are flying incognito, with no support, no backup. Radio silence on our end. Intercom system only."

"Roger," George affirmed.

"Downside: we have no armament, no ammo. Upside, as you saw in training, the Black Widow has the stuff to leave Japanese fighters in the dust. That's our trump card, especially with no armament. Keep a close watch for any raiders. Early sighting is our best escape. Forecast is clear blue skies most of the way. Perfect for photo-recon. Repeat: keep in mind we got no defense. No cover."

107

"Roger," George affirmed again.

Craig fired up the engines and waited until they were at operating temperature. He received clearance for takeoff from the airfield crew. Chocks removed. Engines revved up for takeoff. Breaks let go. The Black Widow shot down the runway, caught the headwind for a perfect liftoff. She climbed to 30,000 feet before leveling off.

Soon, Craig brought the Black Widow down to "wave-top height" to avoid enemy radar for the run to Japan.

"Miraculous," Craig shouted. "Beautiful, sleek as a hawk's flight from a Nebraska corn field. Damn fine plane. We're good for 2,249 miles."

"Sir, I have something I'd like to discuss with you," George said.

"Fire away," Craig said.

"Last week, when you went home to visit your wife, my flight instructor told me about your son. That he died in combat on Okinawa. I'm so sorry. So sorry, sir. I had no idea."

"Thank you, George. Thank you," Craig said, eyes suddenly swelled with tears. "Losing Thomas was horrible. Our only son. This war. We are blessed with two lovely daughters, Emily, who's expecting our first grandchild in October, Philomena, our youngest child, unmarried. Thank God they're both safe. Life goes on all day, every day. God's will be done.

"We knew it could happen. Thomas did, too. But he wanted to serve our country in this time of war, and help end it. But life is in God's hands, not ours. When the death of a loved one strikes home, it's devastating. Your boy is gone. Your hopes and dreams for him … We miss him, oh my God, so much. Stella grieves every day for the beautiful boy she carried nine months in her womb, and birthed on a beautiful, sunny day in January.

"As a career military officer, I was not able to spend as much time with him, my daughters, and my wife as I would have liked. But Stella and I have always been very close. Over the years, we constantly wrote and talked about him, and Emily, and Philomena. His grandparents on my side and Stella's helped daily with household chores and raising two spunky little girls and Tommy.

"George, you are about the same age as Thomas. When I watched you pitch for your team, I was struck by how similar you two are. Determination, keen attention to detail, academic prowess. Yes, I examined your school records from San Francisco—the local library knows your reading interests. I received testimony on your moral courage in the face of sick modern lures, love of your family and country, loyalty to friends and right causes.

"Thomas was the same.

"Something you may not know is that the US Government does not allow Japanese American citizens to join the war and serve on missions like this one. They can be infantry soldiers, but not fly a plane like a Lightning or this Black Widow, or operate other advanced equipment across all military branches.

"As you know, they keep your people penned up in camps around the country, like the camp your family was sent to. Understandable in this war? Not what I'd support. Only time will tell if it was the right call. Doubtful in my opinion.

"For a time before the attack on Pearl Harbor, you enrolled in the Civilian Pilot Training Program at San Jose State Teachers College. My hero, Mathias Hanson, taught there. He knew you well. Said he'd never had a better student in any class, and all practical training exercises. His word settled the 'who,' for my search. I just had to find you, and hoped for a yes from you."

George said, "I remember Professor Hanson. Great sense of humor, strict, sharp as a tack. Learned so much from him."

Craig continued, "Right fine man, Hanson is. Because of my experience and success flying photo-recon missions in Germany, I volunteered and was accepted for this mission. But, I told the highest-ranking officials that I would do it only if I could take a qualified Japanese-American soldier as my copilot. I had trained hundreds of you guys before the war, and they'd be flying aces today, helping us win the war. Loyal to the max. And know the land and culture, and can speak the language.

"'Not gonna happen,' they said.

"I reasoned with myself prior to going into the meeting to press for your assignment. Hoped for the best.

"Prayed, 'Lord God help us, all of your people. We are mortals. Failing human beings. Yet, you created us in your likeness. Somehow we must prove worthy of your love. And end this war.'

"Then, I walked into the most important meeting of my military career. I let my thoughts fly, with reason, as is my way in personal trials.

"'Gentlemen, fellow officers, throughout time, millions of soldiers, mostly young folks, served and died on either side of countless battlefields. Thermopylae, Changping, Tours, Hattin, Yorktown, Gettysburg. Last year, Normandy. Now, we are planning the atomic bombing of Japan. World War II, a most dreadful war, and not over by any calculation.

110

We have thousands of dead and injured soldiers in Europe, still coming home. Thousands dead and wounded coming home from the battles in the Pacific. Cool heads gotta prevail. We have to make the right decisions, no matter how unpopular. Gotta pick battles we can win and save lives. Get the best men. Give 'em the best tools. And turn 'em loose on the enemy. We must understand, and respect the suffering, the loss of loved ones forever by families, neighbors, and whole cities and towns across the country. Mothers, fathers, sisters, brothers, wives, and husbands. Some of you, like me, have lost your sons and other family and friends in this war. The devastation is mounting. For survivors, the heart-wrenching loss of loved ones can never be alleviated.'

"At the end of my argument before the leadership, I said, 'I will get the intelligence we need on this mission, so help me God.'

"The brass fumed and cursed at the request for you to join me. They were afraid, I suppose, of somebody higher up getting wind of it and denying them promotions. Such is the stodgy military establishment. I stood my ground. Pulled strings beforehand. Called on the bigwigs whose asses I'd saved last year in Europe and recently here in the Pacific.

"My request was approved, but on one condition: that your name would not appear on the flight orders. I said, 'Okay, you can take my name off the list, too, if you like. But I need that soldier. I trained him for this mission. We must win this war. Must be better as a people. Must be smarter than the enemy.'

"That's how I got you, George. You and I will live or die on this mission. I believe we will win the war, soon, and live to tell our families what we did. I promised your mother and father to bring you back alive. I will keep my promise."

George responded, "Thank you, Sir. I am very grateful that you chose me. Deeply humbled. I will help you complete this mission and we'll see the end of Imperial Japan together."

Both men settled into the tight quarters of their cockpit seats for the long flight. From time to time they went over details of the mission to get it right: orders from headquarters, features on the maps, compass settings for every change of course, prevailing winds, critical marks and notes by George, Craig, and command, and likely places where they may encounter fire from anti-aircraft batteries on the ground, and in the air by Japanese Zeros and other fighters.

"05:03 JST ten miles southeast of Kagoshima, Japan," George announced.

Craig ordered, "George, light up the cameras. Time and date stamp should be on 'em. Roll 'em."

"Roger. Cameras marked and rolling," George shouted in acknowledgement.

Craig shouted, "We are at 30,003 feet, max, and holding, can probably go higher, since we are so light. May have to. That should be just above their guns' maximum effective range. Should give cameras good image definition."

"God save us from anti-aircraft guns on shore and inland. Hopefully, nobody gets lucky down there," Craig said.

"Japanese radio operators screaming about imminent bombardment. Requesting anti-aircraft fire immediately. Requests approved," George said, relaying the Japanese radio communications.

Within seconds fire flashes from the Type 99 88 mm AA guns lit up on the ground. Immediately, the projectiles exploded in multiple salvos below and around the plane. Clearly, the anti-aircraft guns had the Black Widow's position, speed, and direction of travel. Then, an anti-aircraft shell exploded at their altitude, but too far to port side.

"We got lucky. Enough of that crap! Gotta scoot fast. Those guns have an effective range of 34,000 feet. Higher than our ceiling of 30,003 feet," Craig shouted.

"No kidding. That shell shook the hell out of our bird! Hurt my ear drums," George added, his voice getting hoarse from shouting.

The Black Widow moved fast, 376 mph. More anti-aircraft shells exploded far to port and starboard, as the plane sped away.

"We might have taken shrapnel from that last one, Sir! Don't know where or how bad," George reported.

"Yeah. Hope it's minor. Pray it's not worse."

"Sir, our position is now over Kumamoto."

Craig kept the Black Widow at 30,000 feet.

"Anti-aircraft guns silent, Sir."

"Keep the cameras rolling. Never know what we might find down there," Craig said.

"Roger. Kagoshima coming up on port. Anti-aircraft guns firing again!"

"Gonna be a bumpy ride the whole way, I'm afraid," Craig shouted.

"Nagasaki in view, port side, Sir. Five Franks coming at us fast on starboard!"

"Roger. Franks. A serious plane, but I think we can dodge this threat. Taking her all the way up again for safety."

"Sir, we took coupla hits on starboard fuselage, tail, and wing from the lead Frank's machine gunfire," George said.

"Roger," Craig acknowledged.

The Black Widow swiftly, gracefully shot up at a 2,500-feet-per-minute rate of climb. Hit new ceiling of 34,000 feet, left the Franks behind.

"Keep an eye out for Franks, George. I don't think this is the last we'll see of them."

"Roger. Coming up on Fukuoka, on port side. Anti-aircraft guns firing a barrage, but blowing under us."

"Turning east to get Kokura," Craig said.

"Kokura off starboard, Sir."

"Going to get the best photos of this city and the next," Craig said.

"Hiroshima coming directly under us now, Sir," George reported. "Now over Osaka. Anti-aircraft guns firing. Three Franks coming at us on starboard side!"

"Roger. Going up."

At the new ceiling again, the Black Widow began to vibrate.

"What's that, Sir?"

"Don't know. Can be an issue . . . Now it's settling down, thank God."

"Okay. Nagoya going in the camera now, port side, Sir."

"Roger."

"Tokyo's ahead," George reported.

"Going back down to 30,000 for best photos."

"We are over Yokohama, Sir."

"Roger. Banking hard to port, heading over Tokyo."

"Sir, AA guns firing big time now. Exploding below us. Holy crap! Three Franks starboard. Closing in fast!"

"Roger." Craig immediately put the Black Widow into a steep climb.

114

"We may have got some hits again," George reported.

"Roger. Ishikawa's next. Then north to Aomori."

"Hida Range ahead, Sir."

"Roger. Japanese Hida Range of mountains are about 10,000 feet. We are set to clear them."

Suddenly the left engine sputtered. Then, the right engine began a coughing fit.

"Black Widow can fly with one engine, but it's not looking good for us, George."

"Foothills dead ahead, mountain peaks coming, west coast, but we're also getting some weather, Sir."

The sky turned to heavy cloud cover, light rain, and thick fog. Visibility was less than three miles. Lightning and thunder signaled they were heading into a serious storm.

"George, scan the map for any kind of landing area. I got gauges showing issues with the engines, they're still turning okay, but I'm hoping at least one recovers soon!"

"I'm on it. Nothing nearby, Sir. Mountains, we can clear 'em, then seacoast approximately 100 miles west, northwest."

"Holy crap, Sir! There's a Zero far out to starboard."

"Okay, here's what we're gonna do. Mark our location on the map. Leave it in the plane."

"Roger."

"The plane's losing power faster than I hoped. I'm slowing it down some more for us to bail out. You, then me. I'll try ditching it in the ocean, if I can get over these mountains. This bird can be a bitch to get out of. But you practiced the technique. Get ready. Parachute on. Bail out tight, like a ball, so you fall straight down. On my order."

"Roger. I'm ready, Sir."

"I will find you, George. We're gonna make it outta here one way or another. God be with you, son," were Graig's last words to George. Then, "Bail!"

George released his safety belt and tore himself out of the cockpit. He slid headfirst with the wind pushing him off the trailing edge of the wing, down and away from the horizontal stabilizer. He kept his arms and legs tucked in. It worked. Clear of the plane, he pulled the ripcord handle and the chute opened.

The next instant he listened to the dampening roar of the engines, and watched the Black Widow fly away. Miraculously, it soon recovered normal engine sound, went into a steep climb, and left the Zero behind.

"Thank God, Sir, our mission just might succeed. Hope the Zero doesn't find me hanging around," George chuckled.

He fell through the rain and fog. Glided swiftly downward. Nothing visible around or below.

No Zero.

He could barely make out his immediate surroundings due to the lingering rain and fog. Vision became better the farther he dropped. A thick forest was all around. His chute did not get tangled in treetops, fortunately.

He prepared for contact. Down hard—on dirt! Went into the parachute landing fall. Recovered uninjured.

He landed, with great fortune, straddling a level section on a mountain path, with one foot on either side. The path meandered up steeply fifty yards behind him, and down steeply fifty yards in front of him. A stream was gurgling and splashing through rocks on the left side of the path.

George gathered up the parachute, walked into the underbrush on the right side of the path, opposite the stream. He clambered around large boulders and fallen trees, until he came to a small open space in the edge habitat suitable for hiding. Used his parachute for a makeshift mattress and blanket. "This will do for now," George concluded. "I can adjust the hiding place tomorrow when there's more light." The last thing he did was set up concealed quick-exit routes, one front and one rear.

# — 16 —

SECONDS after George bailed, Craig, struggled with the controls, and the Black Widow recovered fully.

A miracle.

That was only an instant before he planned to bail out. The Zero was firing its guns, but still out of range.

"Come on, baby, climb!"

The Black Widow's Pratt & Whitney R-2800 Double Wasp engines responded magnificently. Craig leveled out above the Zero's ceiling and flew at top speed to Vladivostok without incident. He waited there for a crew to inspect and repair the plane. Refueled, he flew back to the base.

When Craig landed the plane on June 8, 1945, technicians removed and processed the reconnaissance film, delivered it to command headquarters.

In his debriefing, Craig gave a full account. At the end, he said, "Last thing, with that engine trouble, we had a Zero on us." He reported the location on the map where George bailed out. "He'll be waiting for rescue on the ground. I can parachute in and help him walk out to a waiting sub."

In the middle of a war, in the frenetic effort to put together a catastrophic attack against the enemy, the first of its kind in the history of the world, some things drop out. Despite Craig's loud protestations and pleas,

Headquarters Command decided that George would have to sit tight for now.

Craig's heart dropped like a 150 lb. blacksmith's anvil knocked off a stump. He felt faint. He left the meeting deeply troubled, and looked up the base chaplain, Brother Gildard Buvala, OFM. They prayed together for George's safety on the mountain in Japan, and for his rescue. Craig wept for George. War had made them adopted father and son. Brother Gildard, eyes full of tears, hugged and blessed him.

Outside the chaplain's tent, walking aimlessly, Craig recalled his ancestor and namesake of his son, Thomas Bradley, Rifleman, Stirling's Division, Spencer's Regiment, Valley Forge. Craig stumbled on a round stone in the sand walkway, righted himself, leaned against a com pole to regain balance, then hung his head in the deepest sorrow of the ages.

"War was easier back then, right, Thomas? And all the ages before?" Craig mused. "Surely not. Ever. War is so goddamned ugly, whenever, wherever, period. Deadly, awful, horrible. We're in the middle of it. Cain, festering with envy, killed Abel, his brother. Why? God accepted Abel's sacrifice, but not his?

"What is man? Lord God help us!

"But at times people must take up arms and fight against an enemy determined to destroy them. At those times, as now, I believe, Lord, war is necessary to protect the innocent, and secure freedom, civilization, and humanity, now and for future generations. Lord God! If ever the flickering candle is blown out . . .

"We've answered our country's calls for defense of life and liberty. With mortal sacrifice. God bless my son,

Thomas. Rest in peace, Thomas. I love you. I miss you so much.

"And, God, save George."

Brother Gildard happened by, put his arm around Craig's shoulders and walked him to the mess hall. They prayed over supper, for Thomas's soul, for George's safe return, and for an end to the war.

At 1910 that evening, Craig received orders to immediately join a top-secret meeting using his recon photos to help prepare for dropping atomic bombs on one or two Japanese cities. First choices became Kokura and Hiroshima. It was now two months nearly to the day the war with Japan would be brought to a devastating end.

# — 17 —

ALWAYS ready to comfort and help the needy, Brother Blaine had pledged to Olivia, Stella, and the Young Mission on that terrible day to serve as their spiritual guide. And to help them with Jedediah's passing in the best way.

He organized parishioners, townspeople, local VFW, and the media to provide food, home upkeep, and funeral services. They tackled house cleaning, lawn and garden care, and home repairs without affecting the family's need for privacy.

Someone answered the phones, another collected and organized all the sympathy cards. Another led vigils, rosary services, and prayers of remembrance at church. Someone stepped up to arrange for private and group visits with Olivia and Stella. Several experienced widows and veterans met with Olivia and Stella to help with body transfer, the mortician's services, choosing a casket, burial plot and headstone. Deal with military services and benefits. And set up the funeral Mass and graveside committal.

Olivia and Stella, always kept in the loop, were so grateful and relieved for their kindness.

Hana stayed with Stella every day and night for the next month.

The day after notification, Olivia's sister, Emma, and her husband, Gordon Stanton, booked a hotel room, and came to visit with their children, Carla, Montgomery, and Etana. Their home was several miles away across the valley. The whole mission prayed with Brother Blaine over the noontime meal, a healing, loving family tradition.

After lunch, all the teens broke away from the adults to be with Stella in her bedroom. Etana cranked up Stella's "ancient" Kenwood KR-V5560 Stereo Receiver, Technics turntable SL1200 with Bose Intermediate Audio Series speakers—a gift from Dad years ago. Dad, Uncle Jed, had converted each of them into polished audiophiles. "Nothing can play music like vinyl," Etana recalled Uncle Jed's words softly.

They took turns with the magic of changing the vinyl albums and flipping sides for the LPs, and gently dropping the needle arm for the finest landing. Listened to Stella's favorites, playing low in the background Ludvig van Beethoven's Symphony No. 9, Franz Schubert's Symphony No. 8 "Unfinished," Edvard Grieg's Peer Gynt Suite No. 1, and many more from Uncle Jed's huge collection. Albums were stored in an old cedar blanket chest, stacked on edge, upright, alphabetically, by composer.

Talked about life, and growing older, school and their friends. Reminisced about their wonderful adventures over the years as cousins, with Stella, Olivia, Jed, and all their parents and grandparents. Worked from time to time on a 1,000-piece jigsaw puzzle. Ran like a wild stampede of mustangs downstairs and outside to practice soccer in the yard. Curled up to read books of their own choosing from the Youngs' library shelves. And they read books they brought along in backpacks recommended by the Stanton Academy for Humanity.

At the end of the day, they all slept over in Stella's room. Heads buried in fluffed-up, king-sized pillows. Exhausted teen cousins, legs and arms akimbo, bodies scattered about haphazard under comforters on the carpeted floor.

They had slept over in each other's bedrooms since they were toddlers.

Every morning before dawn the teens cleaned up the house, rearranged furniture, and set up the dining room table for plates, silverware, and food servings. The parishioners' cleanup detail had nothing to do. The young folks also guided the mission for meals, and cleaned up afterwards. They worked a valet service at the driveway, parked and retrieved cars on the street. And cut and trimmed the lawn.

In between times, they recalled learning how to do so many things from Uncle Jed. Staying busy with chores and talking about stuff with her loving cousins, helped Stella embrace her personal grief. Before retiring at the end of the day, all their thoughts flowed back to Uncle Jed, their dearest cousin, Stella, and Aunt Olivia. And they cried tears of sadness for this great loss each night before falling asleep.

Hana's parents, Evan and Isa Sanada, her grandparents, Jonas and Audra Sanada, and Stella's maternal grandparents, Marcus Stanton and Charlotte Rose Stanton, and, Louis and Tyra Young, Jedediah's parents, visited every day, bringing fresh, cleaned and pressed clothes, snack food and drinks. And gave the warmest hugs and kisses in the world to all in the family. Especially, Olivia and Stella.

The big family of Youngs and Sanadas was as close and loving as families can be. They had always celebrated events together. Now, as one family, together with Olivia and Stella, they would soon say the saddest, final goodbye to their adored Jedediah. The time for Jedediah's wake, funeral Mass, and burial came faster than the little mission expected.

On the morning of the funeral, Brother Blaine knocked on the front door of the Youngs' home. Stella and Hana let him in. The house was filled with family and friends. They were all helping to set a tone that was uplifting, warm and respectful. Turn by turn, they gave Olivia and Stella the warmest, most sincere hugs, kisses, and fervent promises to help with anything they might need.

Standing at the edge of the gathering, Brother Blaine waited for a time when he could speak privately with Olivia and Stella. Hana, sensing his interest, squeezed through the gathering and brought out mom and daughter. Brother Blaine put his arms around them and whispered his private thoughts, wishes, prayers, and blessings to them. He had baptized Jedediah, Olivia, and Stella, and had given them all the sacraments, including marrying Jedediah and Olivia. Except, until now, the last rites. Tears of sadness, joy, and thanksgiving flowed from their eyes.

"I will go now and prepare the church for Jedediah's funeral Mass. God be with you," Brother Blaine said. He bowed and departed.

St. Ann's Catholic Church, located in a wooded acreage at the north edge of town, was built in 1865, at the end of the Civil War. It is the oldest church in the region. The architectural style is early Romanesque, later called Gothic. Local stone carvers, masons, and carpenters of the day,

126

Italian, German, Irish immigrants, and recently freed African slaves, built their church in the 900 AD European architecture.

St, Ann's majestic towers, colossal, thick walls, round and arcading arches, decorated piers, and double-barrel vaults, gave the clergy and laity a most sacred gathering place.

The traditional Mass was said in Latin every Sunday, and the other sacraments were also said in Latin. The sacred rites and traditions, majestic altar, with the celebrant facing the tabernacle, had never been altered after the Second Vatican Council, which ran from 1962 through 1965. Parishioners followed the liturgy in Roman Missals—the 1962 English to Latin Edition—stacked at the entrance to pews.

The huge pipe organ in the choir loft, mirrored the beautiful altar in sound and sight.

Sheltered in St. Ann's hallowed milieu, the faithful could pray, grieve, confess, contemplate, sing sacred hymns, dream, experience joy and fulfillment, be inspired, and give thanks to God for all his blessings. In the decades since opening its doors, St. Ann's was also a sacred retreat from war's aftermath.

On this day, Brother Blaine appointed himself bell-ringer, calling all the townspeople to Jedediah's funeral Mass. He walked, feeling so much grief, from the choir loft up the dozen oak steps with four landings, to the bell-ringing chamber. A solitary thick, braided bell pull was held on the side wall by an iron loop. The rope was tethered to the headstock for an immense bronze bell seventy-five feet up in the church tower. He took hold of the bell pull with both hands. Paused to pray aloud the Ave Maria. Then, he pulled the rope down slowly for the first ring.

The bell clanged, and then swung its great weight back, pendulously, to clang again. Brother Blaine pulled the bell to ring forty-five times — Jedediah's years on earth.

When the hearse pulled up to the curb at the front door of St. Ann's, Evan, Hana, Carla, Montgomery, Etana, and Major Sawyer were waiting as pallbearers. They took places on either side of Jedediah's coffin. Grabbed a lug, in turn. And gently lifted the coffin from the rails. Lieutenants Blakely and Garvey trailed.

When Hana, Carla, Montgomery, and Etana grabbed the lugs, they were struck immediately by the heavy weight of Jedediah's coffin. Switched to both hands. Each looked deeply into one another's eyes, red-swollen and teared up. Their hearts were overwhelmed with sorrow, their deepest sense of loss in life, so far. Nothing could have prepared them for this.

The pallbearers carried the grave mournfulness of the day, along with their beloved Jedediah's body, up three wide, worn, sandstone steps, into the church. Once inside the narthex, the foyer, they gently rested the coffin on a wheeled catafalque.

All the pews in St. Ann's were filled end to end. The foyer was packed, as were the choir loft, and the side aisles.

The great oak entrance doors were opened wide, as were the inner doors to the huge nave, with its sturdy oak pews and honed Carrara marble aisles. Worshipers stood crowded on the entrance steps, and out on the wide sidewalks and lawn surrounding St. Ann's.

The people who arrived late, had to park their cars blocks distant, and many chose to sit in their cars.

Anticipating a large turnout, students from the Academy for Humanity worked with Brother Blaine and an anchor from the local TV station to provide a live broadcast of the whole service. Everyone would have a close-up view.

The faithful in St. Ann's watched in broken-hearted silence as the pallbearers solemnly guided the casket carrying Jedediah's body down the center aisle, to rest before the communion rail and steps up to the sanctuary.

The church bell ceased ringing.

Olivia and Stella sat in the first pew, by the center aisle, on Mary's side, left of the sanctuary. Isa, Evan, and Hana, Emma, Gordon and Carla, Montgomery, and Etana sat in the pew behind Olivia and Stella. Grandparents Louis and Tyra Young, Marcus Stanton and Charlotte Rose Stanton, and Emily and Jonas Sanada sat in the second pew behind mom and daughter.

Dressed in their finest suits, they all held hands devoutly.

Major Sawyer and lieutenants Blakely and Garvey sat in the pew behind the grandparents. A dozen other officers and enlisted men, who had served with Jedediah in the war, sat to the left of them. All the soldiers wore dress blues.

Hana saw Brother Blaine dressed in his vestments at the doorway to the sacristy. The service was about to begin.

She chanced a long glance back into the church. Was overwhelmed at the number of people there. She was especially surprised and proud to see students, instructors, administrators, parents, and donors from the Academy for Humanity. "How wonderful for Stella and Olivia! So much love and care from our school, and so many relatives, friends, and people from town," she thought.

As she returned her focus to the front, she paused to see Stella and Olivia embracing, crying softly, kissing away tears, saying the most precious words for Jedediah, and giving back looks with nods of thanks to their whole family and the faithful gathering.

Two acolytes, carrying lit candle lighters, walked solemnly out of the sacristy and turned to face the center of the altar. They genuflected, then went up marble steps to light three candles in tall stands, on either side of the tabernacle. They stepped down from the altar, genuflected again, and returned to the sacristy.

The Mass began with resounding organ music and the parish choir singing, "Exaudi Nos/Hear Us, O Lord."

Brother Blaine walked solemnly out of the sacristy, accompanied by four acolytes. One acolyte, in the lead, held the processional cross with both hands, and placed it in a brass base on the sanctuary floor left of the altar. The next carried wine and water in glass cruets, which were put on a side table, next to the lavabo and manuterge—a towel, a pitcher of water, and a small basin. The third, carried a golden chalice and tabernacle key, genuflected before the altar, walked up the steps, set them in the center, bowed, and walked down again. The fourth, carried the large Roman Missal, with red leather binding and gold-edged pages. The acolyte, following the same ritual, placed the Missal on a wooden stand, left of center on the altar.

The ceremony followed the rite for a traditional Catholic Sunday Latin Mass. Brother Blaine made revisions to the ordinary service for this funeral. He selected readings from scripture keyed to Jedediah's life, his love for Olivia, for his daughter, Stella, the Young and Sanada families, and the hundreds of family and friends in St. Ann's on this day.

Communion and all the liturgies completed for the Order of the Mass, Brother Blaine paused, bowed and kissed the altar. He walked down the steps, turned to the tabernacle, genuflected, turned to face the laity, and went to stand before Jedediah's closed coffin. He put his two hands softly on the casket. Closed his eyes. Then, he placed a neatly folded linen napkin on the head of the coffin.

In his rich baritone voice, Brother Blaine prayed aloud:

"Dearest husband, father, brother, uncle, captain, and friend, Jedediah Louis Young.

"You are our beloved hero. There is no burden we won't carry for you. For Olivia and Stella, you are the most loving and loved Jed and Daddy. You are their rock. And, in truth, you are the rock for this whole family, our parish, this loving community, and our nation.

"You sacrificed your life for us. For your squad in battle. For freedom the world over. The enemy took your life from us. But God has taken your soul to heaven to join the angels, saints, and all who have gone before us.

"Today, we will lay your body, quietly and softly, to rest in the earth.

"Let us look to Holy Scripture for understanding, truth, light, and hope. God said these words to Adam after he and Eve ate the forbidden fruit, Genesis 3:18–19 in the Hebrew Bible:

Cursed be the soil for your sake,
with pangs shall you eat from it all the days of your life.
Thorn and thistle shall it sprout for you
and you shall eat the plants of the field.
By the sweat of your brow shall you eat bread
till you return to the soil,
for from there were you taken,
for dust you are
and to dust shall you return.

"Lord in heaven, ever since leaving the Garden of Eden, our hands have worked this earth, as you commanded us. All day, every day, regardless of the world's troubles, the plowman turns packed dirt and sand, and with the harrow, renders it into loose, life-giving soil. The fertile earth is planted with grain from the last harvest. Drenched with rainfall and sunlight, grain becomes plants to feed on the rich soil, to multiply into thousands on thousands of grains, nourishing our bodies to live hundreds more tomorrows.

"Eating our harvest gives hope to our hearts and souls for an eternity with you.

"We were given these words of hope and promise from Isaiah 58:10–11, in the Hebrew Bible:

> And you proffer your bread to the hungry,
>      and sate the appetite of the afflicted.
> Then your light shall dawn in the dark,
>      and your gloom shall be like the noon.
> And the LORD shall guide you always
>      and sate your appetite in arid land,
>      and your bones He shall strengthen,
> and you shall be like a well-moistened garden
>      and like a water source
>      whose waters do not fail.

"Now, let us turn to the apostle John for the words Christ spoke to his disciples 14:1 – 8, in the Saint John's Bible.

"The hour had come when Jesus would die on the cross, leave this world and return to the Father. All of the disciples were afraid.

"Simon Peter asked Jesus where he was going.

"Jesus answered that they cannot follow him now, but they will follow him afterward.

Do not let your hearts be troubled. Believe in God, believe also in me. In my father's house there are many dwelling places. If it were not so, would I have told you that I go to prepare a place for you? And if I go and prepare a place for you, I will come again and will take you to myself, so that where I am, there you may be also.
And you know the way to the place where I am going."
Thomas said to him, 'Lord, we do not know where you are going. How can we know the way?'
Jesus said to him, "I am the way, and the truth, and the life. No one comes to the father except through me. If you know me, you will know my father also. From now on you do know him and have seen him.

"Beloved Jedediah, we will do our best to follow your example, in keeping with sacred scripture and tradition, to make a good life for ourselves.

"And we will work to make the world a better place for others.

"God, hear us. We love and miss our Jedediah. We remember him since his first coming into the world, now, and always, and forever. Amen."

As Brother Blaine concluded the eulogy, he closed his eyes and bowed to kiss the wood on the casket.

Two acolytes approached the coffin from the sanctuary. One carried the aspergillum, a brass ball filled with holy water, with a handle. The other carried the thurible, sending up clouds of fragrant, burning incense.

133

Brother Blaine, speaking prayers in Latin, with a quiet voice, walked twice around the casket. First to say rites to bless the body and casket reverently with holy water, and then with incense.

When the Mass was ended, he walked to where Olivia and Stella were standing, and hugged them one by one. Then, stretched his long arms around both, to hug them tight. All were shaking and swaying gently while crying. He kissed their cheeks and foreheads. Held them close a little longer.

Looking heavenward, he said for all to hear, "God, receive into your loving embrace, our husband, father, son and brother, Jedediah. Look ever so kindly upon Olivia and Stella, who have lost their life's love so early. Bless them with your grace. Guide our humble parish and community in giving this little family all the love and care that can only flow from your blessings. Amen."

Brother Blaine's immediate private thought was that he had not cried so many tears since he buried his parents, ten years past.

The entire assembly wept tears of sadness.

Brother Blaine blessed everyone:

May almighty God bless you,
The Father, and the Son, and the Holy Spirit.
Amen.

Years later, parishioners would recall this funeral Mass as the most solemn and uplifting ever attended.

A choir of Franciscan friars led by Brother Cyrus Wolverley, OFM, raised their voices to chant "Libera me Domine/Deliver me," an ancient poem asking God to have mercy upon the soul of the deceased on Judgement Day.

134

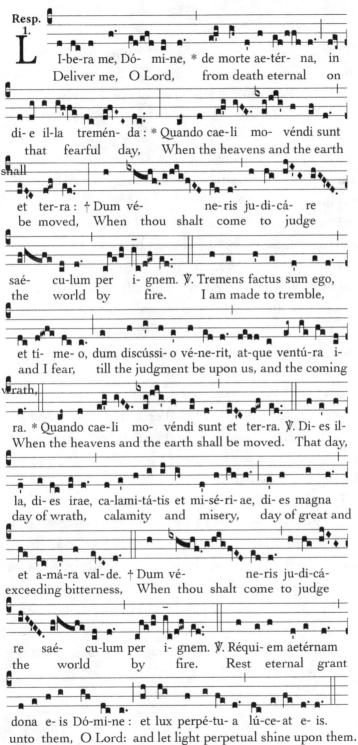

**Resp. 1.**

LÍbera me, Dómine, * de morte aetérna, in
Deliver me, O Lord, from death eternal on

di- e il-la tremén- da : * Quando cae-li mo- véndi sunt
that fearful day, When the heavens and the earth

et ter-ra : † Dum vé- ne-ris ju-di-cá- re
shall be moved, When thou shalt come to judge

saé- cu-lum per i- gnem. ℣. Tremens factus sum ego,
the world by fire. I am made to tremble,

et tí- me- o, dum discússi- o vé-ne-rit, at-que ventú-ra i-
and I fear, till the judgment be upon us, and the coming

ra. * Quando cae-li mo- véndi sunt et ter-ra. ℣. Di- es il-
wrath, When the heavens and the earth shall be moved. That day,

la, di- es irae, ca-lami-tá-tis et mi-sé-ri- ae, di- es magna
day of wrath, calamity and misery, day of great and

et a-má-ra val-de. † Dum vé- ne-ris ju-di-cá-
exceeding bitterness, When thou shalt come to judge

re saé- cu-lum per i- gnem. ℣. Réqui- em aetérnam
the world by fire. Rest eternal grant

dona e- is Dó-mi-ne : et lux perpé-tu- a lú-ce-at e- is.
unto them, O Lord: and let light perpetual shine upon them.

*Repetitur* Líbera me *usque ad* ℣. Tremens.

The pallbearers took hold of the lugs on Jedediah's casket to begin the procession out of St. Ann's. Placed it in the hearse. A funeral attendant drove the vehicle to the cemetery on St. Ann's east lawn.

The entire assembly processed slowly out of the nave, passed through the church's massive oak doors, and walked to the gravesite in the cemetery for Jedediah's committal.

After Brother Blaine completed religious rites, Lieutenant Garvey put a polished bugle to his lips and played the most reverential "Taps" anyone ever heard. A squad of soldiers fired three rifle volleys. Major Sawyer ordered the other soldiers to remove the flag from the coffin and fold it. Crying tears of sadness, he presented Olivia and Stella with the American flag.

Before leaving St. Ann's Cemetery, the Bradleys, Sanadas, and Youngs walked to the burial plots of their other deceased relatives. Brother Blaine joined them. Each of them carried a flower they drew from the top of Jedediah's casket to place on the headstone of a relative who preceded Jedediah.

The close-knit family gathering paused at each granite headstone to recall and share fond memories of the departed. Placed a flower gently on the stone. Prayed for their souls and the souls of all the faithful who were called home to God.

Weekly, after Sunday Mass, the family would visit Jed's grave, pray for his soul and the souls of all the faithful departed, and place a single white rose atop the headstone.

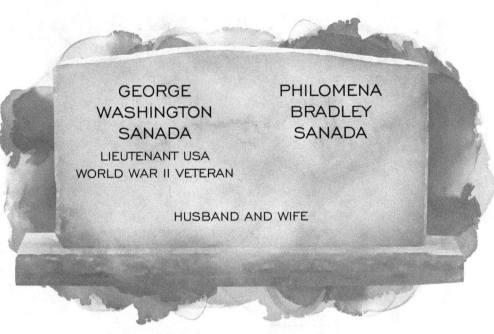

GEORGE
WASHINGTON
SANADA
LIEUTENANT USA
WORLD WAR II VETERAN

PHILOMENA
BRADLEY
SANADA

HUSBAND AND WIFE

Great-Grandfather
of Hana.

Great-Grandmother
of Stella.

AKIRO SANADA     SAKURA SANADA

HUSBAND AND WIFE

George's father.
Great-great-grandfather
of Stella.

George's mother.
Great-great-grandmother
of Stella.

CRAIG ALEXANDER
BRADLEY

STELLA
BRADLEY

MAJOR USA
WORLD WAR II VETERAN

HUSBAND AND WIFE

Great-Grandfather
of Stella.

Great-Grandmother
of Stella.

THOMAS NELSON
BRADLEY

1ST LIEUTENANT
KIA BATTLE OF OKINAWA.
BELOVED SON

SCARLETT
BRADLEY

BELOVED
DAUGHTER

THOMAS BRADLEY

RIFLEMAN
WAR OF INDEPENDENCE
VALLEY FORGE

Ancestor of the Bradley family.

Brother Blaine drew the family together at the cemetery gate. He asked them to join him in the Lord's Prayer.

Our Father who art in heaven,
hallowed be Thy name,
Thy kingdom come,
Thy will be done on earth
as it is in heaven;
give us this day our daily bread;
and forgive us our trespasses
as we forgive those
who trespass against us;
and lead us not into temptation,
but deliver us from evil.
For Thine is the kingdom
and the power and the glory
forever and ever.
Amen.

Then, he blessed everyone.

Holding Olivia and Stella close, the mournful family walked slowly to the church.

In the basement was a large hall, where St. Ann's Ladies Guild had organized a luncheon of soup and sandwiches, coffee, and soft drinks for all.

# — 18 —

ALL the family came together at the Sanada country home to hold a surprise party celebrating the seventeenth birthday for the girls.

They gave Hana her sixth-year voucher as a resident in the Academy for Humanity, new fall and winter clothes, tickets to a concert by her favorite musician, and a lime-green sling bag filled with essential tools for personal safety and gardening.

She was completely caught by surprise. All the gifts were things on her Need to Get list. She'd outgrown most of her clothes, like every year. The concert tickets were only a dream until now. The sling bag filled a big need.

She had earned the bag and tools by working in the garden since she was a toddler. Inside were a first aid kit, flashlight, mini garden tool set, multi-tool, fire starter kit, spool of parachute cord, and a water bottle. Two "energy bars," Hana's favorite chocolate candy bar. Also, a special tool: a leather-sheathed farmer's dagger for chopping off cabbage heads, carrot tops, Brussels sprouts, tree limbs, and vines.

When she unwrapped the dagger, Hana shouted with joy, "Exactly like yours, Papa! I've used it in the garden every day for years."

"Happy birthday, Hana!" They all shouted in celebration. She went around and hugged everyone.

"That dagger cuts just about everything down to size," Jonas said. "It'll do double service for defending yourself, if ever you should need it."

Charlotte said, "Stella, you are a precious, dear friend of Hana, and you are an adored child, cousin and grandchild in our family. Born on the same day in June to your wonderful mother, Olivia, and your adored father, Jedediah."

A pause for mourning.

"We are so, so sorry for Jedediah's passing. He's looking down on this birthday celebration now. Your father, and the love of your life, Olivia, are an inspiration to us all, and to the whole country. Captain Jedediah Young is a modern-day hero to everyone.

"Stella, you help us so much. And we love you, like our own granddaughter.

"And Olivia, you are a daughter to us.

"We love you both so much.

"Today is your birthday, Stella. Papa and I want you to have this present."

She handed the present to Stella. The box was covered in white wrapping paper with a crimson ribbon and a large crimson bow. Stella opened the box.

Inside was the same sling bag, in desert camo, her signature color. She unzipped the bag and pulled out the card listing her sixth-year voucher for a resident in the Academy for Humanity.

The sling bag contained the same tools for personal safety and gardening that Hana received.

In the box were new fall and winter clothes, including some in camo. Tickets to the same concert by their favorite musician.

A separate surprise red envelope held all arrangements for Stella, Hana, Isa, Olivia, and all the cousins to vacation for a week in February in the Bahamas.

Tears of joy trickled down Stella's cheeks.

"Oh my God! This is so kind, so thoughtful of you. Thank you," Stella said. She went around to hug and kiss her mom and grandparents, adopted grandparents and parents, cousins and Hana.

"A worker should have the best tools for laboring in the Garden of Earth," Jonas said.

"You've earned them, working side by side with us, Stella. And excelling in the Academy. All the gifts are so much love, so much gratefulness for you, our lovely child. We love you so much, and will throughout time."

Hana said, "You are my bestie, my sister, Stella. I'm so glad for you."

"And you are my sister, my bestie, always, Hana," Stella said.

Then, Stella stood, drew her dagger from its sheath, and shouted, "To arms, Washington!"

In sync, Hana stood, drew her dagger, clashed Stella's dagger, and echoing Stella, shouted, "To arms, Stella Emilia Young, my bestie!"

The whole birthday party laughed heartily. Hugs and kisses all around.

"Time for chocolate cake, sodas, and vanilla ice cream," Olivia proclaimed joyfully.

Later that evening Jonas told part of a somber, fascinating family history to the birthday party.

"Your great-grandfathers, Lieutenant George Washington Sanada and Major Craig Alexander Bradley, flew a secret reconnaissance mission over Japan, weeks before we dropped the atomic bombs on Hiroshima and Nagasaki, ending that horrible war.

"Let's pause the story here."

The party reverently bowed their heads in prayer for the suffering, the loss, and the deaths of soldiers and civilians who died in the war in Japan, Europe, North Africa, the Pacific Islands, and the United States.

Olivia, a deacon at church, prayed aloud, "God, we beseech you in utmost humility. We ask your forgiveness for all people for the horrors committed in that war, and for all wars before and since. . . . We know evil rises up from time to time. We must have the courage to know evil for what it is, and defeat evil. Lest it destroy us, your people, and your covenant with mankind since creation. God, bless and keep all people throughout the world. Amen."

"Amen," the party prayed in unison.

A reverent pause.

"The story continues like this," Jonas said.

"On a sunny day in the spring of 1966, a black 1962 Chevy Biscayne taxi pulled up to George Sanada's driveway. Some of the family stood on our front porch to see who had come to visit us—in a taxi.

"You never saw a taxi way out here.

"The driver got out, walked around to the passenger side rear door, and opened it. Out stepped two very handsome men, one older, one younger, dressed in the finest suits we'd ever seen.

"Then, the taxi driver opened the car's trunk.

"The younger man reached into the trunk to bring out a long, slender case.

"He approached the porch and said, 'I am Haruki Sanada.' Gesturing to the older man, he said, 'This is my father, Kenshin Sanada. Are you George Washington Sanada?'".

"'Yes, I am. Oh my God! And I recognize both of you. What a wonderful surprise. Welcome to our home in America,'" George answered with a broad smile.

"'Philomena, tell Mom and Dad to come on the porch.'"

"George's parents, Akiro and Sakura Sanada, were now in their late seventies. They had sold the Sanada Clothier business in San Francisco the previous year, and moved in with George and Philomena, and their newborn son, Evan."

"'Please forgive us for this unannounced arrival,'" Haruki stated. "'Governments, here and at home, are still not so friendly to the ways and needs of good, free people. It delayed our correspondence and travel from Japan. And arrival here at your home in America. But, we do not complain. It is what it it is, as Americans are fond of saying. Sad, but true.

"'Is Major Bradley here, also?'" Haruki inquired.

"'Philomena, would you please call the Bradleys?'" George asked.

"'Yeah,'" Philomena said.

"Turning to Haruki, George continued, 'They live just down the street.'"

In minutes, the Bradleys arrived.

After warm bows, hugs, and handshakes all around, Haruki Sanada spoke, "'My father wants you, George Sanada and Craig Bradley, to have this case of two samurai katana swords. They were used by our ancestor, Sanada Nobushige, to defend our ancient clan and lord from our enemies four hundred years ago.'"

"Then, he handed the case to his father. Kenshin Sanada bowed, and in turn held the case out horizontally with both hands.

145

"He said in a strong Japanese-American accent, "'I present this to you as a token of our family's deepest gratitude for your bravery in saving all of us from almost certain death. Also, for bringing us safely out of the cave in the forest, our secret place of hiding from the Imperial Japanese Army, in 1945.'"

"After a hastily prepared feast by Philomena and George, Haruki, Kenshin, and the taxi driver departed with gifts from George and Craig to take back home to Japan. The visitors couldn't stay long because they had business meetings arranged with clients in Boston, New York, Miami, St. Louis, and Chicago."

When the seventeenth birthday party for the girls was ending, Jonas brought out the ancient, ornate wooden box, about three feet long, by six inches wide, and four inches deep. He had never shown this heirloom previously. It had been stored away in the attic since arriving.

"Stella, there's a secret latch to open this case. Would you press your finger gently on this small, gold leaf, right here," Jonas asked, pointing with his index finger.

"Okay, Grandad Jonas," Stella said.

Instantly, the top of the case popped open. The inside panels, lid, and base were lined in rich, ancient, crimson silk, with a dragon motif. The box released a rich aroma of ginger and anise.

Jonas explained, "In this case, are the two, Japanese katana swords, once used by a samurai warrior in our family. They are encased in wooden sheaths decorated with animals. One a ferocious boar, the other a savage wolf. If the case is opened by a thief or someone not in the Sanada family, a curse to extinction falls upon him and his family throughout time."

He grabbed the handle of one sword, pulled it out of the case, held it up, and slowly drew the blade out of its sheath.

Everyone was astonished at its beauty.

Jonas added, 'The blades are twenty-eight inches long, curved upward slightly, and made of hardened, razor-sharp steel, according to ancient recipes. The neatly corded grips are long, for two-handed fighting."

"Now, they pass down to you. Happy birthday, my lovely grandchildren, Hana and Stella," Jonas concluded.

# — 19 —

DAY One 0317.

A swarm of tiger mosquitos found the heat from George's body a perfect target for an early morning meal, especially his exposed ears and face.

Swatted 'em away.

"Time? 03:17. Ugh. Wet. Chilly."

Yawned and stretched each arm and leg separately, so as not to make a sound kicking underbrush or dislodging rocks.

"Damned uncomfortable mattress. Couple of rocks did a number on my back.

"Cold. Wet pants. I'm shivering."

He pulled the jacket collar around his ears. Sat up.

In the dim light, he made mental notes of every object that came into view, 360 degrees around. As the light increased, he added more detail to the map. The slow, downward-sloping mountain path was the most prominent feature. He linked everything to the path.

Four Japanese hondo deer, antler-less, approached the path below him from his side. Slow-walked, noiseless, crossed the path and stream, disappeared like ghosts. A bug-eyed dormouse scurried upside down on a tree limb over his head. Half an hour later a black Asian moon bear, all but impossible to see, followed the hondo deer.

149

"Probably searching for the same food," he reasoned.

A white-backed woodpecker broke the morning silence, pecking for insects on a dead tree limb high up, across the stream. "Early bird gets the . . . bug for breakfast. Thank God for beautiful, innocent wildlife," he thought.

George checked his equipment, touching each: dog tags on chain around neck, taped for silence, canteen full of water on belt, 5 emergency ration Hershey's chocolate bars in right front pants pocket, three rice cakes from Mom in right jacket pocket, one red Yakima apple picked from the crate in the mess tent in left jacket pocket, basic first aid kit left shirt breast pocket, compass and fire starter kit right shirt breast pocket, parachute, now his flimsy mattress, TL-29 pocket knife hanging from a loop on front left belt, Binocular M13A 6x30 with strap on the ground at his right hip, leather flight helmet on top of the binocs, ANJ-3 leather flight jacket, underclothes, pants, socks, boots, .45-caliber Colt M1911 pistol, cocked and locked in leather holster on right hip with two full spare magazines in pouches, 7 rounds each, pistol belt, wallet in front left pants pocket, pocket-sized Hebrew Bible and New Testament in the left inside breast pocket he'd sewn on his fatigue jacket.

"Seems damned picky, I suppose, but gotta know what's here, in case I need any one thing in a pinch. Gotta keep busy, mentally and physically, too," George reassured himself.

He pulled out the compass and determined that the section of mountain path before him ran east to west, same as the last leg of their flight yesterday. The forest canopy prevented using higher or more distant points for bearings.

"That will have to do. The Zero's pilot surely spotted me bailing out and reported where. Could have a visitor or two. Sit tight for now. See what's here."

Sleep came.

Day Two 0515.

Get up.

A rivulet, arm's length away on his right side, slow-trickled seep water to the mountain stream. George used his fist to make a depression in the flowage large enough to refill his canteen for fresh water, when the puddle cleared.

Misty, rainy morning.

Movement up the path.

Twelve adult Japanese peasants, and one husky lead man, all wearing drab jackets and pants, walked slowly, single file, strung out, down the long, meandering, narrow mountain path. Sometimes they came into view, often they were hidden by overhanging foliage.

George pulled up the binocs.

Peering through the leaves and branches, he studied the peasants' movements. The lead peasant slowly turned left and walked stealthily into the brush at the stream edge. Up the path, each person stepped off the path at a point known to them. They crossed the stream and disappeared, like the hondo deer.

George caught sight of them again. They continued a slow, silent walk to a secluded meadow a stone's throw away.

In silence and in slow motion, they tended fish traps in the stream, small game animal traps in hollow logs, tree trunks, and burrows. They cultivated vegetable gardens scattered about. At the far end of the meadow, was a shallow

151

marsh fed by a spring higher up the mountainside. There was an earthen dam at a slightly lower elevation to regulate water levels for rice. Plowing, germination, seedling growth, planting, and harvesting.

Numerous dead trees lent natural overhead camouflage throughout the garden area. Their gardens were varied, discrete, and meticulously cared for.

All day long, George studied the peasants collecting and gutting fish from the traps and re-baiting them. Same with the small game traps. They dumped scraps into several depressions they had dug in the ground. There to decompose into fertilizer for later seasons.

Everyone tended the garden and cared for the land. Plowing and raking the soil with handmade tools, and pulling weeds. Worked the rice paddy. No slacking. No haste. No talking. A hand signal now and then. Like the moon bear, dormouse, and hondo deer, they foraged in silence, worked the soil, the stream, and the marsh, harvesting food all day long.

At twilight, the peasants gathered up the harvest in shoulder bags. They reversed course, with the husky man in the lead again, and walked silently back up the path. Disappeared in the mist and foliage.

Before darkness settled in, George cleared emergency exits for himself in front to go up the mountain path, another for down the path, in the rear to go downhill off the path, and one exit at the rear to go directly uphill.

Darkness came early due to an overcast sky, mist, and drizzling rain. Before he laid down for the night, he used the TL-29's screwdriver blade to dig up a couple of fist-sized stones and move them to the side.

"This night's rest should be a tad more comfortable."

152

Pulled out a rice cake from Mom. "Yum. I love you, Mom."

And a government-issue chocolate candy bar. "Not so tasty." Took a swig from the canteen to wash them down.

Sleep came.

Day Three 0503.

George stretched, sat, ate another rice cake, quenched his thirst, stood, stepped aside, relieved himself. Sat back down.

Sun's rays, ever so slowly, increasingly, shined through huge billowing white clouds to light up the forest.

Steam was rising. Burned off by the sun.

About the same time as yesterday, but now more visible, the peasants appeared, walking slowly, silently down the path. They followed the same procedure. The same order.

This morning, three elderly people led, far ahead of the others: two men first and then one woman behind. After them came four other adults, the husky leader, and today, five teens.

"More than twelve people up there," George pondered. "They appear at dawn each day, slow-moving, silent, and indistinct. Pass through tree trunks, branches, leaves, boulders, on wet mountain soil, to labor a simple life in the forest. A well-worked routine. Expert care for the land, planting and harvesting their food. Day by day.

"Who are they? Why are they here? Japan's at war?" George had considered these questions day and night since the first discovery.

"Puzzling. Fascinating. Good. Natural. Sacred. Beautiful.

153

"Like a dreamland. The Garden of Eden. Paradise recovered. The rest of the world is flaming mad, but nowhere hereabouts."

When the sun began to slide behind the mountain, the peasants collected their harvest and slowly, silently, walked up the path. The temptation to greet them, know them, follow them up the path was overwhelming.

"I'd really like to talk with them. Not now. Not yet," he counseled himself.

"How am I gonna get outta here? When? Where to? Secluded. Sitting, stretching, waiting, listening. What for? I don't yet know. Seeing nature's beauty, and these people going about their daily work together. To plow, plant, cultivate, and harvest food the way God intended, all day. What could be more pleasing, more human? Staggering contrast in a world wracked by this hellish war.

"Mom, Dad, I love you, and hope you are well. Craig, I pray you ditched the plane or made it to Vladivostok safely. I love you all. I will get back home."

George took the apple from his jacket pocket and used the TL-29 to slice off pieces for quiet chewing. "So good." He plucked seven seeds out of the carpels, put them in the jacket pocket with the Bible, and buried the core in the soil. "Some day I'll plant these seeds for an apple orchard."

A drink from the canteen and a rice cake for dinner. Sleep came.

Day Four 0248.

A huge tiger, with wide, shimmering green eyes, leapt down from an overhead tree limb, through the dark night

154

sky, and viciously attacked him. Its huge jaws, opened wide, released a stench like rotting meat. Choked his breathing.

Sharp fangs tore off his face. All four paws, with yellowed claws the size of bale hooks, ripped his arms, sides, back, and legs to ribbons of skin and muscle. A sudden bite and jerk of the tiger's head tore off his scalp. A second more and it would rip out his throat and stomach, spilling his blood and guts down the mountain to the stream.

"God help me! I can't move! So hot. Can't breathe. Licking my blood and sweat pouring out everywhere," George mumbled.

All at once, the enormous cat stood stock still. Glared into his face, its nose inches away. The beast's lungs swelled massively, drew in the late nighttime air, and exhaled a forceful blue, fire-tinged, putrid breath. A terrifying, massive flaring.

The beast circled around him, and then stood astride him, head-to-toe. Looked away to the south. Growled violently, in the manner of a disturbed big cat. Looked north, then east, then west. Paused at each compass point. And then turned its gaze south again. Looked down into George's eyes. Slowly moved its broad head in a circle, now lovingly, as if to caress its newborn cub. The long, stiff whiskers on the cat's face and chin inclined forward to gently comb George's hair, forehead, ears, eyes, nose, chin, and neck. The fearsome beast sensed what was happening to him and around them.

Then paused. Snarled loudly. Turned its head up to gaze gloomily at the dark sky.

A moment passed.

Then, the gigantic tiger melted away.

"I'm touching my face. I'm still alive. A nightmare! Jesus, help me!" George, abruptly conscious, sat bolt upright, in a full body sweat.

"Oh my God! Horrible. Get up."

George eased himself upright, stood for a while, shook loose his arm and leg muscles. Arched his back forward, all around, backward. Twice again.

Then, sat down. Thanks to the Japanese tiger nightmare, he came in touch with his impassioned instinct to survive.

Breathed deeply, exhaled slowly. Became calm once again.

The Waxing Gibbous moon, shining steely blue light, was suddenly hidden by a slow-moving, dark cloud.

Murkiness reigned everywhere, causing a chilling interlude.

Moments later the cloud passed by and the moon again lit up the forest with its cool metallic glow.

An indistinct drone far in the distance, behind and overhead, gained definition.

George knew the sound: a Japanese plane. It flew in a northerly direction, and completed a turn directly overhead. Continued flying due east.

"Zero's pilot reported," George reasoned.

Presently, there was a loud thud on the path, and "Oof."

A minute later George could see a parachute, descending into the same area, rapidly, catching tree branches, snapping limbs, and collapsing on the mountain path.

The second thing to drop out of the sky with a parachute was a Japanese soldier. He stood over the motionless lump on the path. A teammate, his partner, whose chute never opened.

The second soldier spoke Japanese in muffled anger, "Damn it! You sick coward. You son of a bitch! Afraid the war's ending, eh? We're gonna lose? We got monstrous losses everywhere now. You would rather commit suicide than help win the war. Help find the American enemy. Capture and kill him. You leave the work to me? Bastard. Asshole. I hope you rot in Jigoku."

George spoke Japanese fluently, so he understood everything said by the soldier. They were sent here to capture and kill him. Torture him for thrills. But one assassin had had enough of the war and killed himself.

George stood up silently, slowly. Studied options for his next move. Said in silence, "Recap: today, in the early morning darkness, two Japanese soldiers on a mission to kill me landed on the path. One dead, one alive. Absolutely everything I choose to do depends on every next little thing."

He took a long, quiet, deep breath. Right-hand fingers touched the Bible in his left breast pocket. Felt the apple seeds. He exhaled slowly. "Now, everything must be deliberate and silent," George commanded himself. Fingertips unbuttoned the leather cover-flap for the Colt pistol on his right hip. He was confident of his first and follow-up shots. An expert marksman out to fifty yards, and then some.

The Japanese assassin continued cursing. Gathered up his parachute, extricated cords from the tree branches, and dropped it all in a crude pile on the path. Next, he kicked the corpse hard, one foot after another. Dragged the dead body to the stream-side of the path. Rolled it over the stream bank, out of easy sighting. "Serves you right, you sick asshole," he pronounced in a hushed voice. He retrieved his own parachute for bedding, and walked to the same side of the path George was on, some yards farther up.

Hungry, the assassin sat down on the mountainside and promptly opened one of his five food ration packets. Before his flight, he had assembled them from an open "Polished Rice Combination Case." He also brought along several rice cakes left over from past days. Ration packets included the usual: polished rice, dehydrated miso paste, vitamin B supplementary food, vitamins A and D tablets, powdered tea to supply vitamin C, and a portion of fuel and matches. The fuel he stashed for later to warm meals in daylight. Matches into his shirt pocket for lighting cigarettes. Rice and miso paste saved for breakfast tomorrow morning. He dumped the powdered tea into his canteen, let it cold-steep. Ate a rice cake. Drank the tea to wash down the vitamin tablets. Paused. Stared straight ahead. Nodded sleepily several times. He settled into the brushy, rocky ground on the hillside to sleep. Grumbled. Shifted positions.

"Shit! Damned rocks!" The assassin grumbled. "Bugs up my nose! Ears! Damn it," he cursed quietly. He sat up. Struck a match. Lit up a Japanese Golden Bat cigarette.

Downwind, George saw the flame, the bright-red burning ash, and caught the rank smoke.

When the first Golden Bat was a bare ember, the assassin lit up a second from the live butt, and continued smoking. Fell asleep sitting, hands in his lap. The whole, red-hot ash on the Bat dropped, tumbled down, slowly burned through the cloth at the crotch of his pants. Seared the head of his penis.

"Shit! Damn it!" the assassin seethed in muffled anger. Abruptly stood up, while shaking the burning cigarette ash from his crotch. Patted out his smoldering pants. Spat

158

on his fingers and shoved them down his pants to soothe his burned penis head. Lay down again. Passed out. Snored loudly.

George nearly retched from the putrid smell. Golden Bat cigarette smoke, mixed with burning trousers, and scorched human skin. Dozed now and again.

Sleep never came.

Day Five 0517.

George had been awake, off and on, all night. He peered through the early morning mist for an hour after the very barest daylight lit up the forest.

The assassin rustled in his sleep on the stony bed. Moaned and groaned. He stood up, stretched. Faced downhill. Opened his pants and pulled out his penis to pee. Forced out a howler fart. Inspected his seared penis head. "Ugh, burned deep. Pus oozing out." Applied his spit. Smeared it around. Squeezed the penis head. Sighed in relief. Bent forward and closed his pants.

A movement caught his eye.

He turned his head to look up the forest path. The first elderly peasant man walked down the path, out of the mist and into the dim morning light, unaware of the danger he faced. The second elderly man and the woman followed the first at their usual twenty-foot intervals. The lead team was far ahead of the other gardeners.

"What the hell!" the assassin said, loud enough for all to hear. He burst through the brambles. Strutted hurriedly onto the path, his 8x22mm Nambu pistol in his right hand pointed directly at them. Waved his left arm erratically.

"Stop!" he commanded.

The first peasant halted. Faced the assassin, four feet in front of him. All the peasants stopped walking the instant the assassin shouted the order.

The nine peasants farther up the path, swiftly, silently disappeared into the underbrush.

George did not move or make a sound. "Watch. Listen. Wait. Stay calm. Make a plan," he could hear Craig whisper in his ear.

"Get in a line! Now!" the assassin ordered. "The punishment for deserters and traitors is death!"

The peasants stood shoulder-to-shoulder, one foot apart, in a line across the path, facing the assassin. Two men on the left, the woman on the right.

The assassin walked over and stood in front of the woman.

"What is your name!" he demanded. "Look at me when I give orders!"

The woman gazed very slightly, obliquely, past him down the path.

"You insolent old bitch! I said look at me!"

Her gaze remained fixed away down the path. Her face placid.

In a flash, the assassin hit her head on the left side with the pistol, so hard that blood streamed down from deep gashes on her scalp, welled into her eyes and ears, and drip, drip, dripped from her earlobe, nose, and chin into the soil. The assassin watched her attentively, with grim amusement. Eyeballed the woman's blood oozing from her wounds, flowing down her body, to soak her clothes red, and puddle in the soil at her feet. He showed extreme irritation. Hatred. Only more cruelty could follow.

"You answer me! Now! Your name! Why are you here? Not working in a factory? Okay, bitch, chew on that. I got something special for you after I interrogate the two old bastards with you."

He walked in front of the man in the middle of the line. "That old hag your wife?" the assassin screamed, laughing hysterically. "My lucky guess, eh? Answer me! You cowardly old fool. Idiot. Useless cockhold!" The assassin bent close to the elderly peasant's face and screamed, "Where are you hiding the American?"

The peasant stood calmly, gazing past the assassin down the path, seeing nothing, showing no emotion.

The assassin noticed. "Just like your slut wife, eh. Insolent bastard! The American! Where is he?"

In the blink of an eye, the assassin pistol-whipped the second peasant on both sides of his head. Red blood gushed from the wounds. Splattered on the leaves, sticks, and grass. Soaked up by the soil. The assassin laughed menacingly. "You like that, asshole? Wait till I finish your whore-wife."

The assassin strutted to the third peasant.

George's mind was racing.

An uncanny mist had settled upon the mountainside, but held, like a leaden curtain. Did not stir. In the pale morning light, trees, trail, stream, and actors in the tableau were fixed, like an eerie daguerreotype.

George had seen and heard enough to know the assassin's MO. Was confident about the next steps the little martinet would take to get his jollies, his personally seasoned prize. George chose the closest route from his position to the mountain path. Oblique, cleared of brush. Slowly drew the Colt pistol half out of the holster.

161

"Gotta be a better way. One shot, all cover blown, for miles around." Paused. "Not another Gunfight at the OK Corral," he summed up.

George recalled, "A nun from elementary school, fourth grade, Sister Mary Paulus. God bless her. They were all Sister Marys. She always had us print JMJ at the top of every paper: for Jesus, Mary, and Joseph, to protect us. Must have worked. Got me this far."

"JMJ," he mouthed reverently.

Then, George recalled Deuteronomy 31:6, the Hebrew Bible.

Be strong and stalwart. Do not fear and do not dread them, for the LORD your God, He it is Who goes with you. He will not let go of you and He will not forsake you.

Mouthed a silent "Amen."

George looked to the ground. At his feet were the two stones he dug out of the soil that had caused him such misery the first night. "Appear to be volcanic rhyolite, worn smooth and rounded by Mother Nature over millennia," he noted. A plan fell into place instantly. Picked up the stones. "Size, about right." Tossed them up, one by one. "Heft, about right. Round enough. Not a Spalding, but hell, I started by throwing rocks not half this good," he reminisced. Put the first choice in his right hand. Second stuffed in his left pants pocket over his wallet. Noiselessly slid off the jacket and binoculars. Laid them on the ground at his feet. "Eyes open wide. Totally study the scene," he cautioned.

Darkly silent as the ghostly hondo deer the first morning, George creeped on the escape route he'd made from his hideout to the center of the mountain path. Passed silently through the trailside brush. Took a position about sixty feet behind the assassin. Waited for the signal.

The gaze of the peasants changed for an instant, ever so subtly, from the assassin. Their eyes infused with the light of hope. They had watched George appear, like a noiseless morning shadow, to step fearless out of the brush onto the path, directly behind the assassin.

George read their eyes intently. And they his. They discreetly shifted their vision smoothly from the assassin's eyes to George's and caught his silent command, "Speak with your eyes." The peasants acknowledged his game call with blinks. With life or death imminent on this mountain trail, the peasants instantly grasped George's strategy: "Catchers: send me the signal rapierlike, portending certain death."

The assassin walked up to the third peasant. Immediately whacked him violently on the left side of his head. Red blood flowed down his face, soaked into the soil at his feet. Like the others, he stared ahead, didn't flinch.

"Another stubborn bastard! What's your name? Why are you here?" the assassin demanded, then punched the pistol barrel hard into the peasant's chest. Drew blood. Shouted inches from the peasant's face, "Where are you hiding the American? Tell me. Now! You perverted shit!"

No reply.

The assassin turned and walked back. Paused to stare into the middle peasant's eyes. His gestures and movements bespoke rage. Stopped in front of the elderly peasant woman. Glared at her. "One of you will crack. Always ends this way. Weaklings win. Ha ha ha ha," he insulted them loudly. Clearly, he'd carried out this deadly routine with captives, more than once before. He was not a worthy Japanese soldier or enemy. Picked by superiors for a barbaric craft. He was a satanic tool.

The assassin stared fixedly into the woman's eyes. He slowly re-holstered the pistol held in his right hand. From a scabbard held by a belt at his waist, he then drew a Japanese tanto dagger. Put the silvery, razor-sharp blade under her chin. In a cold, sinister voice, he said, "You disgust me, traitor. Old hag. You got one last chance. Answer my questions, or prepare to die!

"No answer?

"I will choose how! Here?" Moving the blade from her right to her left ear, suggesting slashing her throat.

"Here?" Moving the blade across her stomach to disembowel her.

"Or, maybe you'd like it here, up from your nasty crotch? My choice," pressing the blade's tip hard onto her pubic bone, drawing blood. "Lower, maybe?"

Catchers' signals given. George returned them with a well-known, slight tip of his head, prepared to wind up for the pitch. Quick as lightning, all the peasants dropped into the crouch position.

"What the hell are you imbeciles doing?" the little martinet screeched. His orders, once given, can never be disobeyed! He rapidly tossed up three delicious options in his sick brain: slit all their throats with the tanto knife, blow out their brains with the pistol, or, best, carve them up alive one by one, to make them beg him for mercy. Strange that! The peasants' eyes were no longer gazing into a mystical distance. Instead they were focused intently on something particular, behind him. He turned around to look where the peasants eyes led him. Spotted

George, the American. Dropped the tanto knife and drew his pistol. As he brought the gun up to aim, George's 96-mph rhyolite fastball immediately slammed into the assassin's forehead to bury itself in his skull. He dropped like a stone. Dead.

No one moved or uttered a sound.

Time passed.

George listened. Surveyed the area for any other threats. Slowly looked right, left, behind, above, like the great American bald eagle patiently, wisely searching for threats or prey.

Insects resumed buzzing, roaming for mates and bloody bites. Songbirds chirped, staked out their territories, courted. Woodpeckers rattled on dead tree limbs high up, across the stream, seeking insects to eat. Clear, cold water in the mountain stream, flowed freely from high up, burbled, crashed, splashed through rocks, fallen limbs and logs, fish swimming about, on its ancient, meandering way to the Pacific Ocean.

All was quiet. Peace had returned to the mountain's forest path.

Satisfied that there were no other threats, George slowly turned his focus forward, and walked up to the crouching peasants. "I will do you no harm," he said softly in Japanese. "Please, dress your wounds as best you can in the stream. Then, we will talk."

The elderly peasants stood, bowed to George, and walked to the stream, holding hands for balance.

# — 20 —

LAST year, winter came early to Eridu Springs. Early and harsh. Wicked cold northwesterly winds blew from Canada. In frosty weather-speak, "Alberta Clippers" roared into the region again and again. From mid-October to March 20, first day of spring. Week after week, below-freezing temperatures held sway.

Dark billowy clouds broke over that dreaded horizon from where the winds came. They brought humungous storms that buried the land in snow for hundreds of miles around.

The deep, rich black soil was frozen to the greatest depth ever recorded by farmers and the local weather station. The annual "January Thaw" lasted only two days, and brought some relief and joy to hearts of families hunkered down for the duration. But the rock-hard ground did not thaw. Farmers remember such things.

More hardship was in store for the Gordon and Emma Stanton Farm family.

The Stantons were no strangers to extreme weather of all kinds. They were proud of their heritage, toughness against all odds. In this time of dire need, they helped neighbors who were less fortunate, with shelter, food and clothing.

Gordon and Emma Stanton lived in the Stanton Family House with their children, Carla, Montgomery, and Etana.

All three teens were enrolled as resident students at the Stanton Academy for Humanity. Twelve girls, who were also resident students at the Academy, lived in the Stanton Family House. Savior, the family's famous German Shepard, was everyone's favorite family member.

At the core of the Stantons' home life was caring for all the children, and farming 250 acres that Gordon and Emma leased from the Stanton Academy for Humanity.

Gordon's ancestor, Ebenezer Stanton, answered the notice he received from a rider on a watershed day in April, 1775, to fight in the American War for Independence from England. He said a tearful goodbye to his wife, Anna, and their two-month old son, Marcus. He rode away on their only horse, Bucephalus, named after the most famous horse of Alexander the Great. As ordered by his commander, Ebenezer Stanton arrived on the road from Cambridge to Concord, Massachusetts. He was armed with his short hanger sword, an iron-headed tomahawk, Pennsylvania long rifle, and accoutrements. After the Battles of Lexington and Concord, he served in several local militias, and finally in the army under George Washington. At war's end, after the Treaty of Paris on September 3, 1783, Bucephalus carried Ebenezer home to continue farming with his wife and young family.

In recent years, the house was enlarged and renovated. Later it was renamed the Stanton Family House, one of twelve Family Houses in the Stanton Academy for Humanity.

The annual ten-acre garden and orchard that Gordon and Emma Stanton tended was legendary, providing bushels of vegetables and fruits for the Stanton Family House. When the gardens of neighbors and friends didn't produce enough, the Stantons provided. They sold twice that much or more to the Academy. The farm also sold products to local markets, and at their own roadside stand down by the mailbox on the county road.

Their food supply and animals held up well that winter, bad as it was. No one in the Stanton Family House, or among the animals, got sick.

In February, four ewes brought surprises, each birthing twins—eight black, button-nosed lambs. Students from campus visited often to care for them, play with them, and for the pure joy of tending the little darlings. Just to sit back and marvel at their cuteness and crazy antics.

"God's creation is beautiful and plentiful. We are grateful, Lord, for what we have. Thank you, for all our blessings. Amen." Gordon's prayer when it was his turn before supper.

In wintertime, on many days after chores and studies were done, Gordon and Emma spent time relaxing by the wood stove in the large family room—with their three kids, twelve girls from the Academy, and Savior.

Wind howled menacingly outside, family life inside was warm and cozy. They talked about the day's events, things they loved doing, their fears and worries, and dreams. Friends. National and international news.

The twelve resident girls talked about their own families and friends living in other towns and states. Their aunts and uncles and grandparents. Letters, texts, photos, and videos from home. Birthdays and anniversaries. Reports of illness and death.

And the instructors, and their many friends in the Stanton Academy for Humanity.

They cracked jokes and laughed until their bellies ached, even if retold a dozen times before.

The home had a well-stocked library off the family room. The whole family would read literature, history, the

Bible aloud for all. Other times alone, privately, curled up on a sofa. Talked about a myriad of world events, cultures and discoveries. They enacted scenes from plays, duked it out with board games and charades, or put puzzles together for the umpteenth time.

"We have lots to be thankful for," Emma would say with arms outstretched before they went to bed. "I love you all. Sleep well, children."

"We love you, too, Mom and Dad. Thank you for all you do for us," the kids said in a chorus.

Emma and Gordon remained in the family room until the kids were asleep. They cuddled up on the sofa, fitted like two spoons, under a throw, for warmth.

They drank a glass of wine or two, talked about the kids, the day, the farm, their dreams, and kissed lovingly before going to their bedroom.

The winter gave way to spring on the Stanton farm, as always, in its own time, and in its own way. No season was the same year to year. No season can be rushed. Only endured and worked. On dark, frigid nights, Gordon and Emma prayed that they had made the necessary preparations, stocked enough food, checked and rechecked the equipment, and stacked the woodpile high. Mother Nature does not bargain.

Some years, harvests were plentiful. Occasionally, harvests were disastrous. Most years the harvest was just good enough. There was, though, the little matter of getting all work done with Mother Nature's erratic surprises. And other unexpected, live events.

One day a week, ahead of this planting season, Gordon spent an hour, in a personal, traditional way, studying the moisture content and temperature of soil in their four large grain fields. He'd select a spot and stab a thermometer into the soil to get a reading. Dig shallow holes with a trowel in low places, especially, to expose roots, dirt and decaying matter. Then, he'd grab a fistful, squeeze it with his fingers and smell it. The moisture content was always too high. Smell was good, though.

Every year Gordon strove to get a true sense, like farmers did thousands of years before him, for the year's first day to start plowing. He couldn't plow too early, clod up the mucky soil, and risk getting the tractor and plow stuck in the field. A springtime plowing disaster.

"Nope, not yet, but soon. Soon," he concluded each day.

Two weeks earlier, when the frost was finally out of all the ground, he drew soil samples and brought them to the Stanton Academy's lab to be tested by students for nitrogen, phosphorus, potassium, pH, calcium, magnesium, organic matter and copper, zinc, iron, and manganese. The results came back yesterday, showing excellent conditions for the grains he would plant in the four fields.

"You can't rush nature. You have to love her like a beautiful woman. She comes through in her own time, in her own way. Often with great surprises. There's no wrong or right to nature. You gotta stay up to date in agricultural science. That's all we have, and it ain't certain by any means, besides traditions handed down generation after generation. A ten-thousand-year, ongoing process, in God's design. Keep accurate records on grains, crop growing histories on your land, soils, and rainfall, temperature, varying seasonal deviations, consequences, and on and on.

"Nature doesn't follow science. To the absolute contrary. Science is only a useful, manmade method of continuously inquiring about constantly evolving events and elements in the natural world. Our beliefs, our hopes, and our dreams are continuously evolving on this land, in our families, and communities. Nature is God's handiwork unfolding as sublime creation—beyond human knowing. All that we can do is try to know her, and always respect her. Prepare the best we can every day for whatever may come. And pray that we get things right for her.

"God willing," Gordon reflected out loud.

Late that afternoon, Gordon was on his knees in Grain Field 4, where he'd stuck the trowel in the soil again to take a sample for moisture content. Savior stood nearby. Watched Gordon's every move. Wagged her tail back and forth rhythmically. Breathed with her tongue out. Waited patiently.

A cool east wind blew sleet in Gordon's face. Batting his eyes, he stood up, wiped his brow, squeezed the soil, sniffed it, and threw it into the wind. The wind carried the particles away in a magical dispersion.

"There it is! Savior!"

"You betcha," Savior barked.

"Tomorrow, Emma, I will plow our fields," Gordon proclaimed aloud joyfully, as though she was by his side listening.

"I heard that!" Emma's voice came from his cellphone, laughing loudly. "I heard it all, Lover Boy!"

She took great delight in catching her husband forgetting to end a phone call to her.

"Gotcha again! Ha ha."

"Emma, you're amazing, my beautiful bride. I love you."

In the background, Savior barked, "Hello."

"Hi, Savior," Emma responded.

"I'll be home soon for dinner," Gordon said, and ended the call. He noticed next to no battery life remaining on his phone.

Next morning at 3:00 a.m., Emma awoke, reached over and grabbed Gordon in a special way that said, "Honey, let's make love."

In the early morning darkness, in the act of eternal love, husband and wife gave one another the gift of sacred connubial bliss. A most profound sleep came upon the lovers.

At 4:00 a.m., the alarm on Emma's cellphone chimed, "Time to rise and shine!"

She shook Gordon awake.

He said sleepily, "Again?"

"I would love to, Lover Boy, but the dawn's calling us."

Gordon went to the bathroom, showered, shaved, and dressed.

Emma pulled on her knee-length flannel nightie, got the coffee brewing and made a breakfast of fruit, yogurt, hard-boiled eggs, and toast for herself and Gordon. She filled a large Thermos with black coffee, and assembled two lunchmeat sandwiches, an apple, and a granola bar for Gordon's meals. Stored them in his insulated lunch bag.

Then, checking the week's menu posted on the fridge for the family, she gathered ingredients for the fifteen kids' breakfast, and set them on the countertop. Stacked plates and cups close by, and laid out boxes with silverware and napkins.

Savior sat on her behind nearby, waiting for her breakfast. She knew Emma always gave her a treat before setting out her meal.

"Here, baby." Emma flourished the Milk-Bone. Savior downed the treat, then began crunching her main meal and lapped up water.,

Gordon sat at the breakfast bar, thinking about his first day of plowing this spring. Emma poured coffee into two mugs for them, set out their breakfast, then sat down next to her husband. She wrapped her arms around his neck, gently put her head on his shoulder, and whispered, "I love you, Gordon."

"I love you, too, Emma. You're my best friend. My beautiful bride." They finished the breakfast meal.

Gordon grabbed the Thermos and lunch bag, and passionately hugged and kissed Emma. With a quick look into Savior's eyes, he walked to the breezeway. Savior knew the routine, and followed. Gordon grabbed his cap, Savior's lunch, and opened the door. Outside, a cold darkness before dawn.

"Bye, you sneaky little sweetheart. I love you. See you for supper," Gordon said.

"You're my Lover Boy," Emma said, hiking up the nightie with both hands. Her beautiful, delicate, areolae, mons pubis, and delicate feminine curves showing delightfully.

Gordon beamed, blew her a kiss through a wide smile.

"I love you, too, Emma," he said.

Savior jumped into the morning darkness. Gordon closed the door. Slightly cold and damp outside. No breeze.

The evening before, Gordon had hooked the Deere up to the 3-bottom plow, greased all fittings, and filled the tank with diesel. Now, he climbed into the cab and turned the switch to light up the glow plugs. Seconds later, plugs heated, he turned the switch all the way to start. The

174

Deere's three powerful cylinders exploded in sequence. Lights on.

Typical for morning weather in spring, a heavy fog covered the land. The sun would burn it off in a couple of hours. Gordon let the engine warm up. Looked at Savior waiting on the ground and said, "Are we ready to plow all day, girl?"

Savior barked, "You betcha!"

In a few minutes they were in Field 1. Gordon drove the Deere midfield, aligned it with the edge of the field, lowered the plow, and started cutting the first furrow of the season. Savior kept pace at a safe distance, left of the Deere.

By noon, they had a good-sized swath of the field plowed. Gordon stopped plowing and turned off the engine. He grabbed his lunch and a water bottle, the canvas bag with Savior's food, and climbed down from the cab. He walked back to the plowed sod, grabbed a handful of dirt and tossed it into the wind.

"As good as can be expected, Savior."

"You betcha," Savior barked in agreement.

"Let's eat lunch."

Gordon sat crosslegged on the ground, using the Deere's large rear tire for a backrest. He opened Savior's bag and took out two shallow pans. He filled one with water from the plastic bottle, and the other with dog food.

"Eat up, Savior, we're doin' a lot a plowin' before dark sets in."

Gordon opened his lunch bag. Inside, at the top, was a love note from Emma. "Hope plowing the field isn't better than plowing me, Lover Boy! Tee-hee!"

Savior barked loud, "Whoo hoo!"

"Hey, Savior, that's between me and my wife!"

Savior barked again, louder, "Whoo hoo! Whoo hoo!"

"You're right, girl. A woman's love is a precious gift for her husband. No reason to hide it."

Lunch finished, Gordon lovingly petted Savior's head and back. He picked up the bags and bowls, and climbed into the cab.

"Savior, here we go again, girl." With that, he fired up the Deere and resumed plowing. After two passes, Savior stood where the Deere would pass, barking at the course ahead. Gordon knew she had found stones that should be removed from the field. He throttled back the Deere's engine to idle and put the transmission in neutral. Climbed down, grabbed his pickaxe and went to see what Savior found.

"What you got here, girl? Oh, my, two football-sized stones."

"Yep," Savior barked in agreement.

Gordon used the pickaxe to dislodge both stones buried in the dirt. He muscled one up, carried it to the tractor, and dumped it into the large plastic barrel wired onto the weight on the front of the tractor.

"Heavy sucker," he judged.

When he walked back for the second stone, he felt a slight pain in his left shoulder, that moved gradually to his upper arm. He felt woozy, breathing was difficult, like something was pressing onto his chest. He stumbled and fell with his left arm and shoulder full into the furrow.

"A heart attack?" he mouthed weakly.

Struggled to get his cellphone from his rear pants pocket.

"Can't get it. Oh, shit. It's dead. Savior!"

She was right there in front of his face. Intense eyes.

"Savior, fetch Emma," he said weakly. Then, his whole body relaxed.

Savior ran to the Stanton Family House faster than she'd ever run in competitions or combat. At the house, Savior bolted through the doggie door to find Emma carrying a basket of washed and dried laundry up the basement stairs. Savior's loud, continual barking signaled to Emma that Gordon was in trouble. She dropped the basket. Speed-dialed 911, ran out the back door, and jumped on the Gator, parked by the family's picnic tables. Talked to 911 dispatch about emergency status, likely issue, location. Fired up the Gator, shoved it into gear, and sped away to Field 1.

Savior was already halfway to the field.

The sun shined bright and warm through a cloudless sky. Gordon breathed easy, tucked in the furrow. Focused his eyes intently on the smoothed, dark brownish black soil, just turned over by the plow. Inches from his face.

"Rich soil here, any plowman would be proud to work, sow in wheat, corn, and soybeans," he thought.

The Deere, in idle, rumbled, and rattled in the background. Music to farmers. An earthworm poked its mouth out of the shiny dark brown dirt near the top ridge. Repeated its muscular expansions and contractions until most of its body was hanging out, blindly twisting and curling, searching for more loam to munch on.

"You're an inspiration, little red wriggler worm. So small, among all God's creatures. Your kind do so much, all day, every day, to open up the soil. Eating and fertilizing soil as you go. Forgotten by many, in the dark below, beyond plowing and harrowing, up here in the sunshine. We're one in the dirt. Honored to meet you today, so low

177

in the furrow, eye to eye, earthworm, my humble friend," Gordon said quietly.

The worm fell into the furrow. Burrowed a new channel. Disappeared to continue eating decaying roots and leaves, and aerating the soil. "Look at that! The awesome digging power of a simple earthworm. I expect to join you soon, little buddy. I mean, alive, with my tractor and plow. Gotta get outta this heart attack first," Gordon observed.

Springtime mosquitoes found him, buzzed his ears. A cloud of gnats fought to enter both nostrils. He sneezed them out, again and again. White-winged moths flitted over the plowed ridges in the distance.

He dared not move.

"Dear God, here I am, Gordon Stanton. I've fallen sick. My work's only just begun. These fields need plowing, harrowing, sowed with wheat, drenched in rain. And charged with bright, warm sunshine. To sprout and grow to harvest time. Bless and protect my lovely wife and children. Amen."

He snoozed.

Savior, racing top speed from the Stanton Family House, made an abrupt stop at Gordon's head. Sniffed his nose and eyes. Licked his cheek, and barked good news repeatedly.

Emma stopped the Gator at the Deere's front wheel. Ran to Gordon's side. Sirens blared, coming closer and closer.

"Oh, baby, can you hear me?"

"I'm here, Emma, my love. Savior fetched you."

She held his hand, and kissed it and his cheek, lips and forehead, repeatedly. Held his hand in hers lovingly, pressed it into her breasts, and squeezed gently from both sides.

178

"I love you, Baby. Hang on. Hang on. Gordon, my Lover Boy. Please stay with me. God, please help us." Tears ran down her cheeks.

Rob Fogarty, the senior EMT in town, swooped in and took over with his team. In one minute, they had Gordon out of the furrow, onto the gurney. One tall EMT, freed momentarily, reached up and turned off the Deere. Rob installed an IV, hooked up sensors, and the team shoved a worried but smiling Gordon through the back doors of the ambulance. Emma climbed in, still wearing her nightie.

"Savior, go home, girl!" Emma shouted kindly.

Emma texted, "Carla, Dad's had a heart attack. Going to St. Lukes. Take over the house. Bring clothes for me to the hospital. Pray for Dad!"

Doors closed, the ambulance charged over the unplowed field, lights flashing, sirens wailing. A short time later, four nurses in the emergency room slid Gordon from the gurney, naked on his bare back, onto the chilly slab of the operating table.

Heart bypass surgery, three days in the hospital, drug therapy, and physical therapy.

Done.

Brother Blaine visited daily to bless him and give him communion.

Gordon was released in good health, considering what happened.

Back home, in five weeks, he was his old self.

Emma, Carla, Montgomery, and Etana thanked God that their husband and father returned to them. The twelve resident students had prayed for Gordon, and now were full of joy for him and the Stanton family.

They gave untold hours helping him recover at home.

179

The whole Academy community gave thanks to God for Gordon's recovery.

Neighboring farmers plowed the Stanton fields and garden. They planted Gordon's grains in the fields, and started early spring vegetables in the garden. They fed the farm animals, watered them, and cleaned their stalls and feed lots beautifully.

When Gordon's primary physician pronounced him "fit as a fiddle," Emma and the whole Stanton Family House provided a "Thanksgiving Roasted Pig Dinner" for all the EMTs, neighbors, friends, students, instructors, as well as administrators in the Academy community, and Brother Blaine.

Savior was awarded special honors for saving Gordon's life. One of many awards hanging over the fireplace mantel that she received while on tour in Afghanistan.

"Thanks. You betcha," she barked.

## — 21 —

GEORGE knelt down slow and easy, sat on his ankles, and let out a sigh of relief. "God is good," he mouthed. He studied the second stone he still carried, now in his right hand, in case the first missed the target. "Would fly just as true," he said smiling. Then, he pressed and ground the stone into the loose soil until only the bare top was visible.

"Like planting Japanese spider lily bulbs in my parents' garden back home in San Francisco. I love you, Mom and Dad."

Many soft footsteps approached ahead.

When George looked up, the husky peasant was leading all the other peasants down the path. He directed the first team of three to care for the wounded. Directed another team to remove the dead body and equipment. "Bury it. Never to be found." Next, he directed a team to scour the hillside for any remaining signs or artifacts. They found the assassin's partner and all their equipment. Debris, match, and cigarette butts. And George's stuff. "Give that to him," he said, motioning to George. "Bury the rest."

Then, standing before George, the husky peasant bowed at the waist and said, "Please excuse me." He walked to the stream, where the team was cleaning, suturing, and bandaging the injured. He conferred intimately, quietly,

181

with them. Studied their wounds and dressings. Assured that all would recover, he returned to sit on his ankles in front of George.

"You are the American, the assassin spoke of?" the husky peasant inquired politely, looking into George's eyes.

"I can only reveal my name, rank, date of birth, and serial number, per the 1929 Geneva Convention." George answered flatly in Japanese.

The husky peasant said, "Yes, of course. Excuse me, for causing any confusion. I am not a soldier in the Japanese military. Never have been. I do not intend to make you a prisoner of war. Can't. Won't. Far from it. What you do not know is those three elderly people that the assassin brutally assaulted are my mother, my father, and my uncle. If not for you, they, and possibly my whole family here, would be dead now. We are extremely grateful. You look hungry. We will give you food. Your clothes are wet. We will care for you. We will tell no one that you are here or that we have ever seen you. Your safety and security are equal to ours. My whole family will help protect you. We invite you to stay and help protect us."

The husky man bowed. A tear trickled from his eye, rolled slowly down his cheek, and stopped on his chin.

"I speak the truth to you, even though I do not know who you are. Where you came from. Why you came here. I watched you step fearlessly onto the path of certain death. I was powerless to defend my family. We all were. We had only a slim chance against the automatic pistol. You risked your life to save our lives. Killed the assassin by hurling a native stone into his head. That is proof enough for me to trust you. I am Sanada Kenshin, head of the Sanada clan, from the days of Sanada Nobushige, our

182

revered ancestor four hundred years in the past. Several years ago, I led my family to this peaceful mountain range from our homeland of Osaka, where we lived a slave-life. Walked through frightful nights, frigid air, storms, and risk of capture, imprisonment and execution. First day of the trek, one of our young girls was raped, butchered, and left for dead by a mob of soldiers. Two others died on the journey. God rest their souls. We have enjoyed life here ever since. Yet, we have always known that our retreat from the real world would come to an end. We prayed the end would be peaceful.

"There was never a discovery of our hiding place, until today. I watched the event unfold from where I hid beside the path. I did not know how you got here. Now, I see that you parachuted in, and the assassins, too. The stage was set for a duel between two mortal enemies. Good prevailed over evil. Thanks be to God."

"God works in ways man cannot fathom," George started in Japanese.

Kenshin bowed in agreement.

George could not hold back a slight, warm smile. Kenshin noticed.

"The world is so small. A single event can be good, and can also be bad. Today, it is good. Mr. Sanada, I am a Japanese American. My name is George Washington Sanada, in the English way."

By then, most of the Sanada family had gathered, standing around them, wondering, learning more and more about George, growing joyful, surprised at this miraculous reunion.

Kenshin said to the gathering relatives, "The Sanada family was rescued in World War II Japan by a distant

183

relative from America! He threw one perfect fast ball, with a stone, killed the assassin, and saved the Sanada family. Like David against Goliath!"

George was beside himself. Full of joy, laughter. The family, children, parents, and elders, embraced him. Hugs and kisses all around. He warmly embraced Sanada Kenshin's mother, father and uncle. He asked them about their injuries and apologized for delays that led to more suffering for them.

They hugged him tight and long. Kenshin's mother said for all to hear, "In the face of certain death, George Sanada, you were the only warrior standing on the field of battle who could, and did, destroy the enemy. We suffered some wounds. They will heal with time. George Washington Sanada, you are a modern-day samurai warrior. We love you. We admire you. We thank you."

Sensitive to having a lapse in their security routine, Kenshin ordered the family to complete garden duties at once, and retire at twilight.

Sanada Kenshin led George up the path to the cave. Upon entering, he briefly explained what happened to those who did not go to the garden. He asked the women to prepare hot food for their guest. Had the men get pails of hot and cold water, soap, wash cloths and towels, so George could clean up. And bring dry clothes and sandals to fit. Had the children take his clothes, wash and dry them.

George was famished. He did his best to be polite when eating before his guests, he apologized, confessing that he hadn't eaten for several days. Everyone watched him eat until he was full. No one was offended.

George used the opportunity to speak with the Sanada family. He explained he was their distant relative. That his mother wrote to the family in Japan frequently from the United States before she, his father, Akiro, and he were sent to a concentration camp. Kenshin's mother, father, and uncle remembered the letters George's mother, Sakura, wrote them from America.

He explained he had no classified information to give, and he wouldn't be able to share it even if he did. He graciously accepted their offer to stay with them. Had no way out. Would live with them here in peace and freedom. Help them. Protect them. However long it took.

Sanada Kenshin and his people, to the last one, lovingly accepted George into the family. They sang *"Sakura Sakura Season of Cherry Blossoms,"* a traditional folk song, in honor of George's mother.

# — 22 —

AIRCRAFT very seldom flew over the Sanada sanctuary. But early on a warm, cloudless morning in October 1945, the gardeners heard an airplane slowly approaching from the east. If an aircraft ever approached the valley, their well-practiced safety routine was to squat with drab hoods pulled up to hide their heads and hands. Then wait stock-still until it disappeared over the western mountains.

Today, before the plane came into view, they instantly dropped down. Became motionless. Seen from above, they were several scattered, rotting tree stumps in a remote marsh.

But this airplane slowed when it came overhead. All but hovered there.

A man fell from the plane, his parachute opened, and he glided to the mountain path. The man landed exactly where they watched George challenge the assassin, and save them.

Upon landing, the soldier waved to the plane, gathered up his parachute, with all the lines. Undid his harness and pack of gear and rations. Rolled the chute in a neat bundle, and laid all on the ground at his feet. The plane circled three times, to acknowledge the hand signal from the soldier on the ground, before flying back east.

The parachutist looked all around, slowly, and twice more. Listened to chatter from birds and the buzzing and humming from a myriad of autumn insects. Swift-running water splashed and gurgled in a nearby stream. A woodpecker commenced rat-a-tat-tat-ing on a dead limb farther up the path across the stream.

He knelt down and sat on his ankles. Thought about his son, Thomas, wept, and prayed for his soul in heaven. Then, he asked reverently, "Will I find George alive?" He recited the prayer of Jesus at Gethsemane before he would be crucified, Mathew 26 — 39.

My Father, if it is possible, let this cup pass from me; yet not what I want but what you want.

"George was here. I know. I can feel it," he said softly, hopefully, prayer-like. The soldier lowered his left hand to the ground. Felt the second stone George had buried there. He dug it from the earth with his fingers.

"Interesting," he mused. Wiped it clean. Pondered the unique, fist-sized round rock. Akiro Sanada's touching story came to mind about George's love of baseball, and meeting famous baseball players for the Seals. His great pitching for the Oakland Team in the concentration camp.

"So like a baseball," he thought, reflecting on the game he watched George pitch.

One of the Sanadas in a garden, farthest up and nearest the stream, slipped through the brush to disappear up the path. When she arrived at the cave, she alerted Kenshin and George. All three descended the path stealthily to the point where they could see who had landed, but not be seen.

188

"Major Craig Alexander Bradley!" George erupted in a joyful welcome. "You returned! You found me!"

Both men ran to one another, embraced, and hopped in a circle.

"George." Craig pulled back. Shouted loudly, "The war with Japan is over!"

That announcement brought all the Sanadas to the path from the gardens, rice paddy and the cave. All were incredulous, yet totally relieved. Believing in this miraculous rescue. They sobbed with joy, knelt on the path to give thanks, hugged and kissed and danced as the precious news swept through their minds, hearts, and souls.

Sanada Kenshin ushered everyone up to the cave, where they celebrated all night long, a world at peace once again.

After four weeks of walking, Craig and George led the Sanada family out of the Japanese Hida Range of mountain wilderness to an American base in Tokyo, and real, lasting freedom.

The aftermath of the first atomic bomb dropped August 6, 1945, on Hiroshima, was estimated at 70,000 to 135,000 people dead. With Japan's refusal to surrender, the second bomb was dropped on Nagasaki, not Kokura. Cloud cover spared Kokura, a first-choice site, for the atomic bomb that was dropped on Nagasaki. Kyoto was also spared, because of its cultural significance.

Estimated deaths were 60,000 to 80,000 people.

The extent of destruction made accurate reports impossible of the civilian and military men, women, and children who died. Cause of death was reported as "acute exposure to the blasts and from long-term side effects of radiation."

Two days, two atomic bombs dropped on Japan. To say nothing about multiple prior fire bombings of many other Japanese cities. How much more loss of Japanese citizens and Allied troops would it take to bring the war to its end?

With hindsight, total American troops dead or missing in the Pacific Theater would be 41,592. Wounded 145,706. Casualties of America's allies were also high. Total Japanese combatant deaths were estimated to be 2.1 million. Estimates of Japanese noncombatant deaths range from 500,000 to 1 million. There were many Chinese casualties, also.

Finally, the Japanese emperor, Hirohito, announced on a radio broadcast Japan's surrender at noon, JST, on August 15, 1945. The whole world erupted with relief. And with the deepest sadness for horrendous personal losses.

# — 23 —

D ARIUS, with Harding riding shotgun, parked the Lark on the Loop in front of a very large, imposing barn.

"What you see here," Harding began, before opening his door, "is the original barn built on the Stanton farm. Cornerstone over there has the barn raising on 'Anno Domini July 4, 1777.' One very famous day to build a barn. There's 1,500 acres all around. Owned and worked by one family through the decades.

"Well, there's a lot more to show and talk about. Let's go in the Stanton Family Barn."

Harding led Darius to the side door, opened it, and they entered.

"What's that smell?" Darius asked.

"That's the sweet smell of cut hay. Bales are stacked in the hayloft for feeding our cattle over winter. More in wrapped, round bales stored in the fields. Come back in the spring. summer, and early fall, when our farmers harvest this year's hay. No sweeter aroma on the farm," Harding promised.

"Here come our guides. Darius James, let me introduce two absolutely marvelous instructors. Adira Abrams specializes in the origins of civilization, with a focus on agriculture in the Indus Valley, Mesopotamia, and Egypt. Tahmina Hakimi, another expert in this study area, specializes in the history and practice of breeding plants and animals. Like all instructors here, Adira and Tahmina, also stolen from industry jobs, are the heartbeat of the Academy's theme Agriculture from the Dawn of Civilization."

"Thank you, Mr. Harding," Tahmina said. "We are so pleased to meet you, Darius. Welcome to the Academy."

"Yes," Adira put in, "Mr. Harding has told us so much about you, and your wife, Cherice, and the baby on the way. Welcome to the Stanton Family Barn, where we amaze kids with *Estuaries, Agriculture, and Civilization*."

"Such a pleasure to meet you, also," Darius said. "First time I smelled hay. And my first time in a barn. Don't have these in the City," he said smiling openly, kicking everyone into a laugh.

"Yeah, I hear you. I grew up in the projects in the first circle around Cleveland, Ohio. No barns there either, just projects on projects, abandoned factories and vacant lots," Tahmina added, smiling broadly. "But the sights, smells, and labors on a working farm are primal, and beautiful."

"Would you mind giving Darius a snippet of your study area? We're having lunch in the Lambardi Family House at noon, so we'll want to watch our time," Harding explained.

"Be a pleasure," Tahmina responded. "Before we go any farther, please select a pair of galoshes that fit over your shoes from the rack over there. We'll be walking through some muck. I know how much Mr. Harding loves the sweet smell of poop from our cows, pigs, sheep, and chickens — smeared in the classic Lark."

"Oh, please, please! Galoshes on, yes. Last time, I skipped the galoshes. Had that expensive French perfume in the Lark for a month before it cleared out. Phew!" Harding joked. They all laughed at Harding's goodhearted response to funning.

"While we explain what we have for the students, we'll guide you through the different labs, pens, and meeting areas. Might be a little quick, though," Tahmina continued. "Our study area, *Estuaries, Agriculture, and Civilization*, is organized into six distinct, but interrelated segments listed in this table on the wall:

- *Components and Processes: Air, Water, and Soil.*
- *Abundant Life: Ants, Pollinators, and Earthworms.*
- *Field to Table: Grains Over Millennia.*
- *You Are What You Eat: Responsible Treatment and Use of the Land, Livestock and Poultry.*
- *Look and Feel Your Best: Textiles, Clothing Design, and Fashion.*
- *Making Physical Work Easy: Electricity, Engineering, Mechanics, and Physics.*

"Students at first- and second-year levels take *Components and Processes and Abundant Life*. Third-to-fifth year students take *Field to Table, You Are What You Eat, and Look and Feel Your Best*. Because it's so much more rigorous, *Making Physical Work Easy*, is reserved for sixth-year students. All segments are cumulative, and have knowledge and skills that appeal to everyone. Students' comments bear that out. Segments take place over a three-month period, meeting every school day. Study areas are here at the Stanton Family Barn, the pens, outbuildings, Glacier Pond, and fields on the farm."

Adira moved in as naturally as water flowing in a stream.

"The titles of each study area are reasonably self-explanatory. What may be less evident is how and why we take students, as we do, from *Components and Processes* along to *Making Physical Work Easy*. We teach the real history of farming—agriculture—starting from the natural elements and earliest records," Adira explained.

"We start each study area reminding students that this is *agriculture*, from the Late Latin agricultura, which translated to English means 'cultivation of the land.' It's farming. No farming, no eating. That important. That simple. A fact very nearly hidden in contemporary American society," Adira continued.

"'Food? They make it in the supermarket, right?' In *Field to Table: Grains Over Millennia*, we give each group of three to five students a set of seed packets with five ancient grains: teff from Ethiopia, millet from Africa, buckwheat from Asia, quinoa from Peru and spelt from Europe. There is also one seed packet with modern wheat grains. They study differences between the grains throughout the growing, harvesting, and milling cycle.

"Like you saw in *A Case Study of Glacier Pond*, each group receives a plot of land that they own, but it's in our greenhouse. They have full responsibility to care for their plot until they're finished with the first four segments in *Estuaries, Agriculture, and Civilization*.

"In the beginning, students get a healthy high-tech-supported dose of geography and the earliest civilizations: Indus Valley, the Euphrates and Tigris Rivers, and the Nile River. The Sumerians, and Assyrians, for example.

194

Also, we look deeply into coastal trade from India to Mesopotamia to Egypt. River and overland trade along the Fertile Crescent.

"At this point, they've also plowed their plots, and organized, tagged, and planted their grains, which are sprouting here in the greenhouse."

Tahmina resumed, "Then, we ask the students: why the heck did all these different groups of people settle in these marine, estuarine, and riverine habitats? And, how did they get the grains? Cultivate, harvest, and mill enough of them to feed their families—put food on their tables?

"We turn them loose on the resources: our neighboring farmers, the Academy's library, online, wherever.

"Before long, they've all done enough independent and group research to have discovered this truth: the story of agriculture and civilization is written in conquests of the weak by the strong. Over possession of resources. The knowledge and skills to farm grains and animals, and to mine and fabricate metals from the earth.

"Local and foreign rulers traded with local farmers, but often they took control of the land from desert nomads, herders, and successful, independent and cooperating farmers. Coming upon resistance, while roaming wide across the land, rulers conquered native people and mandated slavery or allegiance, for indigenous people.

"But eventually the local people they'd enslaved were not enough. More slaves were commanded to farm the lands, raise domestic animals, net fishes, mine ores, and feed the extensive and expanding, royal hierarchy. The rulers looked farther abroad to conquer other lands, and capture and enslave more and more people, wherever they could find them.

195

"The passion for empire building caught fire the world over.

"Control the land, enslave the people, make them produce the goods and services. Not only for the ruler's table, but for trade with rulers elsewhere — for profit and power.

"Scraps and crumbs fell from the king's table for the slaves to eat. That was the system of food production throughout the world: slavery, serfdom, indentured servitude. People from every race were enslaved. Tribes, families, and towns not enslaved, lived in extremely remote and unknown or harsh areas. Occasionally, fortunates escaped their ancestral homelands in time to avoid capture, and build a new life elsewhere.

"Some rulers and their handlers were humane. Most were not.

"The abysmal practice has been preserved in stone carvings in ancient Assyria of male slaves tied by their necks to ladder rungs and marched from their homes to the conquering ruler's fields. Their women and children straggled behind, subject to unspeakable abuse and indignity. Anyone who resisted was tortured or slaughtered on the spot. A stark example for wannabe fighters.

"Homeland defenders typically had inferior weapons and defensive strategies. They had what they wanted, and wanted to keep what they had. Wanted to be left alone to pursue their way of life, customs, traditions, religions.

"Moreover, the local tribes themselves fought and killed each other for more land, resources, and slaves to do the work. When battles ended, great or small, the defeated typically had no property, no rights.

"The Biblical story of Cain and Abel, Genesis 4:1–16, coming after Adam and Eve were expelled by God from the Garden of Eden, reminds us that envy of another man's fortunes can drive a man to murder his own brother. Murder, theft, rape, all manner of violence, has been among us since the beginning. Only a covenant, the Ten Commandments given to Moses by God in Exodus 20:1–24, and followed by a people, can protect man from inhumanity to man.

"The same story, from antiquity, is told by people from all ethnic groups and territories across all continents. Asia, Europe, Africa, North America, South America, Australia. Some indigenous local leaders sold out their neighbors to conquerors for profit, and to save their hides.

"Fast-forward to the mid-1800s. President Abraham Lincoln issued the Emancipation Proclamation on January 1, 1863, officially ending slavery in the USA. Took a bloody Civil War to get there. Total Americans who died: 620,000. Some of them former slaves. Most soldiers were poor, whatever their race.

"Other foreign emancipation movements in the 19th century also succeeded.

"We bring the students full circle. Remind them that pursuit of a more perfect civilization never ends. Perfection is not within the grasp of human beings. Ever. Still, we work continuously on the issues of humanity, at home and abroad. That's why the students' commitment, beliefs, knowledge, skills, and investment in justice and morality, are so very important.

"They understand how fortunate we are. The United States was founded on a system of law and order. Government of the people by the people for the people, and for just treatment of the people. Our Constitution and Bill of Rights guarantee all citizens the right to life, liberty, and the pursuit of happiness.

"Our citizens, and new, incoming refugees and legal immigrants, celebrate America as the one country in the world where education, jobs, freedom of speech, religion, and the Bill of Rights, are shared opportunities. America is the land of dreams."

Adira began again. "So, after five comprehensive, literary, historical and scientific studies, the students take up *Making Physical Work Easy: Electricity, Engineering, Mechanics, and Physics*."

The tour returned to the side door of the barn.

Adira concluded the introduction. "But this 'thumbnail sketch' leaves out other important, interwoven details of our scientific studies: mathematics, the tool of science, genetics, breeds of animals and breeding, forecast and measurement of yields, managing soil health, harvest, nutrition, inventions, discoveries, related art and music, etc.

"This is a working farm supporting the Academy and our neighbors. We plow the soil, grow our grain, raise cattle, pigs, sheep, and chickens, and we turn waste into natural, organic fertilizer.

"You had the opportunity today to mingle with our stock, see how we care for them. You visited the milking parlor, butcher shop, machine shop, mechanical design and engineering lab, and maintenance and repair building.

"Scratched the backs of animals. Even got some serious manure on your galoshes. We breed and raise the animals. Slaughter them humanely for the table. Mill the grain. Bake bread. We eat what we grow. Sell the excess. Turn what's scrap back into the soil. We waste nothing.

198

"Tahmina and I, and ten other instructors here, help Sam and Clara and the rest of the Glacier Pond instructors with their work. And they help us over here.

"Our neighbors all around this acreage, own their farms or lease fields from the original Stanton farm. And in farming, as in all of life, unexpected stuff happens. When it does, neighbors lend a hand—including our wonderful students.

"The Academy, in all its study areas, emphasizes a broad, interrelated, and deep education for youngsters. It's scholarly, practical, factual, moral, historical, philosophical—and fun."

Tahmina asked, "What do you say, Mr. Harding? We've given Darius a peek at our labs, instruments, pens, animals, fields, meeting areas, how and why we do our work. Do we have more time?"

"No, it's about noon." Harding said. "Lorenzo and Georgia Lambardi are expecting us in a couple minutes. Students at the Lambardi Family House will be starved, as usual. Thank you so much! Every time I visit here, I come away learning something that's new, or refreshes my memory. Today, it was castrating male animals and controlling the development of different breeds. I'm inspired by the splendid work you do with the students, Adira and Tahmina."

"Thank you, Mr. Harding, for your kind words," Tahmina said. "Oh, lest I forget. Thanks also for the note about castration. There's one more truth, and fact, we're proud to teach students. It's from Genesis 1:27, the Hebrew Bible,

And God created the humans in his image,
In the image of God He created him,
Male and female He created them.


And later, in Genesis 7:1–5, God instructs Noah to load the ark with his household, and all the animals, clean and not clean

Seven pairs, male and female to keep seed alive
over all the earth.


"At the Stanton Academy for Humanity, we apply the true method of science and mathematics to study the natural world. No exceptions. No wokeness whatsoever. No excuses. The real world of God's creation. And the students love it."

Darius said, "Thank you. I'll return for more at a later time. You've put this city boy on a steep learning curve, and it's terrific. Can't thank you enough for taking out time to introduce me to farming."

"Okay! We are very glad you liked it, Darius," Adira said.

Tahmina said aloud, faux seriously, "Hear ye, hear ye, hear ye! Our distinguished guests, Mr. Harding and Mr. James. Before ye go forth, out of the Stanton Family Barn, and step into the Lark, wash the poop off your galoshes here, under the faucet, and return the galoshes to the rack over there to dry with all the fragrant poop scrubbed off. Smelling fresh for the next visitor."

They all burst out laughing.

# — 24 —

THE Lark's engine fired with the slightest turn of the ignition switch, Darius noticed. "Whoa! Unreal. Mr. Harding, who tunes up your car?"

"Learned that skill when I was just a kid. My dad was a factory machine operator. Supported our family. But he was a hot rod wizard throughout his life. Probably where I got my lead foot. On weekends, if we weren't at the racetrack, we were in his garage rebuilding or fine-tuning his red 1932 Ford Deuce coupe. Those were the glory days.

"Oh, Darius, here comes Gordon Stanton with his John Deere tractor and a round bale on the spear. Pull up on the right. I want you to meet him. And Savior, that magnificent German shepherd. Goes everywhere Gordon goes."

The big green tractor pulled onto the grassy inside of the Loop and slowed to allow room for the Lark to pass.

Darius stopped the Lark, and Harding opened his door, and got out. Walked over to the tractor. Savior checked him out.

"Hey, Gordon," Harding said. "Great to see you. Got somebody I want you to meet."

Gordon braked, slowed the diesel engine to idle, put the transmission in park, and climbed down to the ground.

Darius got out of the Lark and shook hands with Gordon. Savior used her nose to thoroughly check out Darius, because he was new to the campus.

"Gordon, this is Darius James, our new theater director and producer."

"Great pleasure to meet you, Darius. Mr. Harding has been searching for you since August last year. Welcome to The Academy. Totally amazed by your work in the City. The students on campus can't wait to work with you. My kids, Carla, Montgomery, and Etana, have been asking about your arrival. Mr. Harding made the announcement in the campus newsletter, "Around the Loop," last December. Got everybody excited.

"A pleasure to meet you, Gordon. You got what I'll always think of as a farmer's handshake: firm and lasting."

"You betcha," Savior barked loudly. They all laughed.

Darius continued, "I got a lot of catching up to do on farms, honest, hard-working people, and the Academy."

"No worries, Darius. Our niche in farming, as the bedrock of learning, will soon be second nature for you. Just wait and see,"

"What can you tell me about this beautiful dog, Savior?" Darius asked.

"Oh, I'm sorry—Savior," Gordon said. "She's my constant companion, and the family's best friend and protector. She served with the U.S. Army's 10th Mountain Division in Afghanistan, but was retired with top honors after being wounded in her left forepaw. 'Come, Savior.' See how she has a slight limp when she walks. We adopted her with great joy two years ago. She came with that fancy, custom-made prosthetic foot, giving her full mobility.

202

"Might take a bit, but, in her own time, she'll accept you," Gordon said, while scratching around her ears and petting her back.

"She's so beautiful," Darius remarked.

"Thanks. Wait til you see her in action."

Then, Gordon said, "I'm running late with work, so please excuse me. Thanks for the intro, Mr. Harding. Darius, welcome to the Academy. You and your wife need help settling in, with the baby coming soon, or whatever, let me know."

With that, Gordon climbed back onto the Deere. Savior seemed to know what was going down, and ran ahead to the barn. Gordon pulled the Deere away at low throttle to deliver the hay bale to hungry cattle in the back lot.

"All the students love Gordon," Harding said, getting back in the Lark. "He has one of those magnetic personalities. His wife, Emma, is the same. Their kids are wonderful. And Savior, she takes care of everybody.

"Truthfully, the kids absolutely admire all our instructors."

"What you see around the Loop are twelve, large Family Houses. Each has a married couple as Family Parents, typically in their 50s and 60s, their kids are grown. They supervise twelve resident students, first year to sixth-year, from all over the country. Boys in six Family Houses and girls in the other six Houses. Staggered around the Loop.

"That brings the resident population to 144. There are usually from 130 to 150 day students, also, who are local, and commute to school. So, in any year, we have from 270 to about 300 students enrolled in the Academy."

"First-year students are twelve years old. From there, the population ranges up to the sixth-year students, who are eighteen years old."

Darius remarked, "Since we arrived, Cherice and I haven't seen anyone on campus hanging on a cell phone. Why is that?"

"Good observation," Harding said. "Our campus rules state that students' cell phones are to be used for emergency calls, only. Resident students who are first to third year, are encouraged to call their parents or guardians at 6:00–700 p.m. every evening. Students in fourth to sixth-years, at 6:00–700 p.m. every Sunday evening. They are teenagers, after all. However, any time parents want to speak with their child, Mrs. Grace makes it happen.

"Instructors are encouraged to carry their cell phones for emergencies, and refrain from calls and texts that are not essential or not work-related.

"We've never had a complaint or issue.

"Everything is in walking distance. Students, faculty, and staff walk to the library, study centers, athletic fields, and so on. Local and state police patrol the campus for safety.

"We have numerous computers on campus for study and research. We have many different athletic, recreational, and artistic performances, ongoing. The kids and adults don't want to waste time on frivolous stuff, or be corrupted by the morally bad stuff that abounds on the Internet.

"Soon after arriving on campus, new students and instructors discover the beauty of this rule: the joy of talking with friends, faculty, and Family House Parents.

"Also, we have a combined firewall and content filter system on campus. It was designed, patented, and maintained by our Internet protection expert, Yuto Tanaka. Our system, the iDome, installed on our server, computers, cell phones, and other equipment, blocks access to or from any Internet source that's not approved. Mobile devices, like cell phones, are controlled by Mobile Device Management software (MDM) for the content filter to apply. Our Parent and Faculty Child Protection Committee works with Yuto to govern legitimate Internet communications, and protect our students. Parents, faculty, students, and staff firmly approve."

Darius said, "That is so good for everyone. There's one more thing on my to-do list. I've got to meet Mr. Tanaka, soon. Changing the topic, does student enrollment rise and fall over the years?"

Harding answered, "We have an abundance of applicants every year. Girls and boys. And, there are now eight other sister schools across the country, with varying themes, but with the same philosophy: Academy for Humanity and Liberal Arts Immersion, with the same policies, and the same general style of instruction:

★ Agriculture from the Dawn of Civilization — that's us

★ History, Development and Use of Technology

★ Human Being: Culture, Religion, Language and Custom

★ Human Spaces: Design of Dwellings, Towns and Cities

★ Critical Elements of Jurisprudence: Greece to the United States of America

★ Medical Science, Discoveries, Practices and Ethics

★ Sources and Uses of Energy and Waste

★ Transportation Through Time and Space

"Thanks to ACLA, a lot of public schools went out of business. The Academy and other private and parochial schools snapped up the buildings. If a student wants to attend an Academy for Humanity, chances are, we'll have an opening at one.

"Up ahead on the right you see balloons on that sign for the Lambardi Family House: Boys to Men. Pull in that driveway. Get ready for a real treat."

Darius rolled the Lark into the drive. He and Harding walked jaunty up the steps onto the covered front porch. Harding rang the doorbell. Instantly, "Wipe Out," the killer 1963 surf rock tune by the Safaris, blasted really loud from overhead stereo speakers. The door opened and Georgia Lambardi greeted them, wearing a strikingly large colorful lei around her neck.

"Welcome to the Lambardi Family House, Mr. Harding and Mr. James!"

Two male students next to Georgia hung aromatic, flowered leis around their necks. The huge dining room beyond was wall-to-wall students, all shouting, "Welcome to the Academy for Humanity, Darius!"

"Wipe Out" continued playing loud in the background.

Harding and Darius, now instant celebraties, were ushered into the center of the dining room. Students were waving and dancing to the music. The music ended, and Georgia stood between Darius and Harding, arms around their waists.

"Welcome to our humble abode," Georgia and the students said as a chorus, shouting, clapping, and waving to them. When the wild welcome quieted down, Georgia said, "Students, please prepare to have lunch with our special guests." On Georgia's signal, the kids sprang into action.

Then, she said to Darius, "In a Family House, on a daily rotating basis, two students who live there have kitchen duty for the day, relieved in time for their study sessions. Work includes food prep, setting tables, and cleanup. Family House Parents do most of the work with planning and preparing breakfast, lunch, snacks, and dinner. Breakfast and dinner meals are for students who live in a Family House. At lunchtime, though, twelve non-resident students arrive who are chosen randomly by Mrs. Grace, and announced a month in advance. A Family House for girls, gets twelve boys for lunch, and a boys' house gets twelve girls. Usually an even mix of ages. Lunches are quick. The students are excited to meet you, Darius."

"Well-organized and sounds like it's gonna be a fun time lunch," Darius observed.

The next minute, Georgia said from the kitchen, "Everyone, please take a seat. Would someone like to ask for God's blessing?"

Stella Young volunteered, "Dear God, we gather at the Academy every day to give thanks for our food. Today, we are grateful to have Mr. Darius James, the newest member of our faculty, join us. Mr. Harding is also with us. Lord, bless this food harvested from our fields and animals. Keep each of us whole. Guide us on the path of life that is often crooked, filled with trials and tribulations. Amen."

"Amen," the others said.

Today's lunch included pasta e fagioli soup and a variety of finger sandwiches with tuna salad, chicken salad, salami, ham, or cheese. Georgia broke in with, "The table is set. Help yourselves, pass platters to your right. Plenty milk, juice, and water in the carafes. Condiments are in the large ramekins. Enjoy."

In just a few minutes, students, House Parents, and guests had their plates filled and were eating. Table manners were observed. Conversations lively, but low-key.

Stella shifted the decorum. "Mr. James, would you tell us about your most challenging stint off Broadway?"

Darius obliged. "Thank you, Stella. There was something challenging about every show, but I'd pick *House for Sale*. After his mother's death, a man travels to his childhood home in Missouri to put it up for sale. He discovers that the house is so much more than a building, a piece of real estate. It is his childhood. Memories of joy, loss, change, learning, dreams, loves, and death all flow together—the essence of human being. I had to do a lot of research about families and childhood in America." At the end of lunchtime, Hana asked, "Have you decided what play you will do for the first performance?"

Smiling coyly, Darius answered, "I have three works in mind that I believe everyone will enjoy. But first, I need to talk with Mr. Harding about their overall fit with the Academy's setting this term, the broader view, and the resources to support the production."

Stella asked, "Do you have a tentative date when work will begin?"

"After the Ides of March," Darius answered, with a smile.

"Okay, lunch is ended," Lorenzo Lambardi announced. "Please bring your plates, silverware, and anything else you can carry, and place them in the plastic lugs on the counter. Thank you. Hope you enjoyed today's lunch. Good luck in your studies this afternoon."

"Molto buono! Buonissimo!" the students shouted as one voice.

# — 25 —

MRS. Grace scheduled dinner for Mr. Harding and Darius on a Saturday evening at 6:00 p.m., at the Family House of Shikhar and Ela Singh. They had immigrated to the United States from India twelve years previously. Their two grown children now had families of their own. Resident students living at their Family House were twelve girls, first-year to sixth-year.

Darius met Harding at the office at 5:45 p.m. Harding rode shotgun, Darius got behind the wheel of the Lark. Pointing, Harding said, "The Singh Family House is there, on the other side of the Loop. Same distance either direction we go."

Darius fired up the Lark and turned right onto the drive. Minutes later he guided the car into the Singhs' driveway. "Girls to Women" was printed in bold letters on the Family House sign. Ten of the girls were waiting for their guests on the porch, dressed in jeans and sweaters or polo shirts. The other two had kitchen duty.

"Welcome to our home, Mr. James and Mr. Harding!" They shouted. The Traditional Indian song: "Ya Allah," from Laya Project, was playing softly in the background. The students led Darius and Harding into the dining room.

Shikhar and Ela Singh, wearing colorful, authentic Indian headdresses and garments, stood at the head of

209

the large dining room table. Cherice James stood next to Ela, Victoria Graves, stood next to Shikhar, and Brother Blaine next to Victoria.

"Welcome to our Family House!" Shikhar said, his arms outstretched. "We are so pleased to meet you, Darius James, and to have you visit again, Mr. Harding. We are also honored to have Cherice James, Victoria Grace, and Brother Blaine join us for dinner.

"Please enjoy the meal we've prepared for you." Ela then described the offering, "We have: Tandoori naan bread, blended black tea with cardamom, cinnamon, cloves, ginger and black peppercorns, Moreish Bengali scotch eggs, spicy pilau rice, mildly spiced curry with a rich yogurt sauce, Tandoori chicken with a rich, buttery sauce, creamy beetroot curry, and chocolate barfi, for dessert."

"Would someone like to volunteer to thank God for these blessings?" Shikhar asked.

"I will," Harper Mathews said, standing next to Darius. She was twelve, a first-year student, and had the same dark brown skin as Darius, Shikar, and Ela.

"Please do," Shikhar said.

Harper began, "Let us pray . . . To the Lord Most High. We thank You for bringing us together today. You have graced us with untold joys and blessings. We give thanks for the goodness shown to us and to our families and friends in the past. We thank you for the nourishments granted us now. And we hope for Your blessings in the years to come. Bless the thoughts we will share with one another tonight. Let us pass on wisdom, care for others, and unchained truth. Guide us as we seek the hard light of understanding, driven by a spirit that abides no darkness, no wrongdoings. A spirit that folds faith, hope, and love for all mankind into good deeds for the well-being of our neighbors the world over. Help us lift all people from suffering and pain to a place of freedom, peace, and joy. We ask all this in Your great name."

"Amen," said everyone.

"Thank you Harper. So beautiful, so fitting," Ela said. "Guests and students, please take a seat. Pass the dishes to the right. Condiments are in the center, as are tea, coffee, juices, milk, and water. There is plenty more food on the counter for everyone. We hope you enjoy this authentic Indian dinner."

For the first several minutes, the only sounds were from scooting chairs, spoons clattering on bowls and dishes, and ladling the delightful food onto plates.

Family Parents, students, and guests filled and refilled their dishes. Conversation was low and polite, but mostly everyone just enjoyed the authentic Indian cuisine.

"Ummm."

"Oh my God.

"So delicious.

"A sumptuous dinner! Thank you, Mr. and Mrs. Singh, and today's kitchen helpers." Harding said after dessert. More words of praise and thanks were said by others around the table.

Darius turned and asked Harper. "Where are you from?"

"South side of Chicago, in Fuller Park," she answered quietly.

"I know where it is. A very rough place. How did you get to the Academy?" Darius asked.

Everyone was listening. Quiet settled on the whole gathering.

Mr. Harding said, "Harper, we all want to hear your story, again. It speaks to the mission, the heart and soul of The Stanton Academy for Humanity. And your arrival."

"Thank you, Mr. Harding. One Sunday last summer, Mama was in the first pew of our church in Fuller Park, praying hard. Like she did every Sunday after Mass. Crying and shaking, with me kneeling beside her. She prayed the Lord would show her a way to get me out of the projects, the murderous streets, and the dead-end public schools. That's when our brother heard her from the sacristy.

"Brother Bartholomew Amani was our pastor, gifted at leading and helping the poor of St. Raphael's. He would call everyone to prayer, lift our hearts to God, and send up our hopes and dreams for salvation on earth. Brother Bartholomew often reminded us, the Lord said,

I am the way, and the truth, and the life. No one comes to the father except through me. If you know me, you will know my father also. From now on you do know him and have seen him.

"That Sunday, he asked me and Mama to pray with him in the sanctuary, by the altar. With his arms around both of us, we said the Hail Mary, Our Father, and Glory Be. He blessed us. We thanked him, and walked home.

"The next Sunday after Mass, Brother Bartholomew held our hands together again at the altar, and said, 'Ms. Kate Mathews, I know you have been praying and hoping for so long to give a better life to your daughter, Harper. I have been praying and searching for you.

"'Recently, I spoke with one of the brothers in a parish out east, Brother Blaine. He told me to enquire about Harper

212

attending the Stanton Academy for Humanity. I did this week. It's a fine parochial school, open to all the faithful, and Harper would live on the campus.'

"That was last August. Brother Bartholomew, Brother Blaine, Mr. Harding, and Mrs. Grace worked with Mama to get vouchers set up for me. Here I am. Mama?"

With tears of pride and joy running down her cheeks, Kate Mathews stepped out of the kitchen, where she worked today to help the Singh Family House Parents with meal preparation. On a rotating basis, she helped all of the other Family House Parents with ordering and food prep across the campus.

The applause was loud and heartwarming. No dry eyes. Everyone stood, clapping, honoring her.

"Thank you. Thank you all. Oh my goodness," Kate said. "I am so blessed, so full of joy for Harper. And so thankful for her new friends, and everyone here. My prayers were answered. Yours were, too. My fervent wish is that all children have a school like this."

Again, the room erupted in applause, and students shouted, "Yay, yay, yay, Ms. Kate!" as she preferred to be called. Ms. Kate walked into the dining room, shook hands and gave hugs. All the students at the Academy knew her, and loved her.

"Thank you, Harper and Ms. Kate, for that touching reminder. And thanks to you, Ms. Kate, for all your help with our dinner. Guests and students, dinner is ended," Ela said. "Kindly take your plates, cups, and silverware to the bus station at the counter. The kitchen crew will take care of the rest. Please enjoy visiting for the rest of the evening."

Darius and Cherice talked at length with many students in the Singh Family House.

"What year are you? Where are you from? How did you get here. What do you like most of all?" They also asked about the students' favorite sports, music, and theater productions.

They learned that every Family House had a similar mixed student population. The kids came from many different backgrounds and many different circumstances.

"There's no quota system at our school," Connor Dunn, a sixth-year student explained. "Mr. Harding, Mrs. Grace, and a team of faculty, parents, and students pore over the applications every year to select kids who will fit in and thrive here. Some are from well-off families. Some come from families living in poverty. Some with darker skin, some with lighter skin. Ancestors came from Asia, Africa, Europe, Mexico, and Central or South America. They arrived recently or long ago. Came through the front door of America from societies and cultures around the world. We all seek the God-given promise from America—freedom for self-determination. Nothing else mattered for my parents, or any other parents," Connor concluded.

Two girls politely nudged close to Mrs. James.

Harper Mathews asked, "Mrs. James? Would you like to see our dormitory?"

"Oh, I'd love to, Harper."

"This is my friend, Raya Carter. We're both first-year students."

"Hi, Raya. Glad to meet you, too," Cherice said.

Harper continued, "We share a dorm with two sixth-year students, Mila Jackson and Riley Wilson. They're on kitchen duty today. Say hi, Mila Jackson and Riley Wilson," Harper loudly introduced them from the dining room, above the other voices.

Mila and Riley turned from their work at the sink and smiled broadly at Harper's recognition. Standing shoulder to shoulder, both girls said, "A one . . . a two . . . a three: Hi, Mr. and Mrs. James!" They bowed gracefully. Then, as if in the Folies Bergère, they waved with their aprons, and sang at the tops of their voices to the Beatles' tune, "She Loves You." "We love you yeah, yeah, yeah, We love you yeah, yeah, yeah, With a love like that you know you should be glad, Yeah, yeah, yeah!"

The whole dinner party erupted in applause and cheers for the kitchen helpers.

"Those two are a scream," Raya said, laughing.

"We'll take you to our dorm, now, Mrs. James," Harper said.

Both girls went to a stairway off the kitchen, and led Cherice to the second floor.

"We have three big dorm rooms up here, four girls in each. Our room is first on the right," Harper said while opening the door.

"This is so nice, so roomy," Cherice noted, when inside.

"Yeah, here's my nook," Harper said with lots of pride, gesturing with her hand. "I have a twin-sized bed, with this closet for my clothes and shoes, a writing table with a drawer and bottom shelf for other stuff, and this chair. My suitcase is under the bed." Waving to the center of the room, Harper added, "Around this open area are the other three nooks. We all share the bathroom."

Raya opened the bathroom door for a view. "Over here's my nook, next to Harper's," Raya said, equally proud.

Cherice noted the concern for respecting each girl's privacy and comfort in the architectural design and lighting for the nooks. She looked at photos in frames on the girls' tables. Asked them to explain the pictures. Harper had recent photos of her and her mom taken around campus, and one of her mom and her grandmother taken before Harper was born. Raya's photos were of her parents and two little brothers at her home not far away. Also on the tables were books for their current study area, their iPads, novels, and other personal things. Both girls had a curiously labeled, green foam box on the bottom shelf of their writing table. Although eager to know, Cherice chose not to ask about that, yet.

"We mostly sleep up here," Harper explained. "Our daily schedule is there on the wall. What we do all day, every day."

Raya and Harper took turns pointing to items and reading the list.

<u>Monday — Tuesday — Thursday — Friday</u>

6:00-7:00 a.m. Wake up, shower, clean dorm room.

7:00-7:30 a.m. Kitchen helpers.

7:30-8:00 a.m. Breakfast.

8:00-12:00 noon. Morning study areas.

12:00 noon-12:30 p.m. Kitchen helpers.

12:30-1:00 p.m. Lunch.

1:00-4:00 p.m. Afternoon Study areas.

4:00-4:30 Afternoon snacks.

4:30-6:00 p.m. Games, gymnastics, track and field, exercises.

6:00-6:30 p.m. Kitchen helpers.

6:30-7:30 p.m. Dinner.

7:30-9:00 p.m. Evening study time for first-to-fourth-year students.

9:00 p.m. Bedtime and lights out for first-to-fourth-year students.

7:30-10:30 p.m. Evening study time for fifth- and sixth-year students.

10:30 p.m. Bedtime and lights out for fifth- and sixth-year students.

## Wednesday and Saturday

6:00-7:00 a.m. Wake up, shower, clean dorm room.

7:00-7:30 a.m. Kitchen helpers.

7:30-8:00 a.m. Breakfast.

8:00-12:00 noon. Morning Study areas.

12:00 noon-12:30 p.m. Kitchen helpers.

12:30-1:00 p.m. Lunch.

1:00-4:00 p.m. Chores campus-wide, by rotating assignment.

1:00-4:00 p.m. Games, gymnastics, track and field, exercises.

4:00-4:30 p.m. Afternoon snacks.

4:30-6:00 p.m. Guest speakers, concerts, performances.

6:00-6:30 p.m. Kitchen helpers.

6:30-7:30 p.m. Dinner.

7:30-9:00 p.m. Evening study time for first-to-fourth-year students.

9:00 p.m. Bedtime and lights out for first-to-fourth-year students.

7:30-10:30 p.m. Evening study time fifth- and sixth-year students.

10:30 p.m. Bedtime and lights out for fifth- and sixth-year students.

<u>Sunday</u>

6:00-7:00 a.m. Wake up, shower, clean dorm room.

7:00-7:30 a.m. Kitchen helpers.

7:30-8:00 a.m. Breakfast.

8:00-12:00 noon. Spiritual events and guidance.

12:00 noon-12:30 p.m. Kitchen helpers.

12:30-1:00 p.m. Lunch.

1:00-4:00 p.m. Unscheduled free time.

4:00-4:30 Afternoon snacks.

4:30-6:00 p.m. Guest speakers, concerts, performances.

6:00-6:30 p.m. Kitchen helpers.

6:30-7:30 p.m. Dinner.

7:30-9:00 p.m. Evening study time for first-to-fourth-year students.

9:00 p.m. Bedtime and lights out for first-to-fourth-year students.

7:30-10:30 p.m. Evening study time fifth- and sixth-year students.

10:30 p.m. Bedtime and lights out for fifth- and sixth-year students.

Visiting hours every Sunday 8:00 a.m. to 6:00 p.m.

"I see why your dorm nooks are mainly for sleeping," Cherice said, laughing. "Your days are filled with learning, and indoor and outside activities. What do you say about the daily schedule?"

Harper and Raya answered at once, "It's terrific!" Harper continued, "We're never bored. The Family Parents, fantastic study areas, sports, our friends,

218

instructors, farmers around the Loop, our chores, our business."

"Tell me," Cherice said, "What are 'chores campus-wide'?"

Raya answered, "Just like kitchen helpers for our daily meals. There's a ton of work to keep the campus clean and well-maintained. We don't have cleaning people do that work. Floors, stairways, bathrooms, windows, meeting rooms, library, every building and the grounds. We all have to do our part to keep our Academy working and beautiful. Mrs. Grace puts the schedule together every two weeks."

Harper threw in, "We do our own laundry in the Family House basement on Saturdays. Also, there's time all day every Sunday for 'Visiting.' That's when a kid's parents and family visit here, go out for lunch or dinner. Or, if their homes are close by, they go home to be with their family for the day. And they often ask kids, like Raya and me, to go along," Harper added.

"And what's this about a business? You're only twelve years old," Cherice inquired with a friendly, wondering smile.

"Yeah, it's really cool," Harper explained. "All first-year students are urged to start a 'small' business with a product or service, keep track of expenses, branding, marketing, advertising, sales, banking, estimating income and profits, taxes, all the knowledge and skills necessary for running a successful small business."

Raya continued, "You can create your own business, or pick one from a past graduate, or take over a business from second-year students. Kids can work together, like we do, or alone. Either way, a sixth-year student is your mentor, guiding your work to success. A special job of all sixth-year students is helping first- and second-year students adjust and do well in the Academy. That's what Mila and Riley do for us. We can't wait to be sixth-year students."

"That's a great feature for both older and younger students. Tell me about your business," Cherice said, now hooked by the business feature and the girls' enthusiasm, "I'm curious."

Harper began, "We are in *Farming Through Time*, the first part, on *Air, Water, and Soil*. So, one day soon after we got here, Ms. Abrams and Ms. Hakimi were telling us how important earthworms are to the health of soil, which is actually a focus in the next segment. Raya's dad is a big-time trout fisherman. When she called home that night and told him about the earthworms, and our assignment to start a business, what did he say, Raya?"

"Dad said," Raya followed, "Hey! There's your business: start a worm farm. Low maintenance. You can spin off lots of products and services. Worms for soil irrigation, solid and liquid natural fertilizer, and especially, worms for fishing. Fishing is popular around here. My buddies and I'll buy your worms and help spread the word about your business.'"

Harper held up the curious green foam box, "Tada! Bodacious Worms! is what we created for our business. We got an artsy friend here at the Academy to do the graphics. Raya and I created the advertising campaign, and branded all the packaging materials."

Raya continued, "Nothing goes to waste at the Academy. We organized our kitchen helpers to collect vegetable trimmings, leftovers, spoiled vegetables, eggshells, shredded brown paper bags, egg cartons, and other things worms love to eat. They tossed that into a garbage can at our

Family House. Once a week we brought the bin to our churning vat in the barn. The vat is actually a large blender. It grinds the pieces into a pulpy mass. We fed the pulp to the worms in feeding tubs. Mr. Walker designed a worm farm tub for us. Ms. Abrams got a plastic fabricator in town to make the tub."

Harper picked up the story, "The worms have voracious appetites. They eat the pulp and produce worm castings—a fantastic solid, natural fertilizer. Another product is 'worm tea,' which is a thick, black liquid fertilizer that drains from the tubs. 'Bodacious Black Gold,' we named it. We were amazed how much food the worms ate, and how fast, and the gobs of castings and tea. We had gallons of products in no time! Since the business was producing, we had to plan it out and do a market survey. We targeted big box stores and mom-and-pop stores in the area for selling our products— sporting goods stores, nurseries, hardware stores."

Raya continued, "We set the launch date, then packaged examples of everything we would sell. Dad brought his truck over and we hit the road for three Saturday afternoons. The response was fantastic. Sold out our stock."

Harper said proudly, "We estimated our profit margin at eight to ten percent! We've learned so much about habitats, soil chemistry, and microscopic animals and plants in nature, how to make and run a business—all from squiggly, little red wiggler worms. Bodacious Worms!"

Raya weighed in with, "It was a lot a work, but we did it. Where do we go from here? Up, and up, and up, in any enterprise we want."

"Are you still doing the business?" Cherice asked.

"We gotta finish school," Harper threw in, laughing. "But, when we reported our results in December, Ms.

Abrams, Mr. Walker, and Mr. Stanton invited us to meet with all the farmers around the Academy to talk about what we did. They're always looking for new ways to use waste and care for the soil. They put our Bodacious Worms to work on the whole farm."

"Yeah, big time," Raya continued. "They worked with sixth-year students in *Making Physical Work Easy* to bring worm farming and composting to full scale at the barn, with machinery they invented, and fully automated, including for processing manure from livestock."

"Once a week," Harper wrapped up, "the kitchen waste from the Family Houses, all the farmers and other neighbors, goes to the vats in the barn for the worms to eat. A whole lotta waste that used to go into garbage disposals. Night and day our little Bodacious Worms work in the dark, turning vegetable scraps into fertilizer. Every day, each worm produces about half its body weight in castings. The sixth-year students also invented equipment to process manure, plus lawn and weed trimmings, into liquid and solid, organic fertilizer. Spread on the fields, plowed in by the farmers, planted with seed. Alpha to Omega and back again. We get new crops to harvest and food for our table."

Cherice exclaimed, "Oh my God! What a story! I absolutely love it! Thank you, girls. This was a special treat . . . Oops! I just felt a big kick," she announced, pressing her hand on her belly. "Now, the baby's wriggling." They all laughed. "We should rejoin the party."

Darius had been wondering where Cherice went, and was a little worried as a husband and soon-to-be father. "Where were you?" he asked Cherice, when she was by his side again.

"Darling," Cherice answered softly, "you won't believe what I learned about the Academy. It's incredible what they do for kids. I'll tell you later, when we're back home."

Then, Mrs. Grace got the attention of Darius and Cherice, "Our students seek a liberal arts education — languages, writing, literature, art, science, mathematics, and philosophy of Western civilization, history and current development of technology. Also, a thorough immersion in Eastern and ancient civilizations, and their cultures, knowledge, and skills. We're reading early applications now for fall enrollment. You'll soon find out, Darius, what they write in their letters of introduction."

Harding was standing nearby. Mrs. Grace grabbed his coat sleeve and asked him to weigh in on a concern occasionally raised by outsiders: "The Academy's curriculum seems busy and rigorous. Is it beyond the students' ability?"

"Glad you asked, Mrs. Grace." Harding, always direct, explained, "Probably a correct observation, from afar. At the Academy, schooling is real life. It should always be presented as such. Protect students from harm? Absolutely. Prevent laziness, fallacy, deceit, dangerous or predatory forces before they take root? Completely. It's a sin against God's creation to parlay wrong, harmful ideas and behaviors in the name of education for children. The mind is infinite — from conception. But bad parenting, servitude, drug abuse, debauchery, immoral influence, socialized dependency, addiction to the Internet, and death can prevent a young mind from learning. Academy students know that life is learning. Living requires work, every day, all day long. Life, like work, is hard. Can be exceedingly difficult, dangerous, and deadly. But the good life is exhilarating. The mind is set free to explore, solve problems, and create beautiful things. The essence of a human being. Create the right environment, like we've done here, and every student will rise up."

Cherice said, "Thank you, Mr. Harding, for those inspiring words. As you know, I'm carrying our first baby, coming into the world soon. Darius and I pray for that kind of learning."

A group of students was waiting patiently close by for the adult talk to end. They wanted to know when Darius would start his first production and what it would be.

His answers were the same as he gave for other audiences: "Thank you for asking. It's in development. You will know soon, real soon."

Of Cherice, the students were curious about her veterinary studies, what prompted her to choose that career, and when she planned to open her practice.

She coyly copied Darius: "Thanks. I'm working on it. You will know soon, real soon." Then, she pressed and rubbed her hands across her belly and announced, "First, we are expecting this baby on February 14, Valentine's Day."

The whole room erupted in applause and congratulations for the young couple.

Sensing that the dinner party was over, or should be, Brother Blaine looked at his watch, and said to himself, "Oh my God, 5:30 Mass for St. Ann's on Sunday morning. Better head home."

"Hello!" Brother Blaine called out to get everyone's attention. He said an evening prayer of thanksgiving, blessed everyone, then, excused himself. Brother Blaine's departure signaled to all visitors how late it was. Goodbyes were said. Thanks given to Shikhar and Ela Singh, and the Singh Family House, for hosting a fine dinner party.

Darius drove the Lark — Cherice in the back seat and Harding riding shotgun — to the Stanton Cottage.

"Mr. Harding," Cherice said when out of the car, "This was a wonderful evening. We are so pleased to be here. Victoria shared with me tonight that you designed the Academy from the ground up. It's genius. Pure genius. A wonderful education for so many kids."

"Thank you, Cherice. It's not something I say. Coming up with a good idea can be easy, but putting that idea into practice? That's where the real important work is done. There are so many talented faculty, staff, parents, students, friends, and donors who make the Academy what it is every day."

"We'll talk more soon," Cherice said.

"Good night, Mr. Harding," Darius said.

"Good night, Mr. and Mrs. James. Your baby just might be kicking tonight."

"It's been kicking for an hour," Cherice said, holding her belly.

They all laughed.

Harding backed the Lark out of the driveway and motored home.

# — 26 —

ON a Friday afternoon, second week in February, Darius met with Harding to discuss using *Antigone* for his performance in May.

Upon hearing the choice, Harding, fixated, said, "Sophocles! One of my all-time favorite tragic playwrights. I recall reading his works in college, and finding such sobering truths about the human condition. Of his works, *Antigone*, *Oedipus Rex*, and *Oedipus at Kolonos*, they are my favorite plays. Darius, *Antigone* is perfect for our times, on so many levels and issues. I'm amazed at your gift for theater. You will help us suspend disbelief, turn a simple stage into a 'place of seeing,' as the Greeks defined theater. And, most of all, when the curtain falls on *Antigone*, we will know who we are as a people, now. And, hopefully, how to become better as people. Send me the budget. I'll run it by the board for approval. It's a pretty sure thing. I'm with you, Darius, all the way. As my dad would say, 'Get crackin'."

"Thank you, Mr. Harding," Darius said. "There's more. By a quirk of fortune in December, an off Broadway theater group I had worked for closed its doors, the Classical Theater Company."

"I remember them from your resume. That's too bad. A real setback for the CTC," Harding added.

Darius continued, "Last week on a call, their manager told me the terrible news. Unless they have to, they don't want to work restaurants, bars, hotels, or Uber people around the metro area. Harsh reality of too many people in theater. The last show they did was *Antigone*. Had rave reviews for a limited run. Then, a plunging internal budget, unsold seats, complaints of high ticket prices around the district. The upshot: wrong economics around the country hit them hard."

Harding recognized the Academy's good fortune and said, "I like where this is going, Darius. Tell me more."

"Yeah," Darius continued. "This could be a great opportunity for us. And a timely rescue for friends in the theater district. It's just what we want, *Antigone*, a turnkey deal. Actors, set, props, costumes, lighting, they know their lines forward and backward. We get rehearsals going. Have students involved. I'll direct. This should light the students' fire. Next season, I'll have the theater department running full on, so students get into plays through history, set design, lighting, and acting."

"Make them an offer they can't refuse. Everybody gets paid, fair and square, including lodging, meals, shipping the set and costumes, and travel up here and back," Harding said. "Three shows over Mother's Day weekend. Friday, Saturday, Sunday. I've already locked in the dates and ticket prices with the manager at the Playhouse in town. I'll get the Chamber behind us, the media, restaurants, hotels, schools and colleges, and shops in the whole county and beyond. This will be a win for everybody.

Darius, overwhelmed with joy, headed for the door, "Alright, Mr. Harding. Thank you so much. I'll contact the manager this afternoon, work up the budget, and get that to you for a contract in the next day or so."

"Hold on, Darius," Harding said with that paternal smile of his. "Speaking of important news, how are Cherice and the baby doing?"

"I don't know much about childbirth stuff, but the doctor said the baby is on schedule for the 14th," Darius said.

Harding returned, "Pretty much all we men can know. Can't really do much, either. It's all about a certain mother doing God's work for creation. That's only a couple days away. Sometimes babies come early, sometimes late, once in a while, on schedule. Might be good to stay close to home until Mom's ready to deliver. You guys don't have a car. Take the Lark home. Tank's filled. Keys are in the ignition. Keep it until the baby's home, and you and Cherice are settled in as first-time parents. Longer. No hurry to return it."

"Mr. Harding, you are so generous. I can't thank you enough," Darius said.

"You are part of the family now, Darius. We're glad to help in any way. Let's get that baby into the world. I know you and Cherice are looking forward to seeing your child's little face for the first time," Harding replied. "We are, too."

Two days later, a six-pound, five-ounce boy, Simon Elijah James, arrived right on time, 3:00 p.m., February 14, at St. Luke's Hospital in Eridu Springs. A Valentine's Day baby.

In the delivery room, first-time Mom and Dad had tears of joy running on their faces. Cherice and Darius were so thrilled.

"He's got your chin," Darius pronounced.

"Yeah, but he has your forehead, for sure. Oh my God, he's smiling!" Cherice said.

"He's so beautiful. I think little Simon looks just like his mother," Darius said, kissing the proud first-time mother, his wife, Cherice, on her lips.

"Congratulations, first-time dad!" she said lovingly.

The next day Cherice's parents, Anders and Ingrid Olsen, came to stay at the Stanton Cottage for the next four weeks, to help Mom and Dad take care of newborn Simon Elijah James.

Their OBGYN doctor told Cherice and Simon to remain in St. Luke's for three days to ensure that first-time mom and baby were healthy, and thriving on their own.

On the Sunday before Cherice's parents would fly back to their home in Wisconsin, Simon was baptized at St. Ann's Church by Brother Blaine. Two other babies of parents in Eridu Springs were also baptized. The faithful gathering of proud parents, grandparents, family and friends stood, holding candles, in their duty as devout witnesses.

Back at the Stanton Cottage, Darius, with help from his father-in-law, put together a very fine brunch for all their friends and family. Many members of the Academy staff and faculty attended.

Harding brought out three bottles of chilled Moet & Chandon Imperial. At a pause in conversations, he popped the first cork and called for a toast. Darius and Anders popped corks on the second and third bottles, and they all began filling glasses.

"Ladies and gentlemen," Harding began, "let's welcome and honor the precious, beautiful, little Simon Elijah James, baptized today, in the faith of our God, our family, and our congregation. Congratulations and best wishes to his parents, Darius and Cherice James, and his grandparents,

Anders and Ingrid Olsen. As your elders, we know that you will face more profound joy and pride, and unknown challenges in the years ahead. We love you very much. Time pushes on, beyond anyone's control. Events will come and go. Sometimes you will be ready, other times not. We know that you will make the right decisions for Simon and your family. Hard as they may be at times. You will do your best to prepare your family for life's journey. Know that all along the way stuff happens. That's normal. Your family, friends, and guests assembled here will give tenderly, lovingly, all the help you may need.

"God bless mom and dad, Cherice and Darius, and their beautiful son, Simon. Our new family at the Stanton Academy."

The first show for *Antigone* would open in only three months. "Mom, Dad," Cherice asked, "would you come to visit again over Mother's Day weekend to help take care of Simon?"

"Would not pass up that offer ever," Anders said. "We get to spoil our grandson and you get to see the first play directed for the Academy by Darius. Get us seats for the Saturday show! We will be here for you."

# — 27 —

THE house lights dimmed, signaling that the performance would begin soon. Characteristic chattering and murmuring of guests became quiet. Two stagehands, hidden from view, parted the curtains just enough to allow one person through — and closed them again.

A spotlight lit up Darius James on stage, stunningly dressed in a trim, black tuxedo. He slowly took in the audience from right to left. Mild, courteous applause began from the more seasoned theatergoers. Loud applause rose up instantly from the Academy's students packed tight in the balcony.

Darius, a poised, polished professional, bowed in a respectful, dignified way. Applause stopped. The audience was seated. Expectant.

"Good evening, everyone. I'm Darius James, director and producer of classical theater at the StantonAcademy for Humanity. This is my first production for the Academy in Eridu Springs. I am extremely pleased to bring you the off-Broadway play *Antigone*, written by the great Greek poet, Sophocles, in 441 BC. And, ladies and gentlemen, I am honored to give you this tragedy, as performed by the renowned New York Classical Theater Company. Enjoy the show!"

233

Darius bowed, the curtains parted, he turned around, and disappeared.

Harding and his wife, Sarah, had arrived at the theater half an hour before doors opened. They had purchased seats in the first row of the balcony for the first night's performance. Harding had been too busy processing student applications on Monday to catch the dress rehearsal, which he'd promised Darius he would attend. After getting past a cranky doorkeeper, they entered the lobby. Sarah pressed a docent for two programs, before they took the stairs to their seats on the balcony level.

After they read biographies of the actors in the New York Classical Theater Company, Sarah said coyly, "Mort, mind if I read the summary, like I did when you took me on our first date to see the opera, *Swan Lake*, at the Met?" Harding looked at his wife and smiled, "I'd love that, dear. My eyes are closed like you asked me to do back then. I'm just gonna 'listen and savor it all, from then and now.'"

## A Summary and Analysis of Sophocles' *Antigone*
## By Dr Oliver Tearle (Loughborough University)

*Antigone* is, after *Oedipus Rex*, the most famous of Sophocles' plays to survive. Written over 2,400 years ago, *Antigone* is one of the finest examples of Greek tragedy: the play explores its central moral issue through its two main characters, Antigone and Creon, and remains as relevant now as it was when Sophocles first wrote it.

The plot or action of *Antigone* follows the events of the Oedipus legend, which Sophocles later told in *Oedipus Rex* and *Oedipus at Colonnus*.

234

The back story is as follows: Oedipus had unwittingly killed his father, Laius, and married his mother, Jocasta. He and Jocasta had had four children together. They had two sons, Eteocles and Polyneices, and two daughters, Antigone and Ismene. After they discovered they were mother and son, Jocasta hanged herself and Oedipus blinded himself and was exiled from Thebes, the city he'd ruled with Jocasta.

Eteocles and Polyneices fell out over which of them should govern Thebes, and they ended up going to war and killing each other. Eteocles defended the city when his brother led an army against it. Creon, Jocasta's brother, became ruler of Thebes now there were no male heirs of Oedipus' bloodline remaining.

Because Eteocles had been governing Thebes when Polyneices killed him, Creon decreed that Eteocles should be buried with full honours, while Polyneices should not be buried at all. In Greek religious terms, this was the equivalent to burying someone outside of a churchyard: it meant their soul would not be accepted into the afterlife.

This is the background to *Antigone*. The action of the play itself begins when Antigone hears of Creon's decision that her brother, Polyneices, will not be buried in consecrated ground. Antigone decides to get hold of her dead brother's body and bury it herself. However, while she is performing a ritual over her brother's body, she is captured.

When she is brought before Creon, Antigone stands up to him, arguing that he has overstepped his remit as ruler of the city, and is attacking fundamental moral values by trying to control Polyneices' fate in the afterlife. Indeed, she argues that such an action amounts to blasphemy against the gods themselves.

As punishment for her defiance, Creon has Antigone imprisoned in a cave with just enough food to keep her alive but make her gradually weaker until she eventually starves to death.

However, Antigone has a useful defender in Haemon, her betrothed, who also happens to be Creon's own son. Yes, Creon has condemned his own would-be daughter-in-law to a horrible death! However, Creon refuses to listen to his son's request and proceeds with the execution. Haemon storms out, telling his father that he will never see him again.

At this point, Tiresias the seer – the one who had revealed the true fate of Oedipus, Antigone's own father, to him in *Oedipus Rex* – intervenes and warns Creon that he is behaving contrary to the will of the gods. Symbolically, Polyneices' unburied corpse is festering, and the stench fills the whole of Thebes. However, like all tyrants, Creon refuses to listen to Tiresias' warning and tries to smear the seer, accusing him of being in the pay of Creon's enemies.

However, privately Creon is worried by Tiresias' words, and knows that the prophet speaks the truth. He resolves to bury the corpse of Polyneices and let Antigone go. But his change of heart is too little, too late: Antigone, rather than suffer a slow and agonising death, has hanged herself (as her mother did before her), and Haemon, Creon's own son and the man who loved Antigone, has killed himself over her corpse.

As if this isn't tragedy enough, Creon's wife, Eurydice, is distraught at news of her son's death, and kills herself, too. At the end of the play, Creon is left standing over the bodies of his wife and son.

### *Antigone*: analysis

*Antigone* raises a number of moral questions which remain as important to us now as they were when Sophocles wrote the play, almost two-and-a-half thousand years ago. What are the limits of a ruler's power? Should there be clear limits? What inalienable freedoms and rights are people afforded?

Like many great works of art, *Antigone* is more complex than a plot summary can convey. For instance, the above summary paints Creon as a tyrannical ruler who drastically – and fatally – oversteps the limits of his power, with consequences both for others and, as is always the case in Greek tragedy, for himself. He has to live with his mistakes, having lost his wife and son because of his tyranny.

As the play emerges, what transforms Creon into a tyrant rather than a judicious politician is his stubbornness, and his refusal to change tack even when all of the evidence points otherwise. If he had initially forbidden the burial of Polyneices because he wished to honour and protect the people he rules, he has now become their worst enemy. When his son entreats him to see sense, he refuses, and loses his son forever.

Then, when Tiresias, who has the gift of prophecy, tells him he's following the wrong course, he secretly *knows* he has made the immoral decision but to save face he refuses to admit it, hoping to undo his decisions quietly without everyone else finding out that he has gone back on his original decree.

Whereas Creon's authority had previously seemed to speak for the whole of Thebes, now it sounds like 'naked self-assertion', the words of a man who is determined to impose his will, even if he knows it's the morally wrong thing to do.

Despite its title, Antigone is really Creon's play more than it is Antigone's. He is the real tragic figure at the centre of the play's action, in that it is his tragic flaw – his inflexibility – which is his undoing, and for which he must undergo suffering or catharsis by the end of the play.

He also speaks more of the play's dialogue than Antigone, who spends much of the second half of the play walled up in a cave before returning as a corpse. In this respect, Antigone is like Shakespeare's Julius Caesar, which may be named after the Roman general but is really the tragedy of Brutus, not Caesar.

Nevertheless, Antigone is one of the most significant female characters in ancient Greek tragedy, and this is one reason why the play has continually proved popular to new generations. The other is that although at first glance the play appears to be about a largely unfashionable clash between civil and religious law, it has endured, and continues to be relevant to modern readers and audiences, because it is really about honouring family in the face of inhumane and unjust – indeed, immoral – laws that forbid such a thing.

It's no accident that the play attracted a twentieth-century writer like Bertolt Brecht, who translated it in the late 1940s: whenever there is tyranny, there will be Antigone to remind us of the importance of doing the right thing.

Harding, with his eyes now open, looked at Sarah, caressed her face with his hands, and they kissed. "Even better than the first time, love," Sarah said softly.

As the curtains began to close on the last act of the play, the house stood and erupted in applause and cheers. The seasoned theatergoers along with the students. After a few minutes of uninterrupted clapping, cheers and bravos, the cast was ready for curtain call. The curtains opened slowly and the audience became ever louder, not stopping. A few minutes later, the curtains closed briefly and then opened again. The cast was standing arm in arm, with Darius in the center.

From stage left, sixth-year Academy students, led by Stella and Hana, carried long-stem red roses to each actor. From stage right, Mrs. Graves walked out to present a huge bouquet of long-stem red roses to Darius. She hugged him, kissed his cheek, then turned to the audience to wave and blow kisses to Cherice, standing in the first row with Olivia. On either side of Cherice and Olivia stood the special guests of the director, Isiah and Ruth Goodman. On either side of the Goodman's, in motorized wheelchairs were Marcus Ebenezer Stanton and his wife, Olivia McIntosh Stanton.

On cue from the left front house floor, the spotlight lit up Harper Mathews, Raya Carter, and Stella Young walking out carrying long-stem white roses. Raya handed a rose to Marcus and to Olivia Stanton. Harper handed a rose to Isiah and to Ruth Goodman, and to Cherice James. Stella gave a white rose to her mother, Olivia Young. The little company hugged and kissed in the spotlight.

Darius and the cast blew kisses into the audience, then bowed slowly and deeply. A tremendous applause erupted that would not stop. The curtains closed a final time. Applause ended in a gentle manner.

# — 28 —

CAPTAIN Marcus Stanton served with the US Army in Vietnam from April 10, 1968, to April 30, 1975. His first assignment was Huey Gunship pilot at Black Horse Base Camp, with the 11th Armored Cavalry Regiment, Colonel George Smith Patton IV, Commander.

Late one afternoon four years later, Marcus returned to camp from a brutal mission north of Dĩ An. Huey took hits from Viet Cong on the ground, shooting AK-47s. Copilot and both door gunners wounded badly. Chopper limped back to base. Deadlined for repairs. Debriefing over, Stanton was dismissed.

Dark cumulonimbus clouds were steadily moving toward the area, portending a storm just before sundown. A merciless, dense mass of steamy tropical air settled in. Marcus showered and changed into cleaned, pressed fatigues. Walked across the parade ground to the officer's canteen tent to have a few beers. PBR, his favorite. "We've Gotta Get Out of this Place" by the Animals, was playing loud from an eight-track tape inside, as it did multiple times every night. Lotta hollering and dancing inside. Two second lieutenants, smoking joints, skipped out the back door arm-in-arm with three prostitutes for boom boom.

Outside the front screen door, a scruffy, wrinkled old private sat on three, stacked-up sandbags. Wafts of his strong, body sweat from jungle heat billowed through the air. Been a long time since he had a shower, shave, and haircut. His bush hat was in tatters, vents blown out. His OD fatigue jacket and pants were frayed, torn, oversized, badly faded, and laterite-stained. Had no dog tags chained around his neck. No name tag, rank or unit insignia sewn on his uniform. Dark-stained, untied, ragged, and warp-soled jungle boots on his feet.

Hanging on a stainless steel chain around his neck, was a Sterling silver pendant of Saint Jude Thaddeus, faithful servant and friend of Jesus, patron saint of desperate situations and hopeless cases. The old private had traded a roadside Vietnamese vendor twenty dollars in MPCs for the medal when walking out of camp on his first patrol.

"Hol' up, Cap'in," the soldier said calmly in a gravelly southern voice. He was old, far beyond his years. Penetrating, bloodshot green eyes. Dark-brown, weather-beaten skin. "Ah believe you' not quite ready ta enter dhis joint taday."

"What did you say, private? Are you drunk? Stand and salute," Marcus, stiffened up, commanded.

The private didn't budge. He replied, "Sir, Ah respects ya as a man dhat Ah nev'r met b'fore. But Ah heard good words 'bout ya. Sincerely. God as ma witness. Ah knows da rules respectin' officers, non-coms an coms... An' da consequences. Ah ain't bein' disrespectful ta ya. Le's put military starch on hol'. Please. Ah wanna talk ta ya man-ta-man fer a bit. If you'll oblige me, as Mama would say."

"Private," Marcus said. "You are a private, right? I can't really tell from your weathered uniform with no rank insignia." The captain, glancing up at dark clouds billowing in the distance, said, "You have a clever way of

242

getting my attention this evening. I'll put formalities aside, this once, for you. I'm listening."

"Here Ah am, Lord," the private recited from scripture. "Cap'in Stanton! Been waitin' here fer ya long time. Some folks claim Ah'm a tetchy ol' grunt. Ah ain't. Ah jus' speaks what's on ma mine', from ma experience. An' Ah has some. Didn't dodge da draf' an' go ta Canada on a rich daddy's tab.

"Ah enlisted 'bout seven year ago, seventeen Ah was, ta serve ma country, when called up. Followed ma family's long history a' service. Proud Revolutionary War an' Civil War roots family. Relatives in World Wars I, II, an' Korea. Massive deadly wars dhey was. Ma uncles, Ned, Clarance, an' Amos, didn' make it home from II. Los' Orville, Quentin, an' Lester on Pork Chop Hill, May '53, Korea.

"Were dhose wars necessary? Yeah. Seems. Sadly so. We ended 'em fer sure. Ah'd a liked ta seen more done early ta prevent 'em. Less killin' on both sides over da time, surely. Easy ta look back on dhose wars an' feel proud a' what our boys did, while dheir buddies was ripped 'part by bullets an' frags, arm's length away. We's Americans. We fight fer our freedom. An' we won't have no dictators or tyranny.

"Eleazar Zechariah, speakin' atcha. Mountaineer from da hollers a' West Virginia. Was a' M-60 machin-gun-totin' grunt fer ma infantry platoon, 1st Cav. Twenty-four year' ol' today. Some birthday, ain't it? Thought Ah'd go fer da career. Re-upped afta' R&R in Hong Kong ta be a lifer. Dhen, Ah was recommended ta Officer Candidate School. Couldn' see me doin' dhat. Returned ta Nam a platoon sergeant. Serve ma country, an' retire in ma late thirties wit' pay an' benefits. If Ah live ta claim 'em. Likely, better dhan workin' da coal mines, like ma relatives an' frien's Ah lef' back home.

"All was reset in a Sông Bé jungle camp two year back when a cherry first sergeant mocked me ever' day since he arrived. Got some kinda kick outta makin' a fool outta me 'cause a' da way Ah look an' talk. Tol' him ta stop doin' dhat. He jus' grinned kinda' funny an' called me a 'dumbass hillbilly.' Ah' had 'nough on da instant. Ain't nobody callin' me, or anyone, dhat.

"Years pas', wit' Mama in da kitchen o' our mountain cabin up da holler, we'd listen ta lotsa fights on radio. Ah 'specially remember da '64 Clay—Liston TKO. Ma uncle, Percy Just, he heard a' ma interest in boxin' an' Liston's fight. Stopped by our home. Gave me his gloves to practice, an' a punchin' bag. Da mice had chewed up da gloves a bit, but Mama sewed up da holes an' worked da leather till dhey was new again. Ah danced 'round in our dirt yard, an' punched da bes' Ah could in da air, an' on da bag, like Ah was Cassius Clay his self. I'd 'float like a butterfly an' sting like a bee.' Good 'nuf lessons an' practice fer me, dhey was.

"Evenin' time. Gettin' dark out. Away from da sleepin' troops. No rules. No refs. Cleaned his clock on da spot. Turned his left jaw inta puzzle pieces. Made him swaller his front teeth. Cracked several ribs. An' dhen some. Ah beat da livin' shit outta him, bes' Ah could. Gave him a lesson he deserved fer a long time from God Almighty.

"Next thing Ah know, Ah'm Article 15'ed, jailed in a shippin' container dhey windowed wit' a torch in camp. Ah was dropped from Platoon Sergeant back ta zero-rank buck private. Had lotta time ta think 'bout punchin' out dhat ignorant-assed white cracka from Chicago. No regrets, tho. Would do it again in a heartbeat. Coulda' killed him. But goin' dhat far was not da Lord's way, in ma mind.

"On da mornin' when ma time in da slammah was up, just b'fore sunup, Ah crawled outta da camo blanket, stretched ma arms an' legs an' back muscles. Ah seen da door was unlocked a'ready. Poked ma head out. Nobody, an' nothin' around. Platoon up and lef' without me. Ah walked away. An' jus' kep' on walkin'. Ah been traipsin' through da jungles, rice paddies, villages, mountains, beaches, an rivers, day an' night, eva' since. Roamin' free in dhis beautiful country. Da whole world's God's creation, a paradise."

Eleazar reached up slowly with his shaky, skin-and-bones, right hand to gently take hold of Captain Stanton's cleaned, heavily starched fatigue jacket—at his stomach.

Captain Stanton backed away slightly, "Excuse me, Private Eleazar Zechariah, I'm sorry you got busted. Whose fault it was, I couldn't judge. Or say you got a bum deal. Wasn't there. I'm not a JAG. But you got no right to hold me here. My friends are waiting for me in the canteen. Let go of my jacket, Private, that's an order."

The private calmly, tenaciously, vice-gripped onto the captain's fatigue jacket with his right index finger and thumb.

One of the captain's friends, at once, appeared like a shadow, and shouted through the screen door, "Hey, Stanton, you ready for beers or not? My round." The captain's attention was riveted firmly by the private's eyes.

"Cap'in Stanton," Private Eleazar Zechariah said, peering deep into his eyes, all the way to his soul. "We been here in Nam since '55. At war since '63. Now it's '72, an' what gives? We got fiyah' powah up da' kazoo. We ain't winnin' nothin'! Ah'm no fool. Always got ma eyes wide open and ma ears cleaned a' taters. Been stompin' all over dhis foreign lan' da'

245

las' coupla' year on ma own. Love Vietnamese people, dheir history, food, culture, religions. Beautiful people. All of 'em. Da Lord's been takin' good care a' me.

"B'fore gettin' busted, when Ah'd come back from patrols, Ah'd fin' Mama had sen' me inta'national newspapa's an' such, exposin' our government's shenanigans. An' history books 'bout Vietnam, goin' back thousands a' years. Reports 'bout da' protesters burnin' Ole Glory, spittin' at, an' cussin' on soldiers returnin' back ta dheir folks after servin' dheir country in a war zone. Many a' da soldiers was all messed up in dheir heads, some more dhen others. Some shot up bad. Legs an' arms gone. Skin burned 'an grafted. Lotta pain. Some wit' no family, or no homes ta go home ta. Suicidin' dheir selves. Families all fucked up on dheir own, an' wit' da mess our nation was in.

"Some homecomin', ain't it? Somethin's gone terribly wrong. Ah lef' America a soldier proud ta serve ma country, when called in ma time. Now, dhere's pampered college kids back home disrespectin' returnin' warriors. Da US military. Da flag we serve. America!

"Ah reads a lot. Thinks a lot. Prays a lot, too. What in da hell's goin' on?"

"It is a curious war, for certain," Captain Stanton averred.

"We just pilin' up American an' Vietnamese boys in body bags, an' lettin' dead Viet Cong boys' rot in da jungle. Fer what? Can't nobody answer dat?

"SECDEF McNamara an' his Ha'vard Whiz Kids at da DOD don' know squat 'bout war. Don' care 'bout Vietnamese people, society, culture or history. Runnin' dhis war like it's dheir business. A single-minded killin' machine an' numbers game, rackin' up profits at dah en' a' da factory assembly line. Watchin' dheir 'vestments

246

in da stock ma'ket goin' down taday, up tamorra'. Always rootin' fer more ups.

"Know what? Dhey's figured out how to up dheir numbers. Been acceptin' recruits dhat can't read or write or speak English. An' wit' low IQs. 'Send 'em out now!' dhey ordered. Firs' ta die in da jungle, dhey was. No su'prise dhere. 'McNamara's Morons,' dhey're call'd. Jus' ta meet da 'manpower 'quirements' dhey sets."

"'We lettin' it be what it is?' as Mama would ask when she called out stupid at town meetin's.

"An' Pres'dent Johnson, playin' da black people an' otha' poor folks ta build his presidential legacy. Da gen'rals, 'crats, pointy-headed academics, an' politicians? All one an' da same. Know-it-alls. Got connections from dheir daddies an' well-placed frien's. Wisdom an' experience from a college sheepskin. No practical experience. Can't change a tire, fix a leakin' faucet, or plow a field. Tellin' us soldiers in dhis jungle war what ta do? What not ta do? An' when? Our boys die, waitin' fer da word from some 'crat half da world away.

"Blood from millions a' innocents around da world is on dheir han's. An' too many of 'em don' care. Dhey's privileged. Dhey's a world away from da bullets, RPGs, an' daily horrors. An' dhey ain't got a conscience, or dhey'd walk away from da Godforsaken cesspool an' grow a spine. A sin against God's children an' His creation. It's written in da Bible, Matthew 18:6.

If any of you put a stumbling block before one of these little ones who believe in me, it would be better for you if a great millstone were fastened around your neck & you were drowned in the depths of the sea.

247

"Chillin' quote from da Savior, 'tis. What goes aroun', comes aroun'. 'We got ta stop da spread a' communism,' dhey's been sayin' since b'fore World War II. Ah sure don' wanna live in dheir tyrannical communism. Want nobody to. Dhat government has slaughtered dheir own people by da millions in Russia, China, Korea, Cuba, South America, an' other countries. University academics roun' da world, Americans too, has sung praises ta communism since before da Russian Revolution. What a beautiful life 'tis. Firs' dhey take out da town an' religious leaders o' da poor people. Dhen all da traditional believers in da countryside who resist communist rule. Mow 'em down wit' machine guns. Natzis used gas ta kill resisters an' innocents. Was more efficient. Horrid, inhumane in any way. Dumped da bodies in a trench.

"We lettin' it be what it is?

"Seems ta me, wit' da ordinance we got, an' wit' proper negotiations, we could a' calmed da spread a' communism in Vietnam long time ago, if we had da right leaders. Might a' been bloodless. Dhere's all kin's a' governments now, an' in da history a' da world. A myriad a' deviations. Not one kind, whatever da foundation. Da government ya has is not necessarily bad. It's da moral integrity a' da people runnin' da government, an' dheir ideas 'bout human rights, without limits. Da backbone an' guts a' da people, da citizens. Dhat's what matta's mos'.

"Tyrants can rot-worm dheir way inta any government, any people, any time. Applies ta our government, our society, too. People ferget dhat. Ah likes our constitutional republic, from da founders, wit' da capitalism. Anybody can make a good life in da USA. We's a free people. Our freedom's a right from God. Governments? Dhey's made

248

up a' men. But mos' every leader don' wan' people dhat's free. Can happen in da US same as anywhere else. Can't rule free people! Gotta kill 'em ta have total control. Or make 'em sheep. Da people dhat's got freedom, dhey's damn lucky. But mus' never sleep on it. Gotta work hard on keepin' it. Be willin' ta fight ta dheir death ta keep it, ever' day. An' always insist on havin' da leas' government possible. In America, where da rule a' law's been sacrosanct since 1789, we don' fight ourselves bloody settlin' differences. We mus' argue da important mattas truthfully in Congress. Deman' fair an' free 'lections ta decide what we gonna do an' where we' goin'. We 'xpect dhat. God help us if we lose dhat only one time.

"An' da, if da people in some othah lan' dhat ain't got freedom a' dheir own, dhey gotta fight like hell ta make dheir own kin' a' freedom. It don' come as a plastic toy in a Cheerios box. Ain't nobody outside can make it happen. An' many gonna die fightin fer it on da badlefiel's' agains' invaders, and dheir own government, dheir own duped kin folk. Like our bloody Civil War. It's damned ugly fightin' fer freedom.

"America's wealth has become an addiction, plain an' simple. A wicked poison. An 'opium' dhat's fuelin' da rich an' powerful. An' stupefien' da masses. Dheir content ta sit on da sidelines, on dheir asses, an' eat cake. Da higher-ups don' care 'bout mindin' da 'store.' Too much a' da 'good life' makes a people immoral, greedy, lazy, an' fergetful. Ordinary folks who's been asleep too long now, dhey'll wake up from dheir rollin', rollickin' drunk when it's too late to recover what dhey had. An da higher-ups knew how ta invest an' read da signs, an' done moved on.

"We lettin' it be what it is?

"Moses, in Exodus 32:19, he saw dhat his firs' time comin' off da mountain. He was rightful angry an' disappointed wit' his people, debauched up as dhey was.

And it happened when he drew near the camp that he saw the calf and the dancing, and Moses's wrath flared, and he flung the tablets from his hand and smashed them at the bottom of the mountain. And he took the calf that they had made and burned it in fire and ground it fine and scattered it over the water and made the Israelites drink it.

"Dhis here war is wrong! Bad fer ever'body an' ever'thing it touches. We should a' neva' come here in da firs' place, if we didn' commit ta en' it morally right—an' fas'. Da Vietnamese people ha' been fightin' fer dheir independence fer 2,000 years agains' one foreign invader afta' 'nother. China, France, Japan, an' now da USA, since at least '55.

"You'd think dhose government folks a' ours would study hard on da history, culture, religions, an' societies a' people dhey gonna deal wit'. Talk to 'em long time, wherever dhey is in da world—b'fore dhey cross 'em. Help 'em find a good solution to dheir differences. No! Dhey's blinded by wieldin' power, God-awful weapons, an' controlin' people. Dhey's hell-bent on hurryin' up da career ladda', an' closin' dheir money-makin' deals.

"We lettin' it be what it is?

"We made boisterous threats dhat's hollow ta da North Vietnamese. We made promises ta da South Vietnamese people we likely won' keep. Dhen what? We jus' pulls out? Let da ones who died wit' us rot away, an' who fought wit' us be at da mercy a' da Viet Cong an' others?

Could be 'notha' violent communist bloodlettin'—now fer loyal, innocent South Vietnamese—men, women, an' children.

"Ah'm afraid we dealt 'em a bad hand, mixin' greed, politics, high-tech weapons, business tycoons, an' ignorance wit' war. Honor thrown out da window by too many of 'em. We went in, blinded by hubris. Inta dhis foreign lan' agains' da well-meanin' Vietnamese people, strugglin' ta fin' dheir destiny.

"Ah believes dhat it's good fereign policy dhat da USA helps our neighbors aroun' da worl' tryin' ta git dheir freedom an' ta keep it. But if we jump on dhat train fer 'em an' dhen jump off b'fore gettin' ta da station?

"We lettin' it be what it is?

"Wit' our fearsome weapons, we makin' da worl' run red wit' da blood a' innocents an' bad guys. If we ain't gonna be honest an' serious in helpin' folks fight a war fer dheir God-given rights, an' fer dheir independence ta da en', better ta let 'em sort out disagreements dhereselves. Or dhey have ta get da hell out somehow, hide in da caves an' hills, arm up, an' live ta fight 'notha' day. It's happened many times b'fore.

"Cap'in, you fly da ultimate war bird. In many a firefight we prayed da Hueys would come in time, while we was sprayin' our las' bullets at da enemy."

Eleazar suffered a flashback. . . . Ah hearin' da choppers comin' in from a long way off. Door gunners is hangin' far out, sweepin' da area wit' dheir M-60s— Tushwitcha- tuswitcha-tushwitcha— Eleazar shouted to his platoon, "Choppers comin' in!" Pilot radioed, "Ruby Belle, light a flare." Eleazar, "Raja'!"—tushwitcha-tushwitcha-tushwitcha— Eleazar, "Flare's lit!"—

tushwitcha-tushwitcha-tushwitcha—"Get ready! Down! Down! Now!"—tushwitcha-tushwitcha-tushwitcha— "Dhey's here! Load up! Da wounded. Dead. Drag 'em. Carry 'em. Come on, Rainey, you's far out. Run in hard! Tucker, Jesus, ya's hit in da right leg, bad. Ah puttin' tourniquet on, okay? Hol' still. Stoner, help me! Take ma M-60 an' ammo, an' Tucker's Thumper an' ammo. Okay, on tight. Bleedin's stopped. Now, Tucker, gimme ya' arm. Keep da leg up! Gotcha. Ya gonna make it. Hang in dhere. Now! Up an' in da chopper! Come on, Crockett, git ya ass in here wit' ya 'Swedish K'! Hurry, ya'll! Hurry up!"—tushwitcha-tushwitcha-tushwitcha— "We're in! Go! Go! Go! Go, pilot!" Eleazar, thumb's up. "We're outta here! Jesus! Lord! God A'mighty! Who all's hit? Medic! Git on 'em! Holy shit, Ah bleedin' from a hole in ma side." Stoner, heard that. Wrapped his right arm around Eleazar's neck and pulled him back to rest his head on Tucker's chest. "Got you, Sergeant Zech. You're going to make it, too. Stay calm. Medic!" Stoner shouted above the roar of the chopper's engine and rotors and the M-60s—tushwitcha-tushwitcha-tushwitcha . . .

"Often dhey came an' saved us. At times dhey was too late fer some, or was not ta be jus' dhen. Had ta lay low an' wait fer rescue latah.

"Fightin' a war ain't a sure thing, evah'.

"Whiz Kiddo Robert Strange McNamara, an' dhose who took ovah' since he lef', dhey gonna fin' out. Dheir war policies, an' systems analysis office in da Pentagon, killed dhem boys on both sides. Prolonged a hated an' unnecessary war wit' bad intentions an' bad policies from da start. May have started a trend.

"Dhey gonna hav' ta answer, like all otha's dhat went b'fore 'em—foreva'—fer dheir sins agains' God, an' God's' creation. If we'd jus' learn from ah' mistakes. An' not ferget da pas', so we don' repeat da mistakes, ovah an' ovah again.

"Lord, God A'mighty! Save our souls!

"War's crazy, Cap'in. On da groun' fer soldiers, total chaos. An' ugly, horrible, death unleashed everywhere. Unbounded. Fogged ove'. Rabid. Bullets 'n frags flyin' ever'where. Blood runnin'. Men's bodies blown ta bits. Absolutely, a soul, an' mind, an' body rippin', mad, hell on earth! Our young men answerin' da call, armed wit' da bes' weapons. Courageous, dhey is. Strong patriots. Fightin' fer freedom fer all. Faithful to dher family, dheir men, da country, belief in God. An' dhey're jus' so young. Ah'm 'fraid we's sacrificin' our bes' sons an' daughters on da altar a' greed.

"War don' foller no rules.

"Cap'in, a Chinese philosopha' an' strategist, Sun Tzu, wrote down long time ago, 'All wa'fare is base' on deception.' He spoke da truth. But, did he mean deceivin' da enemy only? Who owns da army? Who dhey say'n's da enemy? Who's doin' da decievin' now? An' who's bein' deceived here? Sun Tzu raised da ultimate question 'bout war in all times.

"Information comin' inta da Pentagon black box, an' decisions 'bout warrin' goin' out, are hid from We da People by our own government. As if we, da American citizens, can't understand, or be trusted wit' da truth. Dhey's hidin' da truth, an' dhey's lyin' ta us! Ta our country. Ta American citizens! Da government a' da USA s'posed ta answer ta us.

"What da hell's goin' on?

"Decisions 'bout Vietnam, an' otha wars, never should a' been lef' in da hands a' politicians an' bura'crats. Modern-day recipe fer our great American patriots' death.

"We lettin' it be what it is?

"Ma fourth grade teacha', Ms. Everleigh Evans, God bless her, had all a' us kids in da valley memorize dhese here words. Nothin' so sweet, 'ceptin' Da Lord's Prayer.

We the People of the United States, in Order to form a more perfect Union, establish Justice, insure domestic Tranquility, provide for the common defense, promote the general Welfare, and secure the Blessings of Liberty to ourselves and our Posterity, do ordain and establish this Constitution for the United States of America.

"Da Founding Fathers set up da greatest government da world's eva' seen. We got dumb leaders fer too long. Dheir decisions an' policies makin' fer battle losses, bad morale 'cross da troops. An' got lots of 'em killed. An' breedin' chaos, distrust, 'cross da USA. An' da world.

"Da Viet Cong are clever, unpredictable, an' determined ta fight fer dheir rights ta be free a' foreign occupation. Ta become a' independent, respected nation. Pentagon helped make dheir civil war. North 'gains' South Vietnam. Why?

"We lettin' it be what it is?

"Did ya know we fought on da side a' Ho Chi Minh when he was tryin' ta oust da Japanese an' da French back in da 40s an' 50s? Ho Chi Minh wrote President Truman fer help. Was rejected. He went on ta pull da bes' lines from our Declaration a' Independence ta create da Declaration a' Independence a' da Democratic Republic a

254

Vietnam, in 1945! Now, we done made him, an' his army, da enemy.

"Whaddya make a' dat?

"An' da fools in Washington don't care, or dhey'd a stopped it 'afore dhey started it. Da shiny shoes politicians an' ribbon-chesty gen'rals, all one an' da same, dhey is. Wringin' dheir hans', an' screwin' up dheir faces ta lie on TV, like dhere ain' nothin' dhey could do 'bout it. Lookin' dejected. Dhey's da ones dhat made it happen! Maybe somebody grab a Louisville Slugger, swing it 'bout wildly, an' knock sense inta dheir heads. Or hot-tar an' feather 'em, like Mark Twain reported dhey done ta da Royal Nunsuch frauds in *Huck Fin* in da ol' days. Or jus' throw 'em da hell out.

"Respec' fer truth, history, fer all God's children, common sense an' reason, is all dhat's needed. But, ifn' some a' dhem has it, who's got da backbone ta use dhese virtues in Washington, DC, evah?

"Ah've held ya against yer wishes, Cap'in. Hope not too long. Gonna en' ma talk now wit' couple a questions fer ya. Fightin' dhis here war in Vietnam, defendin' America? It's all gaumed up. A total clusterfuck. Whose benefittin'? Da US military industrial complex? Da international banks an' corporations? Billionaires 'round da world? Russia? China?

"An' who's ta say, when dhis here war en's, dhere won' be 'nother wrong war somewhere else in da world? An' dhen, 'nother wrong war in 'nother place, at 'nother time, wit' no end of 'em? Ta ring in more profits on Wall Street? 'Perpetual war,' it's called! Immoral to the nth degree. A long drawn-out slaughter of human beings. Some dhat can't settle dheir differences. Others dhat got no voice

255

on da world stage. Dhey won't give up. Won't come along. Dhey want ta live dheir life as dhey have been fer decades, centuries, or more. Dhey got no place dhey want ta go. Dhey're in da way a' 'progress' of da new world order. Dhey must conform, or be wiped off da face a' da earth.

"An' continual casualties, dhey speaks about. 'Casualties.' Interestin' word. 'A chance occurrence' derived from da late Middle English, ya know. Dhat's what dhey slyly calls counted up hurt an' dead people in da bloody muck, killed by dheir warrin' ways—in dhese wrong wars. Chance occurrence? God A'mighty! A chance occurrence' is da same as boys all shot up in da firefight?

"Are we scarfin' up resources in poor countries? Pumpin' gobs a' money inta makin' war-tech at home? Testin' out our new guns an' otha' murd'rous stuff for killin' people in foreign lan's? Maybe some day domestic, too?

"God help us.

"Usin' up outdated ordinance? Destroyin' towns an' cities?

"Pollutin' forests? Fields? Rivers, ponds, an' lakes? Blowin' da natural landscape unrecognizable, upstream, downstream, ever'where 'bout? Fer what? Ta stuff money inta da pockets a' banks an' elite big money-grubbin', land-stealin', power-holdin' billionaires? Dheir homes, accounts, an' families so cozy, an' secure, an' safe. So is our American patriots called ta fight an' die fer dheir comfort, wine, an' meats? Dheir unlimited satisfaction an' greed? Is dhis a new kinda greed an' colonialism? Da scourge a' all humanity goin' forward?

"Dhey's been talkin' 'bout a 'new world order' since World War I. Modern military, political, an' economic control a' da whole world. Da power-mongers wheel an' deal. Dhey'd divide it all up, like modern-day pirates plunderin'—cause dhat's what dhey is—pirates. Where dhere's profits, dhere's corruption. How deep is da corruption? Where dhat gonna leave da USA?

"Dhey'd trash our government a' da people by da people an' fer da people. 'Cause we in da way a dheir selfish power grab. Dhey can't have people believin' dhey has da right ta be free, armed, and independent from tyranny. Ta control dheir own destiny. People dhat's free have ta fight ta be free forever.

"Ms. Everleigh Evans also made us memorize da mos' worthy line from da Funeral Oration a' Pericles, greatest general in ancient Athens, 431 BC:

Make up your minds that happiness depends on being free, and freedom depends on being courageous.

"Puttin' our soldiers wit' courage on da ground ta fight fer freedom bound ta fail without wise an' honest leaders tellin' why an' showin' how. Da people a' Athens found dhat out, too, aftah Pericles died. An' many 'nothah nation aftah. Seems ta me, at bottom, we's got plenty a' soldiers wit' courage, but we's a long way from fightin' wars fer our national defense—fer freedom—with a true leader.

"We lettin' it be what it is?

"Ain't no red-blooded American wit' an ounce a' sense gonna say 'no' ta protectin' our independence, our national defense of America. Ah believed Ah signed up ta defend Lady Liberty from enemies foreign or domestic. Not ta kill innocent people in poor countries fer oil drillin', minin' heavy, rare earth metals, rubber tappin,' an' such. Suckin' up whatever resources in dheir lands. Tellin' 'em who dheir

257

leaders mus' be. Wheelin' an' dealin' fer control wit' cheats an' halfwit presidents an' gen'rals, ours an' dheirs.

"We lettin' it be what it is?

"On patrol, firs' month in country, ma platoon walked outta da jungle inta full sunlight an' suddenly, we all jus' stopped. We was standin' on a narra', slipp'ry, muddy bank. We watched Vietnamese farmers, men an' women, some yards ta our lef', barefoot, wearin' conical hats an' black pajamas, pant legs rolled up ta dheir knees. Dhey was plowin' dheir rice paddies wit' teams a' oxen. Dhey seemed not ta care we was dhere. Had ta plow all day an' get da rice grains an' sprouts in da beds in time fer da new season.

"Lookin' on da right, 'bout fifty yards off 'cross da water, was 'nother narra', muddy bank. A Montagnard tribe a' twenty-seven was travelin' single file, same direction as us, ta dheir nex' camp. Bare-breasted women an' teen girls carryin' toddlers an' infants, some sucklin'. Ol' men an' ol' women, all wit' cloth wraps coverin' dheir lower front privates. All barefoot. Boys an' men ma age an' olda', was carryin' bows, an' arra's, an' spears, an' huntin' knives. Gutted critters strapped on dheir waists. Dhey jus' looked at us, an' at da farmers plowin' da rice paddies otha' side a' us.

"All dhese native folks, differen' cultures fer sure, not necessarily friends, jus' goin' 'bout livin' ever' day, rain or shine, plowin' fiel's an' paddies, an' plantin', harvestin', an' huntin' dheir food. Jus' ta feed dheir families an' go on livin'. Ah thinks a lot 'bout dhose folks an' dhat rice paddy. It's ever'where here in Vietnam. Tells me somethin' ain't right.

"'Dhere but fer da grace a' God go Ah,' Mama taught me 'bout humility.

258

"Us walkin' between dhem people on da slippery dark gray mud. Wearin' da jungle boots wit' Vibram soles, rip-stop nylon fatigues, flack jackets, helmets, c-rations, automatic guns an' bandoliers a' ammo, radios, grenade launchers. Off in da sky, somewhere else, our jets shootin' out da napalm. Otha' planes dropped Agent Orange defoliant. Hueys wit' Miniguns sprayin' death somethin' wicked. 'Spooky Gunships' wit' 20-mm gatlin' guns an' 150-mm howitzers. Quad fifties. B-52s carpet bombin', an' such.

"Jesus Christ God A'mighty! Dhis little country about da size a' New Mexico? Ordinance from hell, we droppin' on 'em!"

"We lettin' it be what it is?"

"We don't learn dheir language, so we can't even talk to 'em. Don't say, 'How ya doin?' Don' eva' wave to 'em. Or sit down ta supper together. Dhey looks like good folks, same as in ma valley back home in West Virginia. Jus' goin' 'bout dheir plowin' an' harvestin' an' huntin' ever' day. Fishin', too. We jus' keep patrolin' dheir lan's, an' rivers, an' mountains. Killin' da Viet Cong boys."

"Ah don' honestly know if da politicians an' gen'rals drivin' dhis war on da North Vietnamese side is any more moral. Ah pray dhey is. But dhey plant bombs on women an' children ta kill us, an' dhem, too. War is hell-fightin on all sides. Deceivin'. Wastin' innocents. Warrin'. I doubt dhey're any better morally, 'xcept fer one thing: dhey're fightin' fer dheir freedom from invaders. Dhat's us. Dhat's a winnin' game."

Eleazar gently let go of the captain's fatigue jacket. Dropped his arm slowly to his knee. Stared straight ahead, beyond the captain, into inky, swirling clouds, and a blurred yellow sunset.

"No, sir, Ah 'ssure ya, Ah ain't drunk. Don' drink t'all. Or do dope, LSD, heroin, an' such. Lots a US boys do, ya know. Includin' officers.

"Jus' got a lot on ma min' af'er 'bout eight years in Nam, '64 ta now, September '72. Was waitin' here fer ya ta walk by. Wantin' ta share sense, an' reason witcha. Thinkin' it might go up da chain a' command from here an' change things fer da better—from now on. Make some kinda difference wit' life an' death fer civilians an' soldiers on both sides a' wrong wars like dhis one, da world ov'r.

"Ah ain't a peacenik. You got somethin' as god-awful valuable as freedom, ya gotta be willin' ta fight till yer dyin' breath ta keep it, as Ah said b'fore.

"Our wars should be fer defendin' da good ol' USA an' our allies. Wars dhat's wrong-headed, like dhis one, is da worst fer killin' innocents. Breedin' rotten behavior, an' attitudes among soldiers an' youth. Betrayin' allies da world over. An' destroyin' a God-fearin' civilization. History's clear on dhat. Ferget history, an' yer condemned ta repeat it. Da worst of it. Absolutely shameful fer da world's one an' only fought fer an' died fer beacon a' freedom an' hope. A government a' da people, by da people, an' fer da people.

"We might be willin' ta fergive our leaders fer some mistakes ove' time, but neva' ferget 'em. Now, dhey's crossed da line agains' We da People. Dhey covered up da truth. Dhey lied ta us. What else dhey lyin' 'bout? What dhey buryin' as 'classified documents?' Thousands a' our sons an' brothers, sisters, too, been killed fightin' a war in dhis foreign lan' wit' lies an' phony support.

"Fer what?

260

"In da en', Ah say, nothin' but da outright arrogance, greed, foolishness, disdain, an' stupidity a' our leaders. We mus' not let our government fund perpetual, murderous wars, ever again!

"We da People gotta wise up! Else, We da People in da USA are da ones 'sleep at da wheel, by default runnin' a worldwide, human-killin' business. Unjust an' immoral to da nth degree. Blissfully ignorant a' what we're doin' ta da world. Makin' blood money off it. Sippin' martinis in a whorehouse. We da People own everythin', even what we neglect fer laziness. Dhat's what da career politicians know so well. Dhey're blameless elected. Ya see, now? An' da res' a' us are jus' ignorant fools about our own dufus complicity.

"Da unchecked, bad behavior gonna catch up ta us one day. Won' be pretty. Who gonna have our back? God gonna be lookin' da otha' way fer us? No, sir. Dat's not God's way."

"We lettin' it be what it is?"

"Foolish, Ah guess, ta think a washed-up ol' grunt can spout what he thinks is hist'ry, truth, an' wisdom, at twilight, wit' a right fine young officer. B'fore da canteen door, a' all places. Jus' thought Ah'd give it a try. So long Cap'in Stanton. Thank ya fer hearin' me out. Ah ain' right 'bout everythin', but dhere's surely a grain a' truth ta dhis tale an ol' American soldier tellin' ya 'bout wars. I must not forget, Cap'in Stanton, ta ask ya ta read up on da Four Horsemen in da las' book in da Bible, Revelation, 6–8, or da whole book, fer da full prophecy.

"Hope all yer days en' well an' ya gits back home ta yer family in one piece, wit' a soun' mind. An' dhis godfersaken war is ended. An' all future wars like it neva' see da light a' God's nex' day."

261

With those final words, Eleazar stood up, hips weak, from sitting so long on the rock-hard sandbags.

Captain Stanton watched him slowly walk away, feebly, wobbling at his knees, likely suffering war wounds and arthritis. "Private Eleazar Zechariah, your words are truth and wisdom. And not wasted on me. Thank you. And God bless you," Captain Stanton said aloud, respectfully, in farewell.

Eleazar might have heard the captain's farewell. He continued limping slowly on his wayfaring journey, determined to do good, and spread the truth, while gazing steadfastly into the gathering dark clouds.

"Boom!"

An enemy rocket-propelled grenade dropped from the sky into camp. Ripped a three-foot deep crater in the laterite. Shot deadly shrapnel 360 degrees around. And sent up a thirty-foot-high explosion cloud. The advancing storm wind, blowing blustery from the west, dispersed the red dust, wafting to the ground.

Captain Stanton had hit the dirt immediately, instinctively, covering his head with his hands. Lost his hearing for a time. Looked about.

It's said in battle, if you hear an artillery shell whistling overhead, you're damned lucky, because the deadly missile has already passed you. Hit the dirt anyway, in case the next ones strike close. Like a locomotive, "a-rollin' down da track, ya can't hear it 'till it's pas' ya." Eleazar didn't hear an "incoming" warning. The grenade detonated at his last footstep. His body took all the shrapnel in the sector that would have hit Captain Stanton.

Private Eleazar Zechariah's time on Earth ended that dark September evening in Vietnam. His body was a shredded mass of blood and muscle, splintered bone, strings of white sinew. Ragged combat fatigues, and worn-out boots were all dusted with powdery laterite.

Eleazar's Saint Jude medal had settled in a pool of blood between his boots. Captain Stanton knelt down and picked it up. "God bless you, Eleazar Zechariah," he prayed aloud. Then, he sealed the bloody medal in his fist, closed his eyes, and recalled Galatians 6:7.

God is not mocked, for you reap whatever you sow.

"What have we let loose on the world?" Captain Stanton said.

A soldier's partial remains were returned to the USA from Vietnam with no dog tags, and buried at the Tomb of the Unknown Soldier in Arlington, Virginia. His mother never knew that her son, Eleazar Zechariah, died an unsung hero of the fallen in a wrong war.

"We lettin' it be what it is?"

The cost for the Vietnam war was many, many civilians and soldiers, who paid with their lives. Vietnam reported as many as 2,000,000 civilians who died on both sides of their civil war. And about 1,100,000 North Vietnamese and Viet Cong fighters died. The number of South Vietnamese soldiers who died in the war is reported between 200,000 and 250,000.

On the Vietnam Veterans Memorial in Washington, DC, the names of more than 58,300 soldiers, who were killed or missing in action, are engraved chronologically on the day they died in panels of polished black granite. Also, some 5,000 soldiers who died in the war were from allies of the United States: Australia, New Zealand, Republic of (South) Korea, Thailand, and the Philippines. Untold numbers of other combatants and non-combatants from both sides in the war zone suffered throughout their lives from physical, mental, and emotional injuries stemming from the war.

The number of people long-suffering for their dead and wounded sons, daughters, fathers, mothers, brothers, sisters, extended family relatives and friends in the various homelands the world over, is exponential. Millions of family and friends grieve today over their loved ones—men, women, and children—who died or suffered lifelong injuries from the Vietnam War.

# — 29 —

SOME years later.

Stella graduated summa cum laude, with a major in pre-law and a minor in military history and grand strategy, from Hillsdale College. She enlisted in the U.S. Air National Guard while still attending Hillsdale and trained to fly the Sikorsky HH-60 Pave Hawk. She completed numerous insertion and recovery missions for special operations personnel. She married hometown sweetheart, Wyatt Henry, who is now a dentist. After marriage, she obtained a law degree from Yale, specializing in international affairs. Following 10 years of service in the Air Guard, Captain Stella Young resigned her commission. She now serves as the attorney general for the Commonwealth of Virginia.

Hana also graduated from Hillsdale College, tied with Stella for summa cum laude, with a major in biochemistry and a minor in classics. Hana completed her medical training at the Yale School of Medicine for Neurosurgery. She married Karl Schafer, owner of a private research firm specializing in horticulture. She is now a neurosurgeon at Massachusetts General Hospital.

Both women are pregnant with their first child, and they are as close as ever.

The lifelong friends had carved out vacation time once each year for two weeks to finish their book. On the first

265

day to resume work, Stella always recited, "Mrs. Benedictus was right, the sixth-year project at the Academy was one thing, writing the book is another." Hana always enjoined, "Yeah, but we got so much more on our plates now." Today, she rubbed her belly.

At Hana's home late one Sunday evening in August, they were sitting at a table in the family room with the final draft, and selected journals, scraps and bits spread out before them. Their specific task was to review, once again, the wartime journals of their great-grandparents for any overlooked details. With ongoing help from Mrs Benedictus, the book was nearly ready for publication. On the previous Saturday evening, they had just finished yet another "final" draft for the Vietnam War story from Stella's grandfather, Captain Marcus Stanton.

Hana exclaimed, "You scrambling around again, little one?" Her baby's was poking its feet and fists inside her womb.

Stella let fly with, "Is it a boy or girl?"

Hana replied, "Karl and I want the ancient surprise and joy of God's creation to smack us in the face."

Stella said, "Yeah, Wyatt and I are with you guys. God's work is mysterious, uncertain. Bringing a newborn child into the world is humbling, awesome. We want to enjoy the surprise."

Tired from travel, Stella and Hana went to bed early.

Then, the women learned on the next day, Monday, August 30, 2021, along with the rest of the world, that the Biden administration pulled the US troops out of Afghanistan.

After watching multiple broadcasts from different networks throughout the day, Stella asserted quietly,

"Their decisions and failures of preparation on that day alone, led directly to the death of thirteen American soldiers. And death and horrible injuries for hundreds of other soldiers and civilians at the Kabul airport."

Stella was staring into an abyss. She suddenly realized the ramifications of wrong wars for her father, for her mother, for herself, for millions of other patriotic Americans, and people around the world.

Mysteriously, Stella, and her mother, Olivia, did not ever, would not ever, and could not ever contemplate Daddy's death framed as the aftermath of another wrong war—until this moment.

"Eleazar Zechariah was right: few in the government talk frankly and deeply, before armed conflict or in hindsight, about their real justifications and counterarguments for starting a war that goes wrong. In the end, their message is, 'It's over, get used to it,'" she started.

"Who would sign up for that?

"Nor their readiness to accept another American defeat and hasty pullout.

"Who would sign up for that?

"Nor the human suffering from wrong wars, notably from the perspective of the patriotic families of the dead, dying, wounded, and a myriad of people who care for survivors.

"And the lives, loves, hopes, and unfulfilled dreams of the soldiers killed in battles.

"Who would sign up for that?

"Did we do something or not do something to precipitate the aggression, leading up to a wrong war? Did some government official suddenly cut a deal and scrub the war? Did we exhaust options for negotiations to prevent the bad ending of another wrong war? Did our leader actually meet face-to-face and talk with the bellicose leader to ascertain legitimate concerns before committing our troops, all during the war, and before pulling our troops out?

"No one in our government takes responsibility for poor decisions that put our soldiers in harm's way—to explain the attack's impetus for a skirmish, for a specific horrific battle, or for a full-fledged war. They figure soldiers are expendable tools.

"Benghazi happened! Secretary of State Hillary Clinton declared in a congressional hearing on May 8, 2013, 'With all due respect, the fact is we had four dead Americans. . . What difference, at this point does it make?' Then, she and President Obama seized on a sketchy video by an activist American citizen from the Middle East, portraying the prophet Mohammed and his followers as responsible for killing Christians. Totally false. But the claim, issued amid the heat of the international crisis, deflected responsibility for the resulting massacre from the President and Secretary of State to this poor schmuck. CIA intel told them why the terrorist attack occurred in Benghazi, what could have been done to save the day, and who and what was actually responsible—and it wasn't the video producer. Our government owned the refusal of support for four Americans in peril, begging for help, leading to their deaths that night in Benghazi. And our leaders lied about it. Callous and treasonous. And, we still don't know what the President of the United States was doing when Benghazi was going down.

"Who would sign up for that?

"Inferior generals, politicians, and warmongers of whatever stripe run away from honest, public, reflective

268

analysis about the day-to-day carnage, and the truth, about a wrong war's unfolding aftermath.

"Who would sign up for that?

"They stress readiness, troop strength, tolerable casualties, range of weaponry, and such.

"The Biden administration said of their sudden pullout from Afghanistan, it's the other guy's fault. They blamed the war's ugly end on the previous Trump administration. A different political party. A president who was no longer in power, and had stopped the killing of our soldiers during the last eighteen months in office.

"Liers! Cowards!

"This story, the truth about this war's end, like Vietnam under President Nixon, is horrible to consider for the full range of victims, friends and family of the dead and wounded. It's demoralizing for soldiers serving in the field, at home, at bases around the world, and prospective new recruits in our all-volunteer military. And our Gold Star Families. All Americans.

"Are these wrong wars in defense of America and her allies?

"No honest discussion.

"Bad decisions about armed conflict have horrible, wide-ranging, long-lasting and personal consequences for all American families. But that's the most important point: We are supposed to be defending America from enemies at home and abroad, aiding our allies to help preserve their freedom, and safety. That's why our men and women join the armed forces in the first place. They swore the Oath of Enlistment, and willingly put their lives in the line of fire and roadside bombs by the dozens, so that we could enjoy freedom every day. That is America's precious gift to the world.

269

"But, in the light of wrong wars, if patriots hesitate, then what?

"Constant monitoring and checking the numerous bad guys who pose widespread or local threats is critical to prevent cruel and unjust treatment of people powerless to oust invaders.

"That reconnaissance happens.

"Our spies and friendly informants on the ground are essential to knowing day-to-day operations of the enemy in every theater of impending and active warfare. Continuous satellite surveillance of targets and movements on the ground, and all sorts of communications convey up-to-date data to yield a clear, deep, triangulated picture of almost any location, 24/7.

"That reconnaissance happens.

"With our cutting-edge, high-technology tools, combat drones, satellites, and trusted ground sources of our own and our allies, our government should know what's happening in multiple locations worldwide simultaneously, continuously.

"That reconnaissance happens.

"Feed gobs of filtered, organized, and analyzed information up the chain of command so they can make good decisions, order necessary action, eliminate threats, and keep our soldiers out of harm's way.

"That reconnaissance happens.

"Far-fetched? Impossible? I don' think so. Like Eleazar said, 'Ah got ma eyes wide open an' ma ears cleaned a' taters.'

"The US government has been monitoring private direct messages of unnamed, individual social media users, American citizens.

"That reconnaissance happened.

"Who exactly, and how many of our 330-plus million population? And unknown numbers of targeted people around the world. What else lies behind the curtain?

"What the hell is going on?

"'All warfare is based on deception,' as Sun Tzu wisely wrote. He might have meant government, too. Who is the deceiver? Who is being deceived? Who is the real enemy of We the People?

"Ultimately, through apathy and neglect, We the People are to blame."

A torrent of tears flowed from Stella's eyes.

She turned to Hana and asked of her grandfather, "Papa, did we get the story right? So late. The lessons we should take from the Vietnam War? Why they are so important to We the People. And, what has happened to America since Vietnam?

"What about the death and suffering of people around the world from wrong wars by the United States of America, other world powers, Russia and China, lesser world tyrants, drug cartels, vicious, manic bad guys, and villains? The path of wrong wars seemingly has no end. What's next?

"We are supposed to be the leader of the free world, not one of the careless, greedy butchers!

"Oh my God!," she shouted.

"Help me, Hana! What did my daddy die for? Why did I lose my daddy? And so many others lose their loved ones?

"He led his men to fight in battles against the enemy, to bring freedom to the oppressed in Afghanistan. He played soccer with their children. He sat down to enjoy dinners with many Afghan families. He did it all with a

271

fervent hope of saving innocent lives . . . and bringing his team home, alive and unhurt."

Stella, overwhelmed with grief, collapsed, hugging the baby in her womb. Hana caught her fall. Held Stella up, and hugged her. They sobbed uncontrollably over losing, years ago now, a beloved father and uncle, a son, and a husband. Army Captain Jedediah Young, like his buddies, and other soldiers in other wars, are the ultimate fighters and patriots for America. For freedom and justice for all.

Stella looked at Hana through eyes red and swollen with tears, "The war in Afghanistan really was a wrong war! Daddy, Daddy, I love you. Daddy, I miss you so much. And Mom does, too. Our whole family. Oh God!" She sobbed uncontrollably.

## — 30 —

"THE pullout in Afghanistan abandoned to the enemy many American citizens and supporters who were 'noncombatants.' What their fate has been, no one knows. No one is saying," Stella asserted. Then, she asked, "Who wanted to leave behind American civilians and our Afghan supporters? Who? Who chose to abandon our latest military equipment to the enemy? Who?

"The Biden Administration left billions of dollars of equipment on the ground, including firearms, ammunition, thousands of Humvee vehicles, and helicopters. An enumerated total of all abandoned weapons, munitions, and other material has not yet been reported. Nor have the subsequent sales of US war material been revealed. Plunder, to nameless bad guys on the world arms market. Setting the stage for another wrong war somewhere in the world?

"In the mayhem surrounding the last US Air Force C-17 jet to leave Kabul International Airport runway on August 30, 2021, suicide bombers attacked and killed 13 US soldiers. Over 100 Afghan men, women and children were also killed by the bombs. Many more Americans and Afghans suffered horrible injuries from shrapnel.

"US sharpshooters and spotters who covered the rapidly unfolding mayhem, positively identified the bombers, the rapidly unfolding imminent threat, and called for permission to kill the bombers. There was no advance open order for snipers to kill known threats. After the original request by snipers to take out the suicide bombers, there was no return order given to kill them. Tragically, the suicide bombers then reached their targets to detonate the bombs. The snipers assigned to protective duty at the airport suffered terrible wounds, and grieve today for the lost effort to save lives. The families and friends of the patriots and innocents who lost their lives on that day mourn.

"The day of departure in Afghanistan copied the dishonorable American pullout of Vietnam on March 29, 1973, just over forty-eight years earlier. Total American military dead from two decades of war in Afghanistan: 2,353; wounded: 20,149. Thousands of Afghan men, women, and children, combatants and noncombatants, died or were injured in yet another failed wrong war, ostensibly, to free oppressed people.

"Hope that the US would make good on its promises to soldiers, citizens, and allies died on August 30, 2021. The blood of unknown innocents flowed into the soil. The worldwide picture is grim and becoming more appalling due to ongoing bad decisions by incompetent or power-hungry leaders around the world.

"Since the deadly attack on 9/11, 2001, the commitment of the United States to fighting terrorism has grown to seventy-six countries. The three deadliest wars, so far, were in Iraq, Afghanistan, and Pakistan.

"Back home, only days after the Biden administration took office, US southern and northern borders were left wide open to illegal immigrants from around the world, many who were unskilled and illiterate, criminals, fugitive felons, the MS-13 international criminal gang of butchers, Mexican drug cartel operatives, and terrorists from around the world. An honest accounting for the deaths of American citizens from this invasion has not been reported.

"Many illegal border crossers traffic fentanyl and other deadly, illicit drugs. They pour into American communities and streets. Thousands of American youth become addicted and die. The gangs 'procure' children from around the world, illegally pass them across the border as a trafficker's 'children,' and sell them to their agents in American cities. The young girls, notably, are forced to be slaves in a cruel, inescapable sex trade of girls and women.

"Where does it lead?

"Then, the Biden Administration promulgated a new war that opened between Ukraine and Russia. Critics argue that it's really a proxy war between the United States and Russia. China has plans to take over Taiwan, and set up aggressive operations in Africa, South America, and on our front door in Cuba. Palestinians conduct unprovoked and diabolical attacks against Jerusalem, targeting helpless Jewish children, mothers, fathers, and wiping out whole families of innocents. Hawkish, foolish officials and observers talk blithely of an impending World War III, where nuclear weapons may be unleashed by the US and Russia, with China in the wings."

Before he stepped out to continue his mission on Earth, Eleazar Zechariah told Cap'in Stanton to read about the Four Horsemen of the Apocalypse, especially Chapters 6 to 8 in The Book of Revelation in the Holy Bible. Therein the Lamb of God opens the first four of the seven seals, which call forth four awesome beings that ride out on white, red, black, and pale horses, each heralding different and ominous prophesies.

What comes tomorrow?

## — 31 —

ANA knew Stella's remarkable gift for oration when the moment called for a strong voice of truthful dissent. She saw it coming. Stella would speak up when so many others were silent.

The next morning, after a breakfast of coffee, fruit, yogurt and granola, she stated, "After twenty years of war 'for the sake of Enduring Freedom,' our president ended, and classified for the record, yet another wrong war. Abruptly, in ignominious defeat for America.

"The world watched live-streaming video of this pullout of US troops.

"Cowardly. Shamed America, while the eyes of the world watched, and cried.

"Troops were flown out well ahead of flying out all US citizens in the country, and Afghanistan civilians who had served honorably with American and allied forces.

"The president and his administration, gave no clear, thorough, or satisfactory accounting, or explanation to We the People. Our government's war for Enduring Freedom, and everyone it touched, went up in smoke with the last jet's liftoff from Kabul.

"Our whole Stanton-Bradley family is in mourning, like thousands of patriotic families across America. We will try for years, with no end, to understand why we had this war in the first place, if we were not determined to win. We deserve answers.

"What arguments were used, by whom, to start this war? We have the right to know who, who, was in front and behind the scenes, what they said, when, what decisions they pushed for, or approved, and what options were tabled and why? It will do America no good in the present, or ever, to have kiss-and-tell accounts by sycophants and glory hounds. The truth to be held off for protection of 'classified information' claims until twenty to thirty to fifty years from now. By then, the responsible actors will be long dead. And many will not remember or not care.

"Who, including from the presidents on down, over the whole twenty years, made what decisions, on what operations, and for what equipment to deploy, and when?

"2001–2021 'Operation Enduring Freedom,' Afghanistan.

"2003–2011 'Operation Iraqi Freedom,' originally named 'Operation Infinite Justice,' then renamed 'Operation New Dawn,' Iraq.

"2010–2011 'Operation New Dawn,' Iraq.

"Who came up with these titles? Only morons would push out such sanctimonious bullshit for public consumption. Same thing was done in Vietnam. It was an ad campaign worked up by general staff and toadies justifying bloodletting of America's warriors. All are hallowed-sounding titles for recent US conflicts in the Middle East. Hype for the troops. Duping the public. As though the titles themselves held some kind of magic over fighting on the ground. They all led eventually to where we are now: not the promised end, but a terrible lot of bloodshed and loss of life.

"Past presidents: Are you hiding the truth, your culpability? Are you going to wake up and fight for America? Or just gonna continue hobnobbing with billionaires, sitting in lounge chairs at your mansions, and collecting pensions? Teddy Roosevelt never sidelined himself or hid from responsibility! Generals: Where are you in this horrible morass? General Patton would be whipping your asses with a red-hot poker around the Pentagon grounds until you bled to death — or grew balls to do something to end the wrong wars and bring our soldiers home!

"Who dictated the rules of engagement throughout these wars? What were the rules over time? Why were they changed and when? Who exactly pushed for this recent abrupt pullout of our troops from Afghanistan? Who? And why, exactly?

"We've been given exact details for twenty years from several US administrations concerning enemy commanders, and what they have been held responsible for in the wars with Iraq and Afghanistan. What lists detail for We the People the names and history of US officials who failed in their responsibilities for battles, weaponry, ground operations? And how will the current Commander-in-Chief and his administration be held accountable for the shameful pullout, the horrible long-term loss of life from the war in Afghanistan? When?

"Our government made Afghanistan yet another wrong, and costly war!

"We the People must demand open Congressional hearings to expose these politicians, generals, bureaucrats, and lobbyists for their arguments, decisions, and paybacks.

"The ones who did the right things, we must acknowledge and honor them.

"But the ones who made decisions that led to clusterfucks, put soldiers in harm's way, and got them hurt and killed. I can't recall that any big brass were ever called to account, arrested, and brought to trial for their mistakes in battle plans. The high-up brass have no trouble arresting and imprisoning our troops on the ground who might have made bad decisions in the heat of battle. Makes the 'chesties' look good in the press. They're doing something 'honorable' for their friends in the mainstream media. Pushing their long-running, Middle East freedom narrative to a tired and gullible American public.

"It's high time we held senior officers responsible for making bad decisions. And Congress. Get serious, Congress! We must hold you accountable for putting our civilians, allies, and soldiers in harm's way. Leading to thousands of dead and maimed. Do your job!

"Unless We the People act now, our government and the vast military industrial complex, will be the downfall of America as it was meant to be. And as we have known it, sadly, in its decline and fall.

"President Dwight D. Eisenhower spoke these words on January 17, 1961, in his Farewell Address: 'Throughout America's adventure in free government, our basic purposes have been to keep the peace; to foster progress in human achievement, and to enhance liberty, dignity and integrity among people and among nations. To strive for less would be unworthy of a free and religious people. Any failure traceable to arrogance, or our lack of comprehension or readiness to sacrifice would inflict upon us grievous hurt both at home and abroad.'

"Amen.

"At that time, we were already in Vietnam. Eisenhower knew what he was talking about when leaving the White House. He had served as Supreme Commander of Allied Expeditionary Force in Europe during World War II.

"I pray, God, that we put our 'house' in order soon, and Save Our Souls."

A long pause.

Stella had the clear-eyed thinking and the tempered warrior-blood running in her veins, same as her daddy, her papa, mom, and the whole Bradley-Sanada clan throughout their history.

"What is possible? What is right? What is just? What is moral?" Stella asked

Hana added, "Stella, you spoke boldly, truthfully. And nailed it."

Stella felt her heart pounding so powerfully in her chest it might burst. Her baby had boxed and kicked throughout her speech, but at the present time was calm in the womb.

Stella said with robust conviction, "Okay. We focus on the end, the now, but trace back in time for accountability for bad decisions among our elected leaders, appointed officials, and the unelected bureaucrats.

"We don't have a journal from Daddy, but I believe we owe it to him, and the other US soldiers and civilians who were killed or wounded, to follow through. We got leads provided by Papa in his journals from Vietnam, and the whole collection of World War II journals for contrast and comparison. Mindful that this is another time and place."

"Some news sources these days are complicit with the government, to the point of being deceitful, supporting wrong wars. We'll track down the truth-telling sources,

281

like Newsmax, and podcasts by political commentators —
for honesty and attention to detail. ID the frauds and
ass-kissers. In the end, we'll pull together the facts. Build
a coalition of families, like-minded patriots, and moral
politicians. We'll call it, Forward America.

"We will also recognize private individuals and
organizations, like the Fisher House Foundation, Gary
Sinise Foundation, Tunnel to Towers Foundation, and
Folds of Honor Foundation. They unselfishly, generously
honor and provide assistance to the wounded, the fallen,
their families and loved ones, and the Gold Star Families.

"Hana, my dearest friend, the journals we inherited are
so very valuable. We have learned so much. Our research
and writing have come full circle. From a past, that we did
not know, we have come to our present. We got an even
bigger challenge: to use our studies to discover who and
what we are — now. I mean We the People in the United
States of America, from our perspective. Granted, it's only
one family's story in the beginning. But this concerns truth-
telling about modern wars that we need to know, that the
world needs to know. When each story of suffering and loss
is added for the full collection of families undergoing pain
and anguish from wrong wars . . . .

"What is the United States of America doing with our
military might to keep us safe from enemies domestic and
abroad, while protecting our allies?

"Let's face it, we will never get the truth from chesty
generals, Pentagon bureaucrats, lobbyists and the
current administration. Truth will come from the hearts
and souls of patriotic American families, elected and
appointed officials who have a conscience, a backbone,
and our allies.

"There are many stories about these wars out there, but none like this one. We've started it. Looking forward, I believe We the People must put 330 million points of fierce pressure on Congress to conduct thorough investigations, report findings honestly and create laws to end our government's reckless, immoral, self-serving, wrong wars. If we have acted shamefully, we will make a clean breast of it to the world and right our ways.

"The world is a small place, and getting smaller. We are not fooling anyone.

"The time is now for America to create a new schema for reporting on political and military affairs. Rip journalism from the clutches of communists, socialists, and anti-America forces. We must have open public discussion, approval, and oversight on every momentous issue of the day. To hell with top secret classifications that allow government officials, the mainstream media, and big business to hide what's going on and escape accountability."

Hana said, "Stella, I admire your courage and desire to know the truth. I'm totally with you, all the way. When it gets tough to bear, and it will, we'll pause the research, like just now. Reflect. Pray. Cry. Then, pick up the trail when we feel ready."

Both women said, "You're my bestie!" Then, stood and smacked their hands together, like samurai swards drawn for battle.

"Let's get Forward America started," Stella concluded.

# — 32 —

S OME years later.

The sergeant at arms and doorkeeper bellowed from the great doors to the House of Representatives, "Mr. Speaker, the President of the United States!"

A wall of loud approving cheers, joyous shouts, hand claps, and yells broke out in the chamber. It grew thunderous as the second-term president slowly made her way to the rostrum for the State of the Union Address. At every row of seats, regardless of party affiliation, proud and enthusiastic members of Congress crowded to the aisle to speak a few words with her and wish her well. The nine, solemn Supreme Court Justices bowed respectfully and shook her hand. The five, stiffened Joint Chiefs of Staff greeted the first woman president and commander-in-chief with decorum. The various secretaries in the Cabinet welcomed the president warmly, and thanked her for including their requests in this speech.

At the rostrum, President Stella Emilia Young gracefully turned around to hand copies of her speech to the Vice President and the Speaker of the House.

The loud claps and cheers continued. After several minutes of patient appreciation, President Young asked for quiet. Everyone obliged and sat down. However, their standing, loud applause, and cheers of approval frequently interrupted the president's speech.

"Thank you. Thank you. Thank you all very much.

"Mr. Speaker, Mr. Vice President, members of Congress, the first gentleman of the United States, my husband, Wyatt, our three children, Nadetta, Ondrea, and Gabriel, my mother, Olivia, and my dear friend, Hana Sanada-Schafer, distinguished guests, and my fellow citizens:

"Four years ago, you elected me to lead the United States of America. I was deeply honored then. I am extremely honored today for the privilege you gave me, and the trust you placed in me by electing me for a second term as your President.

"During my first campaign, we faced dire conditions as a nation, both at home and abroad. You heartily supported the causes I stood for and the solutions I proposed. You trusted in the style of leadership I hoped to bring to the White House: hard, smart, effective work with no room for nonsense, bolstered by honesty and the drive to hold myself and other government officials accountable for our promises, actions, and results.

"Our slogan was, Restore truth, common sense, morality, and justice to America.

"We won by a landslide back then. Four years later, we won by another landslide. Thank you so much.

"In the days, months, and years since my first term began, hardworking Americans across this nation have stood by me. Congress has stood by me. The Supreme Court and the Joint Chiefs of Staff stood by me. And I have stood with you to 'preserve, protect, and defend the Constitution of the United States.'

"We enacted term limits for Congress: House six terms and Senate three terms. We froze the salaries for members of Congress at $175,000 per annum for the next seven years. Members of Congress, their spouses, and family members are required to report all bonds, stocks, mutual funds, exchange-traded funds, and other sources of income to the IRS at the end of every quarter.

"We established veterans benefits as the only taxpayer-funded health plan for Congress.

"We ended the weaponization of federal departments and agencies against American citizens, against candidates for office, against free and fair elections, against voter ID, and against our legitimate organizations and institutions. We fired the agents who engaged in the clandestine, deep-state control of America. We successfully prosecuted offenders from all departments for treason and lying to the American people, including from the CIA, FBI, IRS, CDC, Department of Homeland Security, Department of Justice, Department of State, National institutes of Health, Environmental Protection Agency, and Congress.

"At long last, We the People have a constitutional republic that is once again of the people, by the people, and for the people.

"We adopted rules and enforcement procedures for decorum for government officials in all official business. We no longer allow: lawless disregard and disrespectful behavior toward the Constitution and the Bill of Rights, toward other members, other branches of government, political parties, and our allies. We do not allow libel and slander, profane language, threats, false narratives, prejudice, lies, and hostility toward others.

"We ended the era of rancorous and abusive behavior and speech by government officials. We treat others as we want them to treat us. We show our citizens, especially our children, that we act respectfully toward one another, even though we may hold widely different opinions on issues.

"We prosecute, convict, and punish elected or appointed government officials who lie to or mislead Congress, or the American people, or leak classified information.

"We reestablished law and order in America. We brought back the blindfolded Lady of Justice to prosecute criminals to the full extent of the law. We impeach federal judges whose decisions about members of juries and their rulings in court are based on prejudice, politics, and ideology, instead of the law.

"Crime of all variations is down significantly across the nation.

"Our parks, monuments, buildings, streets, and cities are clean, safe, and beautiful. Our communities are flourishing. Our farmers are harvesting grain and livestock to help feed us and people around the world. Our men and women in trades are turning out the finest products, goods, and services. Once again, the U.S. is the world's leading oil and natural gas producer. Our small and large businesses are prosperous. The infrastructure is well-maintained and up-to-date.

"Our economy is strong. Americans want to work. They want to support themselves. And they are helping their families and communities pursue the American dream. Unemployment is at the lowest level in seven decades.

"We abolished the U.S. Department of Education and, through alignment with the American Children's

Learning Act, returned responsibility for the education of our youth to their parents, their local communities, and their states.

"We destroyed forever the communist and socialist ideology introduced by our enemies to destroy America from within. Of late, their provocateurs led riots to destroy monuments, federal buildings, police headquarters, cities, and private businesses. Innocent people suffered serious injuries. Some died.

"Violence, mob activities, mayhem, and destruction of property are uncivil, illegal, and destructive. We will not tolerate uncivil behavior and we will prosecute offenders to the full extent of the law.

"We arrested and deported all known illegal immigrants to their country of origin, with the provision that they may apply for legal entry at a later time.

"We restored honor, support, and respect to our police units nationwide. Law enforcement officers serve and protect We the People. Their job is to arrest dangerous individuals on our streets, in our neighborhoods, and in our cities, often putting their lives on the line. Some die in the line of duty.

"We maintained and strengthened our borders and all points of entry to stop illegal border crossings. We ended the constitutional guarantee of citizenship for children of illegal or undocumented immigrants born in the United States.

"Forward America, and other grassroots movements, have succeeded. We put an end to the military-industrial complex of America that for decades has pushed our nation toward wrong wars, having little or nothing to do with our national defense.

"We have lived through these last four years without a war. No soldier has died in combat on my watch, and I intend to continue that record.

"Today, our allies stand with us. Our adversaries respect us. Our enemies know that the response of America and her allies to their persecutions, invasions, and wars against people who cannot defend themselves will bring swift and brutal justice.

"Our central, defensive foreign policy is to maintain productive, continuous open communication with every head of state, and all other political and religious leaders. Face-to-face whenever and wherever possible. We will do everything in our power to listen and understand what they say, and try our best to help settle disagreements on the international stage without firing one shot.

"Our military is the best it has ever been, and second to none in the world, for integrity, equipment, training, strength, and preparedness.

"Our industry is the envy of nations for its flexibility, innovation, high-quality products and services, and timely productivity. American workers reap the benefits.

"We are Americans first. We hope for the best, but we prepare for the worst. Should an enemy try to attack us or our allies, we will retaliate in force immediately."

"The state of the union is strong. Today, America is a vibrant democracy, a constitutional republic, like none the world has ever seen. We owe it to our founders, succeeding generations of Americans, and the whole world, to show that we are not afraid to confront the bad actors, wherever they hide. We will argue ideas with others. Challenge and thoroughly study viewpoints, and resolve disagreements. We will examine issues openly and engage in honest, respectful, and civil discourse. We will determine the merit of everything that comes before us to keep Americans united, safe, moral, honorable, and just. And we will apply these principles to the people around the world.

"This first term bore incredible fruit. I am honored and so grateful to Congress, the courts, my administration, and all the people in this great country for your help with our achievements. It was a struggle, for sure, but like your mama always said ,'Nothing good comes easy, dear. You gotta work long and hard to get that.'

"The only way we can make America safe, secure, respectful, moral, and prosperous is to know and follow our Constitution and Bill of Rights, stand together, and work hard, side by side, to protect this nation of God-given freedom and liberty for all.

"Now, we are set to embark on another four-year journey into the unknown. Like so many brave people who came before us, we will lay down a vision with detailed plans—seeds planted in fertile soil. Our hard work will bear fruit for a harvest that makes life in America good, whole, and secure for every citizen. And prevent the rape of innocence. We will adapt those plans in accordance with ever-unfolding circumstances.

"Next, I will explain my vision for the second term, and the plans I have made, with help from my administration, to lead America forward.

"My vision carries forward the promises made in my first term as your president: to restore truth, common sense, morality, and justice to America. I will begin next week by inviting Americans, representing all different beliefs, professions, and social statuses, to the White House to conduct a national conversation about the most egregious civil rights abuses of our time, at home and abroad—human trafficking and sexual abuse of children.

"First, I will establish the President's Committee on Human Trafficking and Slavery of Adults and Children. Its purpose is to propose measures to clarify, strengthen, and routinely enforce the Trafficking Victims Protection Act of 2000 and its reauthorizations.

"Second, I will establish the President's Committee on Child Sexual Abuse, and Life-Altering Counseling, Surgery, and Medication for Sex Changes of Children. Its purpose is to clarify, strengthen, and routinely enforce the Preventing Child Sex Abuse Act and related laws regarding sexual abuse of children.

"Third, I will ask Congress to send a bill to my desk that puts a knife in the heart of drug trafficking in America, ending a century-long nightmare for parents and victims of illegal drug trade.

"Fourth, I will direct the Department of Defense, the FBI, the CIA, and the Department of Homeland Security to cooperate with their counterparts internationally to identify and bring to justice the leaders of human trafficking and slavery, and the sexual abuse of children.

"Fifth, . . ."